To save her marriage, Laura Harrison accompanies her husband Jack to Indonesia where he is to take over as president of troubled bank; but when her premonitions become reality, events spin out of control.

Laura expects their new home in Jakarta to be a romantic hideaway like something out of a classic Bogart movie. Instead she walks into a house of horrors. White sheets cover Gothic furnishings, and black garments hang in the closets. It's as if the former occupants had fled from some danger. Despite feelings of doom, Laura is determined to make things work. At the local market she's appalled to see a baby orangutan for sale, its mother having been killer by loggers. She resolves to save the endangered primates and their rainforest habitat. As Laura attempts to grow closer to her husband, they become at odds over his shady business dealings. And when his secrets and life of lies are revealed, Laura finds herself alone and responsible for her own destiny.

"...*Ashes in a Coconut* weaves a tale of corruption, betrayal, and ultimately redemption that had me marveling at the resiliency of the characters to the very last page. A wonderful debut!"—*Reyna Marder Gentin, author of Unreasonable Doubts*

"Whet your appetite for the dazzling palette of colors and aromas, the bustling mysterious world of Indonesia...described by author, Bo Kearns, a talented wordsmith and a keen observer....what he paints is the transformation of heart and mind and spirit, an inspiring and sometimes terrifying rebirth. *Ashes in a Coconut* should be on the top of the list for any reader who cares about the planet or the people who inhabit it."—*Daniel Coshnear, Willa Cather Fiction Award winner and author of Jobs & Other Preoccupations and Occupy & Other Love Stories*

"I enjoyed spending time with Jack and Laura as they attempt to mend their marriage and make their way through the Jakarta of 1983, a glamorous and dangerous place of Singapore Slings, shady bankers, mysterious curses, seductive servants, damaged rain forests, magnificent Buddhist temples, and orphaned orangutans."—*Molly Giles, author of Rough Translations, winner of The Flannery O'Connor Prize, the Boston Globe Award, and The Bay Area Book Reviewers' Award*

"*Ashes in a Coconut* fascinated me from the first house on fire to the final coconut. In 1990s Indonesia, a banker fights to save his company and his honor while a strong woman works to overcome American expat stereotypes. Both deal with clashing cultures, political upheaval, and corruption in government and international banking undermining the love they are trying to repair. Kudos to Bo on his debut novel."—*Eric Witchey, Award-winning author of Bull's Labyrinth and Littlest Death*

ASHES IN A COCONUT

Bo Kearns

Moonshine Cove Publishing, LLC
Abbeville, South Carolina U.S.A.
FIRST MOONSHINE COVE EDITION December 2018

This book is a work of fiction. Names, characters, places and incidents are products of the author's imagination or are used fictitiously. Any resemblance to actual events, locales or persons, living or dead, is entirely coincidental.

ISBN: 978-1-945181-50-4
Library of Congress PCN: 2018965025
Copyright Ë 2018 by Robert J. Kearns III

Cover Images public domain, cover design by Shelia Cowley

Dedication

For Patric and Tamsin

About The Author

Bo Kearns lives in the wine country of Sonoma, California where he is a fiction writer, journalist, beekeeper and UC Naturalist. He graduated from the U.S. Naval Academy and following military service he pursued a career in international banking and finance. During that time he had stints in Bahrain, Indonesia and London. In Indonesia, he developed an appreciation and fondness for the country's unique culture of mysticism and magic. And that became the setting of his debut novel *Ashes in a Coconut*. Bo has written short stories that have won awards and been published. He's a feature writer for *NorthBay biz* magazine and the *Sonoma Index-Tribune* newspaper.

Read more about his interests and writing approach at his webpage:

http://bokearns.com

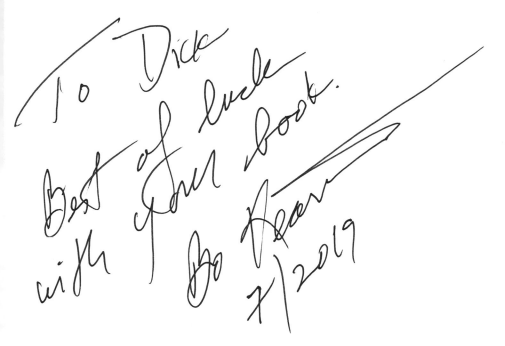

To Dick
Best of luck
with your book.
Bo Hearn
7/2019

ASHES IN A COCONUT

Ashes in a Coconut
September 1983, Bali, Indonesia

In the blistering noonday sun, Laura Harrison stood outside the Denpasar International Airport and fingered the beads on her necklace. Her damp silk blouse clung to her body. In the humidity her red hair curled so that she resembled an adult Little Orphan Annie. She fanned her face wishing she'd worn a wide-brimmed straw hat. And yet she shouldn't have minded the discomfort; she was in Bali. Still, she fretted. The island paradise was only a stopover en route to Jakarta. There she would be beginning a new life in a place she'd never been, leaving everything behind to save her marriage.

Her husband, tall and broad-shouldered, stood beside her. He wore a tropical shirt and exuded confidence.

"Jack, can you hail a cab — preferably one with air conditioning."

"Good luck with that," he said.

Before he could raise his hand, a taxi with the car windows rolled down, pulled up to the curb. Laura grimaced as they climbed in. With their bags in the trunk, they made their way through narrow streets; discreet shrines graced with small floral offerings dotted the roadside. In the distance, young green rice paddies terraced the mountain. After a half hour they arrived at the Seminyak Kebun Resort where a vast manicured lawn and swaying palm trees welcomed them.

"How beautiful!" Laura said. Her spirits rose. "The perfect place for a second honeymoon."

Jack smiled and took her hand.

The couple walked into the large open-air lobby. At the registration desk Laura noticed blossoms in a small woven palm-leaf tray. She picked one up and inhaled the fragrance.

"It's an offering to keep away evil spirits," the clerk said.

"Oh," Laura said. She set the flower down and moved away.

Laura and Jack followed the bellboy to a thatched-roof bungalow that fronted onto a tranquil beach. Inside a four-poster bed covered with mosquito netting dominated the room. Paintings of colorful birds hung on the walls.

Laura walked around admiring, touching. The bathroom, open to the sky, was outside in a small garden. White and purple orchids proliferated, and a showerhead shaped like a dolphin extended from the rock wall. Then Laura noticed movement off to the side. A hammock swung through the air was perfectly still. She got goose bumps watching it. Hugging her arms across her chest, she rushed inside.

Jack, busy unpacking, glanced up. "You okay? You look pale."

Laura dropped her arms to her side. "I'm fine. Must be jet lag."

He pulled a pair of swimming trunks from the suitcase. "Let's go check out the beach. A swim will perk you up," he said.

Laura and Jack walked through the sand to a spot in the shade. Laura set her sunscreen, towel and a book on the lounge chair. Jack picked up the book and looked at the title.

"*Heart of Darkness.* The horror, the horror. I can still remember those lines from high school English class. Gives me the creeps. What possessed you to bring along a book about violence in the tropics?"

"There wasn't a big selection at JFK. It was Joseph Conrad or chick lit."

Jack shrugged and set the book back down. He took Laura's hand and they strolled to the water's edge.

"Looks awfully rough." Laura shouted to be heard above the roar of the waves.

"Reminds me of vacations at the beach when I was a kid. I'd spend the whole day body surfing," Jack said.

Waves rose, crested, and crashed in front of them. Foamy water swirled around their ankles.

"No way I'm swimming," Laura said. "Besides I'm a pool person. You go."

Jack lifted his legs high and ran toward a building wave. As it peaked, he dove through a glistening wall and emerged on the other side. He shook water from his head, grinned, and waved.

Maybe Indonesia will be good for him, Laura thought. Hopefully for both of us.

She wandered to where they had left their belongings. After reading for a while she lay back and closed her eyes. Her thoughts drifted to New York where she had worked as a fashion designer in the garment district striving to achieve recognition. At her debut Fall Fashion Week showing the audience had gasped when her design appeared. The flowing dress was worn by a tall African model. Her dark skin accentuated the rust and marigold colors of the fabrics. As she moved down the runway to the rhythm of David Bowie's "Let's Dance," celebrities in the front row stood and clapped. The buyer from Bloomingdale's placed an order, the biggest of the show. Then that night at dinner, Jack told her about his opportunity to be president of a bank in Indonesia. The news devastated her, and she had to choose — her marriage or her career.

A fly alighted on her arm and she opened her eyes to shoo it away. She saw Jack, now far out. As a wave built behind him, he straightened his arms, lunged forward and rode the crest. The wall of water crashed with a thundering roar. Foam churned and Jack disappeared. Laura gasped and jumped up. She rushed toward the shore and spotted him being tumbled by the heavy surf. A final push from the sea, and he lay lifeless in the sand.

"Jack!" Laura yelled. She ran over, dropped to her knees, and shook him. He didn't move.

Then he flipped over. "I'm alive."

Laura her hand at her throat, glared. "You fool."

Jack reached and pulled her down with him. Traces of a wave washed around them. With Jack's strong arms encircling her, Laura relaxed, and they lay together in the warm salt water.

Back at the room they changed clothes and headed out. White flowers with a yellow center grew in the garden. As they passed, Laura paused to pick one for her hair.

"Let's stop in the gift shop for a minute," she suggested as they entered the lobby.

Inside, the scene resembled a street bazaar. Grotesque Balinese masks and vivid oil paintings of temples, rice paddies, and brown-skinned girls hung on the walls. Statues of Hindu gods with multiple arms and heads of mythical beasts stared from the corners. Laura searched through a pile of sarongs. She selected a solid green one. The color reminded her of the rice paddies they had seen earlier. She also bought a phrase book for Bahasa Indonesia, the language of the country.

In front of the hotel, taxis waited beneath a jacaranda tree blanketed with purple flowers. Jack negotiated the fare to Pura Tanah Lot, the temple Laura read about in her guidebook.

"My name Madé." The middle-aged driver wore a royal-blue polo shirt and a baseball cap. He greeted them with a broad, welcoming smile. "Your first time Bali?"

"It is," Laura replied.

"You from?"

"We're from New York, though we're moving to Jakarta."

"Bali better. Jakarta too many people."

Laura suspected he was right. And she knew many of the too many were poor.

"Lot of American and Australian come to Bali. I speak American English with Australian accent," he said with pride in his voice.

They drove along a narrow, pot-holed road through the rural countryside.

"That Batur," Madé said. He pointed to a volcano in the distance its peak shrouded by vaporous clouds. "Last erupt 1963."

Further on he stopped to let a flock of tall long-necked ducks cross the road. A man wearing a conical bamboo hat shooed them along.

"He take them to paddies. They eat bad bugs and droppings help rice grow," Madé said.

After a half-an-hour drive, they pulled into a parking area.

"We stop here and walk to beach. Not far."

They passed stalls selling T-shirts and gaudy souvenirs. The path ended at the edge of a cliff. Laura stood in awe. Just offshore, perched atop a large black lava rock, sat ancient Pura Tanah Lot. Red bougainvillea cascaded down the cliffs on either side. Tall pagodas rose stark against the blue sky. The scene resembled a delicate watercolor.

"The temple was built in fifteenth century to appease sea gods," Madé said.

Dark stone slabs, covered with green algae and pitted with pools of water, formed the shoreline. An ocean breeze brought the scent of salt and marine life. Jack climbed down among the rocks to take photographs. From a distance the sun's golden rays shimmered about his head like an aura.

"Your husband looks spiritual," Madé said.

Laura laughed. "Jack is many things, but spiritual is not one of them."

Jack returned, winded after the climb. "Beautiful," he said.

"Madé thinks you look spiritual," Laura said.

Jack laughed. "I am."

They left Tanah Lot and headed for Kuta Beach. There a crowd had gathered around a tall multi-tiered structure resembling a huge wedding cake. Painted in bright colors and decorated with strips of gold and silver foil, the tower, about twenty feet high, glittered.

"What's happening?" Laura asked. She leaned forward to get a better glimpse.

"*Ngaben*, cremation."

"Can we watch?" She'd read about the elaborate Bali cremation ceremonies.

"Don't be so morbid, Laura," Jack said.

"Ngaben fun," Madé said. "In Bali, death not sad. It is a time of joy. When person dies, we burn the body to free the soul. They go to better life." He stopped the car. "I ask family if we can join procession. I am sure it be okay."

Laura and Jack got out and the driver disappeared into the crowd.

"They happy you join," he said when he came running back. "But you have to wear sarong." He looked at the couple in their knee-length shorts. "You can buy in shop over there. They cheap." Laura retrieved the sarong she bought at the hotel gift shop from the car and they crossed the street. Inside she tugged at a sarong on the bottom of the stack. "Try this blue one." She wrapped it around Jack's waist. "Cute."

Jack looked in the mirror. "No photos."

Sarong clad, Jack and Laura rejoined Madé. "You look Balinese." He smiled. He pointed to a black and white photograph of a man in uniform on the side of the tower.

"He fight against Dutch in War of Independence in 1945. He sixty-five years old."

The crowd had grown considerably since they arrived. "He must have been well-liked. Look at all the people," Laura said.

"Everyone from his village here."

The women, wearing long geometric patterned skirts, wide sashes, and long- sleeved lace blouses, balanced containers of fruit and flowers on their heads. Several carried poles with yellow-fringed parasols. The gathering stirred in anticipation. Then the body, swaddled in white cloth, appeared. Lifted high, the bundle was passed along by many outstretched brown hands. A man attired in white grasped the body and climbed to the top of the tower and placed the deceased under a canopy. Shirtless young men jerked the bamboo pallet holding the structure onto their shoulders. The man in white garb grasped the side of the tower to keep from falling off. A shout erupted, and a lively procession of several hundred people moved down the street. Laura, Jack, and Madé ran to keep up.

"Remember no crying," Madé said.

Laura wondered if she could do that. She was already saddened by the thought that someone died even though she didn't know him.

"Reminds me of Mardi Gras," Jack said.

"I guess. I've never been," Laura said, struggling not to trip in her sandals.

At a crossroad, the men with the pallet circled three times. The man, still on the tower, tossed rice.

"They spin tower to confuse soul so it does not go back to village. The rice for evil spirits. They stop to eat and do not follow."

The procession resumed down a side street.

"Everyone looks happy," Laura said.

Jack, busy taking photos, nodded.

"Aren't Balinese afraid of dying?" Laura looked at Madé

"Why anyone be afraid to go to better place?"

"But they should be sad. They'll never see their loved ones again."

"They still part of family. We keep small altar for them in our home. We leave offerings — food and flowers. And we pray to them. We remember them all the time. They never go away."

"Westerners don't like to talk about dying," Laura said. "We spend our lives worrying about when it's going to happen."

"Death part of life. Not good to worry. Nothing you can do."

Perhaps that's why the Balinese seem so content, Laura thought. They don't fret about the inevitable.

The procession arrived at the beach, and the men set the pallet down on the sand. A man pulled a live chicken from a sack and tossed it into the air. "That mean release of the soul," Madé said. The ball of black feathers flapped to the ground and darted about, surveying the crowd. The hen then headed straight for Jack, taking refuge under the hem of his sarong. Startled, Jack jumped. The frightened fowl scurried out and hid in a thicket of sea grape.

"I hope that's not like catching the bride's bouquet," Laura said spontaneously. Then she realized the implication.

Jack frowned.

The body was lowered from the tower and placed in an open sarcophagus of wet banana-tree trunks and filled with petrol-soaked wood. A holy man in long, white garments anointed the corpse and women placed offerings of food and flowers alongside.

"Holy water is from Hindu temples. Food is for the soldier in next life," Madé whispered.

Lit with a torch of twigs, the pyre erupted into an orange-and-yellow inferno. White smoke billowed. The fire roared and crackled. In the middle, the body burned. Suddenly, as if the old soldier were alive, the arms rose.

Laura gasped, her hands at her chest.

"Do not be afraid," Madé said. "When fire hot, body act strange. Some believe it is moment when soul leave."

Jack, looking uneasy, stepped back.

"Later, family return here. Boy climb tree for young coconut. At sunset, they cut open and place ashes inside. They put it in ocean and watch it drift away."

Laura pondered the beauty and significance of that scene. She wiped away a tear. "I know I'm not supposed to cry, but that's so beautiful."

On their return to the car, Laura stopped. "Is it okay if I leave an offering?"

"If you like," Madé said. "An offering a sign of respect."

Laura took off her sandals and ran back through the sand. At the edge of the fire, she took the white flower from her hair and tossed it in. She watched the petals curl and disappear in a burst of flame.

***

The following morning Laura awoke to the chirping of birds. Jack stirred beside her. He opened his eyes and caught her looking at him.

"Sleep well?" she asked.

"Not really. The mosquito netting gave me claustrophobia." He moved closer. "And what about you?"

"I think someone died in this room."

"You and your premonitions."

She pulled him close and rested her head beside his. "So why do you put up with me?"

"Must be the sex." He kissed her and laughed.

"Can't you ever be serious?" Laura whacked him with a pillow.

Jack sat up. "Speaking seriously. We shouldn't have gone to that creepy cremation. That's the last thing someone like you needed to see."

"The cremation had nothing to do with my strange feeling. I felt it when we first walked in. Besides, I thought the cremation ceremony was beautiful." She turned her head to look at him. "If I die first, I want you to put me in a coconut."

Chapter 2

Jakarta, on the neighboring island of Java, was only an hour-and-twenty-minute flight away. Laura gazed out the airplane window at the blue sky and white cumulus clouds; the reality of her new life began to set in.

"I wonder what our house will be like," she said to Jack, seated beside her. Though she didn't expect a white picket fence or rambling roses, she did hope to meet other women and make friends nearby. "Too bad we never got the photo the bank supposedly sent."

"Yeah, not sure what happened," Jack said.

"And I wish we could have picked the house out ourselves."

"That would have been ideal, but there's a wait list for decent expat housing. We'll be living in the same place the bank leased for the prior president."

"I know. You told me. You said he left the country mysteriously."

"Family problems, I think."

"Seems odd." Laura frowned. Jack had mentioned his predecessor's abrupt departure before, and she considered it strange, yet hadn't really thought more about it until now. Why did the man leave? She hoped it wasn't anything they would encounter.

They landed, disembarked, and made their way through the airport. Laura glanced around at the throngs of people. She still wasn't reconciled to the idea that Indonesia was to be her new home. She didn't know anyone, couldn't speak the language, and wouldn't be able to work.

Outside the terminal vendors hawked curios: primitive wooden carvings, shadow puppet silhouettes, and cheap batiks. Taxi drivers offering services encircled them. An older man standing in the midst of the crowd held a white cardboard sign and black lettering: *PT Bank AmerIndo*. When Jack waved, he came forward.

"*Selamat pagi,* good morning," he said. He bowed his head toward Jack, not looking at Laura, though she stood between them. She smiled, though not pleased at having been ignored. "Haroon, your driver. Please, follow me." He headed off, brushing locals aside to clear a path. His stature, jerky movements, and strut reminded Laura of a bantam rooster.

Their luggage loaded in the shiny black sedan, they departed the busy airport. They sped past green fields and palm trees on either side. As they approached the town, the traffic and cacophony intensified, the streets a maze of moving, weaving obstacles: bicycles, mopeds, pedal rickshaws, and dilapidated buses with people dangling out the windows, holding onto the sides, and riding on top. Haroon maneuvered expertly through it all. This was not Paris or London. And New York's madness had a purpose. Here confusion and disruption reigned.

Laura took Jack's hand.

"You okay?" he asked.

"Fine."

He gave her hand a squeeze.

"I can't imagine driving here," she said.

"You won't have to. You'll have your own driver."

Though being chauffeured sounded appealing, she was more concerned about what she would do with her time. She had read about an American women's auxiliary with classes in bridge, mahjong, watercolor, yoga — the gamut. Bridge was her mother's game, and she couldn't imagine herself playing mahjong, though she knew nothing about it.

They drove through an area of large colonial Dutch houses set behind high walls. She hoped one of them might be theirs. But Haroon continued on.

Eventually they veered onto a red dirt road. Women clad in bright cloths moved gracefully, balancing baskets and sacks on their heads. A water buffalo stood in the muck, raised its horns, and glared. It was like a living *National Geographic*, she thought.

Further on, after about fifteen minutes, the scenery changed to villages and more poverty.

"Are we close?" she asked Haroon.

"Soon, *nyonya*." Laura had read in her Bahasa phrase book that nyonya meant *madam* or *grandmother.* Though a term of respect, it made her feel old. Jack would be a *tuan*, lord and master. He would revel in this exalted role.

Soon Haroon stopped beside a high stucco wall with a green metal gate. He blew the horn, and a diminutive man appeared and pushed aside the heavy barrier to reveal a white bungalow with a veranda across the front and a red tile roof as if from a fairy tale. Bright red and yellow hibiscus bordered a green lawn. A tree shaded the yard, and a bell-shaped wire cage with a parrot hung from a low branch.

"Jack, look!" Laura hurried out of the car. She loved birds. The parrot hung upside down, twisted its head, and peered at her. "Pretty bird."

"*Nuri,* Nuri!" it screeched.

"His name's Nuri. Means 'parrot' in English," Haroon said.

"As-tri-id, As-tri-id," Nuri squawked.

"What's he saying?" Laura asked.

"Nuri thinks you are Astrid, wife of bank president lived here before."

Laura wondered why Astrid hadn't taken her bird with her. Delighted at seeing such a beautiful creature, she dropped her caution and wedged her finger between the wires to stroke him. Nuri bit her, drawing blood.

"Ouch!" Laura grasped her finger. "Naughty boy," she scolded. "But not your fault. I should have known better. How stupid of me to stick my finger in. I'd be mean-tempered too if I had to live in that little cage. I'll get you something bigger." She took tissue from her purse and pressed it to the bleeding gash, thankful she had gotten a tetanus booster before they left.

"Are you okay?" Jack asked.

"I'm fine." She moved quickly up the path, eager to see inside. She expected an airy, open house with bright sunlight, vibrant colors, sleek rattan furniture, and ceiling fans, like something out of a classic Bogart movie — a romantic tropical hideaway where she and Jack could be happy.

But when Haroon opened the door, she stepped into a dark room and the smell of mildew. Green velvet drapes with yellow fringe covered the windows, and an oil painting of a dour knight in armor on a white stallion gazed down from the wall. The furnishings, covered with white sheets, resembled a gathering of ghosts.

"Oh my God!" Laura said, her hand at her mouth. "How awful."

She crossed the room, pulled back the heavy curtains, and lifted the cloths one at a time, dropping them onto the floor. Dust flew. She uncovered a harp, a small stool, and a music stand with a score. She picked up the sheet of music and read the title: "Masque of the Red Death," by André Caplet. She set it back and moved on to other pieces: a marble-top table, a tarnished candelabra, a worn loveseat, a bust of Freud on the bookshelf. She picked up a framed black-and-white photograph of a family: a man, a woman, and two young children, all in dark attire. They stared unsmiling.

Feeling unsettled, she looked to Jack for reassurance.

"The family who lived here before was European," Jack said.

"European gothic, I'd say."

"Room just needs some rearranging," Jack said, though he too looked troubled.

"Seriously."

She moved through the house, hoping to find more cheerful decor, but found instead oversized, gloomy faux-Venetian furnishings. Black dresses and somber suits hung in the bedroom closet. She jumped when a gecko scampered out from under a pillow on the bed, and in the bathroom she opened a drawer and quickly shut it again at the sight of a giant cockroach, dead on its back.

Dismayed, she wandered into the kitchen where a short, plain-faced girl with braids and wearing a white uniform stood waiting, eyes downcast.

"This is Pua," Haroon said. "She is the nanny. There was a cook here too, but another American family hired her before you came."

"Selamat *siang*, nyonya. Good afternoon," Pua said shyly.

Laura greeted her while wondering why there was a leftover nanny in the house.

Pua whispered to Haroon, who asked Laura, "She wants to know when your children will be arriving."

Taken aback, Laura responded. "We don't have children."

"*Belum*," Pua said.

"What's belum?" Laura asked.

"It means 'not yet,'" Haroon said.

Indonesians favored large families. Children were a sign of good luck and security in one's old age, and there was an expectation that women bear children. But Pua's innocent remark caught Laura off guard. She left the kitchen through French doors opening onto the veranda and a lap pool against the back wall. Jack followed.

"Small," was the best Jack could say.

***

Jack went to take a shower, and Laura returned to the kitchen. Pua wasn't there. Laura rummaged through the cabinets, surprised to find them full of staples and even holding a bottle of gin and another of rum.

Outside she picked limes from a tree, found sparkling water in the refrigerator, and made herself a mojito. As she settled in on the terrace, she thought about Manhattan. At her farewell office party, Grace, her boss, told her she was making a mistake. That she had talent and was throwing it away to go live in a tropical backwater. Thinking of that caused Laura to smile. Grace, a survivor in a brutal business, was not one to mince words. But now was not the time for looking back or second-guessing. Though she was in the country on a spousal visa and wouldn't be able to work, she was determined to be something other than the banker's wife.

A sudden shadow came over her, and she startled. Jack stood behind her, drying his hair with a towel. "You look pensive," he said.

"Thinking about New York."

"I'm sorry." He put his hand on her shoulder.

"Please join me."

Jack dragged over a chair. "I know this hasn't turned out the way you expected. Not a great beginning. We'll get rid of the furniture. That might help."

"Don't bother. If Indonesians celebrate Halloween, we'll be ready."

"Glad you can still joke," he said with a grin.

She rested her head on his shoulder. The humor masked her troubled feelings. And it wasn't just the furniture; she sensed something strange had happened in the house. The feeling was similar to what she experienced at the hotel in Bali. It seemed she was being plagued by feelings of death. She decided not to mention it to Jack. It could just be her adjustment to a different culture.

After a while, Laura went in and began to unpack. With the closets full of someone else's belongings, she wondered where to put her things. Discouraged and not keen to tackle the problem just yet, she wandered to the front room, where she saw Jack and Haroon out on the lawn with a man wearing a sleeveless shirt, dark shorts and sandals. Curious, she went to join them.

Haroon introduced him. "Bambang's the *jaga,* the night watchman. He guards the house from seven at night until early morning, but doesn't speak English."

"Selamat siang," Bambang replied, bowing, shaking her hand. He had a broad grin and a gold front tooth. Laura liked him at once. He would be her incentive to learn Bahasa.

Back inside, Laura asked Jack "Why do we need a night guard?"

"Probably to make expats feel more secure."

Laura had read about the coup in 1965, just twenty years earlier. Some five hundred thousand alleged communists were massacred, and expats fled. Though now all seemed calm, Laura worried.

They sat down to dinner, and Pua brought out two large bowls: one steamed rice, the other vegetables swimming in sauce. "*Gado gado,*" the nanny said softly.

"Looks interesting." Laura spooned a piece of potato into her mouth. "Be careful," she said. "It's spicy."

23

"I heard you calm the spice with rice," Jack said.

"Probably why there's such a big bowl of it." Laura quickly dished some onto her plate. "Pua's probably not used to cooking for Westerners with tender palates."

After they finished their dinner, she told Jack she was going to turn in early.

"I'll be in soon," Jack said. "Just want to read through a few things before I begin the new job."

Laura climbed into bed and fluffed the pillow. She swatted at an irritating mosquito buzzing her head. She lay there, wide-eyed in the unfamiliar surroundings.

When Jack had told her about Indonesia, he said it was her decision. Worried about her fragile marriage and the toll taken by their busy careers, she had thought a leisure life in the topics might bring them closer together. She hoped that would happen.

When Jack crawled into bed beside her, she thought about sex and how comforting it would be to have his arms around her. But too tired, she simply rolled over and dozed off.

At dawn, chants and prayers floated in the bedroom window, "*Allahu akbar* . . . Allahu akbar . . . Allahu akbar."

"What's all the noise?" Jack bolted upright.

"The call to prayer. Isn't it beautiful? We must be living next to a mosque."

Jack flopped back down and pulled the bedding over his head.

Closing her eyes, Laura drifted off again. She dreamed she was atop a camel, riding down Fifth Avenue, her tresses blowing in the breeze. She waved to the normally blasé New Yorkers, who gawked and returned her greeting. Jack on foot, followed. She glanced back and saw his disgruntled face. "Smile, Jack," she shouted, relieved to be home. She passed St. Patrick's Cathedral and saw Pua attired in black, standing on the steps. "Belum, belum, belum," came the servant girl's dirge.

Laura attempted to cover her ears. Desperate to get away, she prodded the camel on. Further ahead she sniffed smoke. The dromedary, suddenly engulfed in a cloud of soot, balked and moved sideways. Laura choked, coughed, and tried to hold on. In a panic, she opened her eyes. The smell wasn't a dream.

"Jack, fire!" she cried as she scrambled out of bed.

He tossed back the sheets. Disoriented, he sprang up and ran to slam shut the open window through which smoke billowed into the room.

Together they stared out at a column of gray rising from the other side of the high wall. It rolled toward their house. Laura grabbed her robe and followed Jack outside. In the garden, Bambang, his head on his chest, slept in a chair propped against a tree. Jack's shout startled him, and he bolted from his seat. The trio walked around the corner of the house and stopped outside the bedroom window. They gazed up at the wall looming before them.

Bambang gestured and spoke in rapid Bahasa. Though the smoke had begun to dissipate, they heard the loud, shrill grind of metal against metal and muffled voices on the other side.

"I'm going over there," Jack said, urgency in his voice.

Laura grabbed his arm. "This is not the time for heroics. We don't speak the language, and who knows what's happening. Let's wait for Haroon. He'll be here soon. He can go with us."

Back inside, Jack changed into a business suit and Laura a skirt and blouse. A breeze had blown the haze away, and they sat on the front veranda to wait for Haroon expected in half an hour to drive Jack to his first day at the office.

"Nervous?" she asked.

"A little. The bank's losing money. New York expects me to turn things around."

Laura looked at him, surprised at the hint of concern. Normally he seemed confident, anxious to take on the world.

"I'm sure it'll work out. Tom wouldn't have sent you here if he didn't think you could handle it." Her comment was mostly just to comfort Jack; she disliked Tom, Jack's boss and head of the international department in New York.

Haroon drove up, and they went to greet him. After relating the morning's strange events, the trio headed out the gate. Heading away from the direction they'd come in the day prior, they stayed close to the wall to avoid the ruts in the middle of the road. She wondered if what they were about to find might explain the prior president's abrupt departure.

At the corner of the wall, Laura and Jack stopped and stared out at a sea of shanties — shanties of corrugated metal, wood, cardboard, and discarded materials of every kind.

"It's a *kampung*, a village. Many people live here," Haroon said.

Laura eyes widened. The patchwork roofs of the hovels seemed to extend forever. She realized their walled house was an oasis in the midst of poverty.

At a nearby white domed mosque, a pencil-thin minaret touched the sky, and a loudspeaker pointed toward their bedroom window.

Laura expected Haroon to lead, but Jack plunged ahead, saying, "This way." He headed down an alleyway.

Squawking chickens and children scattered as they wound their way among the hovels and buildings, and women with babies in their arms gazed from doorways. Laura caught a whiff of sewage. Jack, standing out in his double-breasted suit, led them through the squalor.

The path paralleled the wall beside their house, and Laura searched, though unsure what she searched for. Jack stopped beside a corrugated metal structure, where whiffs of smoke curled from a rusted chimney.

Haroon rapped on the doorframe. A woman emerged, and they conversed. With a curious glance at Jack and Laura, she ushered them in.

"Jack?" Laura, her gaze downcast, followed him.

A fire smoldered in the corner hearth and Laura fanned her face against the heat.

"What do they do here?" Jack asked.

"Tahu factory," Haroon said.

Haroon must have noted the quizzical look on Laura's face. "Same like tofu."

Laura saw children asleep in a side room and realized this was also their home. Burlap sacks of pale-yellow soybeans lay beside an antiquated generator. And frayed electrical wires led to a grinder. Jack walked over and peered inside.

Haroon said. "They put soybeans in the funnel at the top, and the machine grinds them into paste. The paste comes out the bottom, and they cook it over there." He pointed to an oil drum bubbling with yellow liquid. Red coals glowed underneath. "After it cooks, they strain it into those trays to cool it, slice it into squares, and take it to the market."

An old man with a white skullcap shuffled in from the back.

"Pak Hajji's family makes the tofu," Haroon said, introducing him. "And he's the *imam,* the head of the mosque."

"Tell him we've got a problem," Jack said, failing to notice the reverence with which Haroon had addressed Pak Hajji. "There's too much noise and smoke early in the morning. We can't sleep. Can he make the tofu later?"

Haroon translated.

Pak Hajji scowled. Haroon translated his grumbled reply: "They must start at dawn so it's fresh at the market."

"I'll pay him for a year's worth. We'd have peace and quiet and he could spend more time at the mosque."

Haroon conversed with Pak Hajji. "He will sell to you for five million rupiah," Haroon said, his face without expression. Laura didn't think Jack's approach had helped the price.

"Five thousand dollars? I'll give him two hundred."

Haroon translated while the imam listened attentively.

"Two thousand, five hundred dollars," the old man replied in English.

Haroon said that the factory supported Pak Hajji's family and many families in the kampung.

"Okay, I get it. Can he make a cover for the generator and grinder to muffle the noise? And something to block the smoke? Here's twenty-five US dollars for supplies. There's another twenty-five if it works." Jack pulled crisp bills from his wallet.

Haroon spoke again with the old man. "He says okay. It will take him two days."

They made their way back up the alleyway. A pretty little barefoot girl squatted against a wall. Laura felt drawn to hug her, to sink into the wonderment of her large, dark eyes.

At the house, she pulled the shutters against the little girl, the squalor. She thought it odd no one had approached begging for money. Nor had anyone appeared sad. To the contrary, she was the one with a heavy heart.

Jack strode by, and she said, "Pak Hajji didn't seem too friendly, did he?"

"He's probably not happy another infidel moved into the neighborhood."

"Or he was offended by your direct approach."

"You're right, Laura. We're not in New York. I'm going to have to slow down, be more diplomatic. I don't want to be another ugly American."

Laura hadn't expected him to be reflective.

"I'm off to the office. Wish me luck." He gave her a hug, and Laura waved as he drove away. Pua appeared and dragged the metal gate into place, locking her in. The parrot squawked in exclamation of her isolation.

Chapter 3

Jack's career depended on turning around the troubled bank. New York would watch his performance. When he entered the office, the attractive, dark-haired receptionist stood and bowed, her hands clasped. "Selamat pagi, tuan," she said. The delicate innocence of a white flower tucked behind her ear contrasted with her tight skirt.

A short, middle-aged man with thick spectacles and a sparse mustache came out to greet him. He introduced himself as Gunadi, the controller. Jack remembered reading that many Indonesians only went by a single name.

"You met Jasmine?" Gunadi asked glancing toward the receptionist.

"I did," Jack replied. The young woman bowed again. Jack smiled, thinking his head office should consider recruiting in Indonesia.

The two men headed down the corridor. A sporadic tic affected Gunadi's left eye; beneath his arm he carried a file bulging with papers. Jack followed the controller to the president's office, a large room with floor-to-ceiling windows that provided a spectacular view of Jakarta.

Jack looked out at the old city with its whitewashed colonial buildings and terra-cotta roofs. The Dutch colonists named the capital Batavia. On attaining independence in the 1940s, the Indonesians changed it to Jakarta. The Dutch carved wide canals that still remained four hundred years later, though most now lay clogged with refuse. The bank building dominated the skyline, and the vast ocean glistened in the distance.

"Beautiful view," Jack said, and Gunadi nodded.

Standing there, staring out, Jack thought of what lay ahead. If he succeeded in Indonesia, he would likely be Tom's successor as head of the international department, entitled to all the trappings and perks that entailed. He would have attained the status and respect he so desired. Jack smiled and turned from the window.

Indonesian artifacts and framed traditional textiles decorated the office walls, and dark polished hardwood floors added elegance. One wall was covered in a dark blue fabric with a geometric design resembling skeletons. Jack wondered what Laura would think of it. "It's all very nice, Gunadi." The controller smiled, then furrowed his brow. "There is something I need to talk to you about." He glanced at the file under his arm, his nervous tic now more apparent. "But first I should show you around." From Gunadi's demeanor, Jack sensed a problem, but he simply followed him out the door and down the hall to a large area with many desks, mostly occupied. The controller introduced Jack to Imee, the credit manager, a short middle-aged brown-skinned woman with much makeup and dangling silver earrings. Jack picked up on the heavy, sweet scent of her perfume. He knew she must be Filipina. His girlfriend at Columbia before he met Laura had also been named Imee, and she hailed from the Philippines. This Imee had a coquettish smile. Her dark eyes sparkled.

"Seems like everything here is going well," Jack said, shaking hands with Imee. "I reviewed the financials before I left New York. Didn't note any problem loans."

Gunadi cleared his throat. Imee raised her brow.

"It can be tough getting audited statements from borrowers," she said. "Mostly we visit the company and go through the books ourselves. We do credit checks and payment history. But I find my own technique the best. I look the borrower in the eye. If they wince, not a good sign."

"I see." With Gunadi's obvious eye twitch, Jack thought the comment odd, though he doubted Imee noticed the irony.

"Even with that, a few slip through. Have you talked to Mr. Harrison about P. T. Plastiks?" Imee asked Gunadi. Now more concerned, Jack suspected the thick file Gunadi carried information that pertained to the credit manager's comment. Information he wasn't sure he wanted to know.

The controller fidgeted. "Not yet."

The two men walked to the accounting area and on through the rest of the bank. Gunadi introduced Jack to the employees as they went. They greeted him with deference.

"What's the market like?" Jack asked Gunadi as they walked back toward the president's office.

"Competitive. Japanese banks are coming into the country and taking all the business. They're offering lower rates. It's hard to compete."

"How can they make money doing that?"

"After they force all the other banks out, they can do whatever they want."

Back in his office, Jack sat behind the large desk. He motioned for Gunadi to take a seat on the other side.

"What is it you want to talk to me about?"

"Last year the bank made a million-dollar loan to P. T. Plastiks in Bandung. They've defaulted. It was in the report I sent to Mr. O'Dowd in New York. Did he show it to you?"

Jack's eyebrows shot up. He wondered why Tom hadn't mentioned the default. He picked up a paper clip from his desk and twisted it. "This was approved locally?"

"Originated here, but approved in New York. P. T. Plastiks borrowed the money to buy injection-molding equipment for an expansion of their business. After six months they stopped making payments. Said they would send the money soon. We got nothing."

"Check's in the mail."

Gunadi clearly didn't understand the reference. "We sent them letters and called many times, but they never responded. The owner is wealthy and the company large. He has the means to pay us. The bank has a lien on the machinery, so we sent a truck and three men to repossess it. When they arrived, guards confronted them at the gate and wouldn't let them in. I telephoned the head of police in Bandung." Gunadi paused and looked like he was gauging Jack's reaction. Jack motioned him to continue.

"With the help of the police, our men got in, but the equipment was gone. Someone sold it and pocketed the money."

"What are our options?" Jack asked.

"We turned the matter over to our law firm, Perkasa & White. Larry White is handling the case himself. He wants to talk to you. He's hoping you can call him this morning. He said it's urgent." Gunadi handed the thick file across the desk.

"I'll call him right away. Anything else?"

"There's a board meeting next week, and I left some papers on your desk to sign," Gunadi said. "And here is the guest list for your welcome reception this evening." He handed Jack several sheets of paper. "About five hundred have been invited. Many important businessmen, bankers and others will be there."

Jack scanned the list of unfamiliar names, impressed by the sheer number.

"I need to buy one of those batik shirts I understand men wear to these events," Jack said as he perused the list.

"On your way home, Haroon can take you to Blok M, a shopping complex. I've also arranged a staff lunch for you later."

"Thanks." Jack rose and shook Gunadi's hand. "I look forward to working with you." Gunadi seemed efficient, and Jack knew he was going to need a competent, loyal local to help him.

When the controller left, Jack asked his secretary, Wati, to get Larry White on the phone. Once they were connected, Jack recognized Larry's English as American. Midwest, he surmised. "How long have you been here?" he asked the attorney.

"Well, I was in the Peace Corps in Malaysia and I married a local girl there. Went to UC San Diego for my law degree, but we couldn't wait to get back to Asia. Perkasa was looking for someone to move here and help with American firms. That was ten years ago. It's worked out perfectly." He paused, and then asked, "Your wife came with you?"

"She did. Laura had to set aside her own career for a bit — wasn't too happy. But she's a trooper."

"That's the problem. It's almost impossible for expat wives to get a work permit."

"She's resourceful. I'm sure she'll find something to do." Jack hoped he was right.

"I know you're busy," Larry said. "I'll try to be brief. Gunadi's told you about the problem over in Bandung?"

"Doesn't sound good," Jack said.

"This is a perfect example of how difficult it is for foreign firms to do business here. The case is scheduled to go to court next week. I got a call from Judge Hartono. He's been assigned the case. He was quite frank. He wants the bank to pay him thirty million rupiah, or thirty thousand dollars, for a favorable ruling."

Jack rose from his chair. "You must be joking," he said, though he knew Larry wouldn't joke about something so serious. "He called you directly and asked for a bribe? Not even a middleman?"

"Judge Hartono is notorious for this kind of crap."

"Tell him we're an American firm. We don't play that game." Jack attempted to maintain his calm, but his voice rose in frustration. "It's obvious the bank should win. Tell the judge to hear the case."

"I'll pass on your message, but things aren't so simple here."

Jack paced. He clenched and unclenched his fists.

Shortly Larry called back. "Jack, I spoke to the judge. He says he'll take twenty five."

Jack shook his head. "Larry, this is not a negotiation. We're not paying him anything."

"Got it. But don't expect quick resolution. These things tend to drag on. We Americans are not a patient people. Living here takes some adjustment."

Cursing under his breath, Jack hung up. He hadn't expected bribery his first day.

Chapter 4

Late afternoon, Laura heard the crunch of gravel in the drive and a door slam. She ran out and greeted Jack with a hug and a kiss. "A day of isolation turned me into a clinging wife," she said, half joking. She realized that here she would be more dependent on Jack. It felt strange. She had never found herself in that position before.

"That bad, huh?" He put his arm around her waist, and they walked inside. "We need to get ready for our welcoming reception," he said. "Over five hundred people have been invited."

"Really," Laura said not expecting so many.

In the bedroom, Jack hung up his jacket while Laura sat on the edge of the bed, her hands clasped in her lap.

"You seem upset," he said.

"This house is unlucky," she said.

He sat beside her. "I'm sorry you had to be here alone all day in this gloomy place. We agreed to get rid of the furniture. Once you redecorate, you'll feel a lot better."

"It's not the furniture, it's the house. I have a premonition something bad is going to happen."

Jack grasped her hand. "Honey, you need to give it more time. The move has been a big adjustment."

"Did you find out any more about what happened to Astrid and her husband?"

"Didn't ask. I'll check tomorrow."

"Tomorrow? We could be dead by then."

"You're sounding hysterical."

"Sensible is the word I'd use. Promise me you'll find out. It all seems so odd."

She got up and went to the vanity. Though she wanted to say more about her premonition, she had to get ready for the reception. She would speak to him about it at another time. "So how was your first day at the office?"

"Not great. The controller seems capable, so that's good. I met with the rest of staff. They're all nice, but the loan officers seem to be a sleepy bunch. Not a lot of hustle. I know the pace here is slower, but I don't see them bringing in a lot of new business."

Laura, busy brushing her hair, paused to reflect on his comment. It seemed she wasn't the only one needing time to adjust.

"Pak Wulundari, a nice man and one of the local directors, stopped by. You'll meet him tonight," Jack continued sitting on the bed while talking. "And then there's a messy loan situation in Bandung. The borrower defaulted, and the bank's suing. We might have to write off a million bucks. The judge asked for money under the table to settle the case. Can you believe it?"

"Jack, please stay away from that sort of thing."

"Don't worry. The bank's lawyer is handling it. Guy by the name of Larry White. I told him to tell the judge we're an American firm; we don't play that game."

"Why don't you report him to the authorities?"

"He *is* the authority."

"Can't people go to jail for bribery?"

"If they get caught."

Laura watched Jack's reflection in the mirror as he stood up and took off his clothes. "Nice bod," she said.

Jack glanced over his shoulder. "No perving." He walked to the bathroom to take a shower.

"Will the judge be at the reception?" Laura called out, still smiling at his retort.

"His name's on the guest list, but I doubt he'll show up after Larry gave him my message. Though Larry did say he has no scruples."

Laura applied mascara to accentuate her green eyes and added blush to her cheeks. She pulled her hair back into a bun and tucked the stray strands behind her ear.

"So what about you? What did you do all day?" Jack called, his cheerful voice competing with the sound of running water.

"Mostly studied Bahasa and read about the country's customs," Laura replied. Tonight at the reception she hoped to meet other women and discover what they did with their time.

Jack came out of the bathroom, a towel wrapped around his waist. Though Laura knew he had been accustomed to wearing a dark suit and tie for formal functions, he put on a long-sleeved, long-waisted, red, blue, and yellow batik shirt imprinted with roosters and dragons, and a pair of light-colored trousers. "Believe it or not, this is what men here wear to receptions," he said. "I picked it up on the way home. Was the most conservative shirt they had in the shop." With his sandy hair and fit physique, he looked like an aging surfer.

"You're one big splash of color, like a walking Jackson Pollock. The judge should have no trouble finding you."

"Hardly amusing." Jack leaned over her shoulder and glanced in the mirror. He chuckled at the bold shirt.

"I've been trying to decide what I should wear," Laura said. She went to the bed where two cocktail dresses lay side by side. Uncertain as to what Indonesian women wore to such events, she couldn't chose between them. She had the feeling the other women would be well dressed, even glamorous. As the new banker's wife, she thought perhaps she should wear pearls and conservative black, but worried black might imply something ominous. And besides, she wanted to stand out.

She selected the stylish pale-green silk Diane von Fürstenberg wrap dress that matched her eyes and showed off her long, slim legs. From her jewelry box, she retrieved an Italian gold necklace and an ivory boar's tusk bracelet — a present from her father, a prominent Wall Street lawyer. She admired his success and they enjoyed a close relationship. It bothered her that he and Jack didn't get along. When she graduated from Parsons School of Design, her father gave her the bracelet. He said it was lucky. Tonight she didn't want to leave anything to chance.

She glanced in the mirror one last time. Confident with her appearance, she strode down the hall and pirouetted into the living room where Jack sat on the couch.

"Wow!" he said. He stood and pulled her toward him. His hands slid down her backside. "Let's forget the reception."

"Careful, don't rumple me." She laughed and backed away.

He handed her a glass of white wine. "We have a few minutes before we need to go." He led her to the sofa and raised his glass in a toast. "Here's to a happy new life." They clinked glasses.

She leaned over and kissed him. "You look so handsome. I'm proud of you."

When he put his arm around her, she recognized the lust building in his eyes. "Let's go before you get distracted," she said with a laugh. After another sip to calm her nerves, she took his hand and they headed for the front door.

Outside Haroon, in a white jacket, white gloves, and pressed black trousers, stood beside the car.

"Selamat *malam*, good evening," he said.

He's so emotionless, Laura thought.

The driver maneuvered through the narrow streets, where food carts with kerosene lanterns cast an eerie glow. Shadows flickered off whitewashed walls and disappeared into the dark recesses of foliage overhead. A chorus of feral dogs bayed in the distance, and the aroma of sweet tuberose wafted through the air. Villagers peered at them as they drove by in their finery. No quaint cottages marked their way. Laura observed only the poor, and it made her uneasy. The people lived their lives on the edge — the edge of the road. There they cooked, ate, slept, loitered, sold goods, or just squatted and observed. She had never been in place like this. The atmosphere seemed charged and unsettled, as if at any minute something strange might happen.

She startled when Jack spoke. "You okay?" he asked. "You're uncharacteristically quiet."

"Just nerves," she replied. It was true that she was worried she would do something offensive to the culture. She didn't mention her underlying feelings of dread.

By contrast, Jack showed no signs of nervousness. He looked confident. She wished her father Richard were there to see him. He was not pleased when she and Jack got engaged. Jack was from a poor family in North Carolina. He expected her to marry someone with a New England heritage. And he didn't hide his displeasure. After a Thanksgiving dinner in Connecticut, her father told Jack he would never be able to provide for Laura in the manner to which she was accustomed. Laura wondered if Jack might be thinking of that as he rode in a chauffeur-driven sedan on his way to a reception honoring him as the new president of PT Bank AmerIndo.

When they pulled up to the portico of the Hotel Kediri ballroom, he said, "We're here. Let's go in and wow the crowd."

Chapter 5

The hotel doorman attired in a red uniform with a high collar and large brass buttons rushed to open the car door. Laura stepped out, dazzled by billboard-sized floral displays with wide ribbons and greetings in gold and silver proclaiming, *Selamat dating,* or *Welcome, Jack and Laura.* She hadn't expected to see her name there too.

They walked through a passage of blossoms and overpowering fragrance into a huge room with crystal chandeliers suspended from high ceilings. Prisms sparkled in the light. Laura detected an air of excitement as waiters in white jackets scurried about making last-minute preparations.

A thin man walked up to greet them.

"Good evening," Jack said. "Laura, this is Pak Wulundari, a director of the bank and our host. We met earlier today."

"I hope you enjoy your time in Indonesia," Pak Wulundari said.

"Thank you, that's very kind. I'm sure I will. Your country is so fascinating."

"Our guests are beginning to arrive," he said. "Let's stand over by the entry so I can introduce you." Her nervousness heightened, Laura followed.

She stood alongside Pak Wulundari and Jack. She shook hands with the guests while trying to catch the unusual names. Jack had been right about the attire of the men. His batik shirt was one of the more conservative. And, as she had anticipated, the Indonesian women did look glamorous in colorful print dresses, some with their hair styled in a traditional bun set with bejeweled stickpins. She was glad she selected something bold and stylish to wear.

Jack worked the line like a politician. He joked, laughed, and appeared at ease, while a cold draft blew over Laura's bare shoulders.

"This is Wibawa and his wife, Ari. Wibawa was an executive with the national oil company," Pak Wulundari said as he introduced the couple.

"That was a long time ago," Wibawa responded modestly.

Wibawa was considerably older than his wife. Ari had almond-shaped eyes, long lashes, and an unrestrained sensuality. Her high prominent cheeks were rouged, and she wore a turquoise sheath with a slit up one side and a diamond-and-emerald necklace with earrings that matched. Laura thought she might be Chinese.

"How lovely you look," Ari said. She gazed at Laura's boar tusk bracelet. "And what interesting jewelry. Did you kill it yourself?"

"As a matter of fact, I did," Laura said taking an instant dislike to the woman. "It was so exciting."

"How brave you are," Ari replied, her eyes dark like black ice.

When Ari and her husband moved on, Laura leaned over and whispered to Jack, "Interesting couple."

"I heard about Wibawa before we left the States. He's filthy rich. He pilfered billions of the country's oil wealth."

"Why didn't they put him in jail?"

"Because he's a friend of the president."

An older man of medium height and slim build approached and introduced himself to Jack as Judge Hartono. "Larry White gave me your message. I am sorry you feel that way," he said.

Jack ignored the comment and introduced the judge to Laura. Laura had expected someone who asked for money under the table to look sinister. Instead, the judge with a creased face and hair graying at the temples, reminded her of her favorite uncle. Still she was shocked he would allude to a bribe with so many people milling about.

"Are you a golfer?" the judge asked Jack.

"I try."

"I am a member of the Tangerang Golf Club," the judge continued, his manner friendly. "It's a beautiful course on the outskirts of Jakarta. I would like to invite you to play next week as my guest. You might even want to consider a membership. A lot of important business is done there."

"Thank you for the invitation," Jack said. "But I just arrived. Doubt if I will be able to break away for a day of golf any time soon."

"I think you will find it worth your while," the judge said. He turned to Laura. "I hope you enjoy your stay in Indonesia, Mrs. Harrison." He walked off into the crowd.

The ballroom vibrated with laughter, competing conversations, and music long since ignored. "Most of the guests have arrived," Pak Wulundari said. "Why don't you go and enjoy the party."

"Let's split up," Jack suggested to Laura. "We can meet more people."

"Sure," she said.

Jack walked away, and she regretted her hasty reply. Left to fend for herself in a room of strangers, she sought refuge at the buffet, where others gathered. A large ice sculpture in the shape of a mythical bird dominated the long table. Its glistening translucent wings extended over an array of exotic foods: chicken satays, *nasi goring*, giant prawns with a spicy-looking red sauce, and a pyramid of colorful tropical fruit. Guests busily helped themselves, while Laura sampled a few delicacies but didn't take a plate. She looked around and spotted a Western woman in a loose-fitting royal blue caftan standing alone. A mass of yellow curls framed her cherubic face. Laura suspected she might be American and walked over.

"I'm Doreen," the woman said. "We skipped the receiving line. It was long, and I was dying for a drink. Hope you don't mind. I know it's rude, but it's a small expat community here and I knew we'd meet tonight somehow."

"That's quite all right," Laura said, happy to have someone to talk to. Doreen had a distinct drawl — Texas or Oklahoma. Laura suspected she was older than she looked. She envied the way large women could expand into their wrinkles and postpone the ravages of time.

"When I saw you standing over there, I told my Billy you looked like a free spirit," Doreen said. "I told him you should do just fine here."

"Well, thanks," Laura said. She took the remark as a compliment, though wondered what Doreen meant. "Have you lived here long?"

"Long enough, honey," Doreen said. She rattled the ice cubes in her empty glass. Bracelets circled her wrists and clanked as she raised her arm to signal the waiter. "But I can't complain. It's certainly better than Saudi Arabia. That was our first overseas post. Billy's in the oil business. In Saudi Arabia they treat women like dirt. Lucky for us we lived in a compound. We had a grocery store, baseball, sidewalks, ice cream, everything — just like Texas."

"Well, that must have been nice"

"It was okay until once I forgot to cover my arms when I went into town with some other women. The religious police whacked me with a reed. I didn't dare tell Billy about it." Doreen's eyes got big and her facial expressions were exaggerated as she relived her story. "He would have been furious. No tellin' what would have happened."

"Aren't most Indonesians Muslim too?"

"Not the same. They're not so fanatic. They respect all religions. And women." The waiter brought Doreen another drink and she inhaled it as if stranded in a desert. Laura watched the uplifted glass drain and thought perhaps she had stumbled onto the expat woman's secret to survival. She glanced over Doreen's shoulder and spotted Jack huddled in the corner, talking with Ari.

"Doreen, I'd better go rescue my husband. I see him over there. Would you excuse me?"

"No problem. The husbands here go gaga over Asian women. But not my Billy. I keep him happy."

"Thanks for the warning."

"Maybe y'all can come over for a barbeque when you get settled. I'll give you my phone number. Call me if you need anything." Doreen rummaged through her purse, pulled out a piece of paper and a pen, and scribbled her information.

"That's very kind," Laura said and walked away marveling at Doreen's capacity for drink and liking her down-home manner.

Jack and Ari didn't notice Laura approach. "Excuse me, hope I'm not interrupting," she said.

"Not at all," Ari replied. "I was just complimenting Jack on his batik shirt. He looks *soo* Indonesian!"

"Really!" Laura glanced at Jack's blue eyes and sandy hair.

"So, have you settled in?" Ari asked.

"We have," Laura said, not about to divulge her woes to this woman.

Ari retrieved a red card from her silver purse and handed it to Laura. "Call me sometime. We can have tea and go shopping, though there's really not much to buy here. I go to Hong Kong or Singapore for clothes."

Laura glanced at the gold embossed dragon splayed across the top of the card.

"I was born in China in the year of the dragon," Ari said.

Laura's superstitions extended to astrology and the Chinese zodiac. She recalled dragons as being ambitious and dominant. Ready to move on, Laura pleaded hunger. She and Jack excused themselves and wandered over to the buffet.

"I'm hoping you and Ari might become friends," Jack said. "Her husband is one of the most powerful men in the country. I hope to do business with him."

"I suggest you chat with him directly."

"You know what I mean."

Beginning to relax, Laura took a plate and selected a few chicken satays and prawns with red chili sauce.

A tall American man with heavily gelled dark hair approached and greeted them, introducing himself as Larry White, the lawyer. He apologized for being late.

"It was all my fault," said Cindi, his Malaysian wife. "I was playing tennis with my girlfriends, and the match went into overtime. I couldn't leave without a tiebreaker. I hope you'll forgive me."

"Did you win?" Laura asked. She held a skewer, sampling a morsel of satay.

"Of course. I practice a lot. And what about you? Do you play?"

"I'm afraid I don't." Laura finished the satay, picked up a prawn, and dipped it in chili sauce. She took a bite. Overcome by the spice, she choked. Her eyes watered.

"Are you all right?" Jack asked. Laura struggled and her plate tilted. Red blobs dripped onto her dress.

"Oh shit," she muttered under her breath. She set the dish aside, grabbed a napkin and began to rub. The stain spread.

"Sorry," Jack said, glancing at Larry and Cindi. The couple stood transfixed, his mouth agape, her eyes wide, as if they were watching a vaudeville act gone awry. Jack snatched more napkins from the table and handed them to Laura.

"Excuse me," she said. She took them and rushed for the ladies' room.

Inside and relieved to be away from the crowd, Laura leaned against the wall and took a deep breath. Then she spotted Ari standing at a mirror applying lipstick. Laura attempted to take refuge in an empty stall, but Ari spun around and stopped her in her tracks. "Is that blood?"

"Just shrimp sauce."

"What an awful thing to happen. And at your welcoming reception," Ari said. "Those waiters can be so clumsy."

"Unfortunately I spilled it myself."

"Well, I hope you didn't ruin your pretty party dress. That's why I never eat at these events."

Laura went to the washbasin, turned on the tap, wet a paper towel, and blotted the stained fabric.

"Should I find Jack and let him know you're in here?"

"Thank you, but he already knows." Laura wished the woman would leave.

"Well, don't let it upset you. Wouldn't want you to end up like poor Astrid."

Laura stopped what she was doing and glanced up. "What happened to her?" She remembered the photo of the unsmiling family, the harp, and the black dresses in the closet.

"Oh, don't you know? One night when her husband was working late, she slashed her wrist, staggered out to the pool, and fell in. When he came home, he found her floating face down."

Listening to Ari, Laura recalled the macabre sheet music on the stand beside Astrid's harp.

"It was obvious she didn't want to be here," Ari said. "She wanted to go back to Europe, be closer to her children at boarding school. Her husband flew with the body to Austria. They buried her there. He never came back."

"Oh, my God, Didn't she have any friends? Didn't anyone try to help her?"

"It's tough for expat women here. Not much to do. Some become alcoholics, others have affairs, and others leave and go home. Those who do the best have young children. They get nannies and relax. Do you have kids?"

Laura shook her head.

"I wouldn't worry. You have such a sense of humor. You'll do okay." She turned and drifted toward the door.

Laura continued trying to eradicate the stain on the front of her dress. Exasperated and preoccupied with thoughts of Astrid, she gave up. She placed her purse to conceal the obvious and went to find Jack. She searched the crowd and felt uneasy as the eyes tracked her. She spotted him talking to Wibawa.

"Sorry to interrupt," she said. "Jack, can we speak for a minute?" He nodded to Wibawa and excused himself.

"I need to go home and change. I'll have Haroon take me, Please stay. I'll be back as soon as I can."

"Laura, you can't just take off in the middle of the party. We're the guests of honor."

She moved her purse aside to display the large, wet stained spot.

He grimaced. "What a mess."

"Sympathy would be nice."

"Sorry, honey. You're right. Changing is a good idea."

Laura left him and maneuvered her way through the crowd and out the main ballroom door. Alone on the portico, she stood beside a floral wreath with a banner that proclaimed, *Welcome, Jack and*

Laura. She wondered if there had been a banner for Astrid and her husband. And she wondered if her premonition about the house pertained to Astrid's suicide.

Haroon pulled up to the curb and hopped out to open the car door.

"Tuan?" he asked as she climbed in.

"Still here. I'm going home to change. I spilled something on my dress."

At the house Bambang opened the gate and Haroon drove through. Laura got out and stood there for a moment. Previously, the abode had resembled a quaint cottage. Now, knowing what happened to Astrid, it appeared dark and menacing. She rushed inside and changed quickly. Before leaving she stopped at the edge of the pool and looked down into the still water. She pictured Astrid floating in a sea of blood. In the living room, she picked up the haunting sheet music from the stand. She shuddered and quickly stuck it in a drawer.

Laura returned to the ballroom in a black dress more reflective of her somber mood. She no longer cared if there were a bad connotation associated with the color. Besides, what other disaster could possibly befall her in one evening? She also replaced the boar tusk bracelet with pearls. She wondered where her father got the idea the tusk brought luck. She strode in, shoulders back and head high. She hoped she appeared self-assured and didn't betray the butterflies that fluttered within. She worried not that others might notice she had on a different dress but that they would notice she had been away so long.

She cringed when she spotted Ari headed her way.

"Oh, you're back. And you have on another outfit — black," Ari said. Her eyes wandered from hem to shoulder. "So sensible! If you spill something, no one will notice."

"Who knows what might happen next," Laura said. "I have extra outfits in the car just in case."

"Oh, Laurie, you're so admirable. After what you did, you can still joke."

"Actually, it's Laura."

"I'm sorry," With her hand at her mouth, Ari feigned embarrassment. "I thought Americans liked nicknames."

"Perhaps when we get to know each other better. Then you can be Ava and I'll be Laurie."

Ari laughed. "You're such fun. I can tell we're going to be friends."

I wouldn't count on it. She glanced around for Jack and saw him with a group of men near the bar.

"Excuse me, Ari. I want to let Jack know I'm back."

Laura walked off and as she wended her way, an Indonesian woman stopped her. "Are you all right?" the woman asked. "I saw what happened. You've changed your attire so quickly and unobtrusively."

"I'm fine," Laura said, startled, her mind not in the moment. "Thank you for asking and noticing."

The attractive woman, a bit younger than Laura, was taller than most other Indonesians in the room. Laura was just under six feet in heels. She and the woman were about the same height. "I'm glad. Others might not have handled it so well. I'm Sarinah, by the way," she said, her English unaccented.

Laura relaxed, thinking her earlier profane outburst must have gone unnoticed. Or perhaps Sarinah had heard and hadn't given it a second thought. Laura remembered seeing her pass through the receiving line with a handsome Caucasian man.

"We have something in common," Sarinah said. "We're both attracted to bankers. My fiancé Harold is the representative for The Royal Bank of Canada in Jakarta." *She's so gracious.* "Do you have a career?" Laura asked.

"I studied child development and education. I'm hoping to start a literacy program for children in the kampungs, but I haven't been able to find a suitable place."

Laura recalled the pretty little girl sitting beside the pathway in the village. How wonderful it would be if she had access to a program like Sarinah's. "Good for you," Laura said, impressed by Sarinah's desire to help others.

"And what about you?" Sarinah asked.

"I was a fashion designer in New York."

"How exciting." Sarinah's eyes sparkled. "But what are you going to do here? It's impossible for expat wives to work."

Laura winced.

"I'm sorry. There are other things to do. You just need to know where to look. With your interest in fashion, you should check out the Museum Tekstil. The old batiks are beautiful. You might get some ideas."

Laura perked up. She had read about the museum and wanted to go there.

"I'll give you my card," Sarinah said. "Give me a call. I would be happy to go with you."

How perfect. Laura took Sarinah's card, excused herself, and went to meet Jack.

"You're back," he said. "Everything okay?"

"Fine."

He didn't comment on her different dress. "A glass of wine?" he asked. "You probably need it."

She sighed. "That would be nice."

He signaled a waiter with a tray of glasses, took a white wine, and handed it to her. He grabbed a red for himself.

"Sorry I missed so much of the party."

"Accidents happen. From now on, skip the shrimp and the sauce."

"Jack, did you know about Astrid?"

"Who's Astrid?"

"Your predecessor's wife. She drowned in the pool at our house, apparently a suicide."

"What? You're kidding."

"Why didn't you tell me?"

"Because I didn't know."

Laura studied Jack's face. She wondered if he intentionally hadn't mentioned Astrid, concerned she wouldn't come with him if she had known. From his expression she couldn't be sure.

"Maybe her husband wants all their things that are still in the house," she said.

"I'll check with New York."

They mingled with the guests until most had left, then went to thank Pak Wulundari for hosting the reception. Laura hoped he hadn't observed the spicy sauce disaster and her absence. Jet-lagged and exhausted from all of the stress since their arrival just two days ago, she was ready to go back to the house she now feared. Outside, Haroon waited with the car.

They drove away and Jack took her hand. "Nice event, don't you think?"

"Very. Indonesians are so gracious. And I made a few friends. Sarina — she's very nice, and her fiancé is a banker. She's going to take me to the textile museum. And Doreen from Texas. She's nice too, though I suspect she has a drinking problem." Laura leaned her head on his shoulder.

"What about Ari?" Jack asked.

"The dragon lady? You can't be serious." Laura glanced up at him.

"Your friendship with her could lead to lots of business for the bank."

"You're on your own there."

For a while they rode in silence. Jack gazed out the window until Laura spoke.

"I hope you're not considering playing golf with the judge."

"Actually I wasn't going to originally, but now I think I might."

Laura clutched his arm. "Leave the problem to Larry White. He's the lawyer."

"Larry's been here too long. He thinks like a local. I want to meet Judge Hartono myself."

"Jack, you can't just come riding in on your white horse and expect to change a culture overnight."

"I'm not talking about changing a culture. I'm talking about one man. I need to know what I'm up against.

Chapter 6

Aroused by the noise of the tofu factory, Laura got up and went to the living room. She stood beside the harp and plucked a few strings with her fingers. She imagined Astrid playing the mournful song about death before she slashed her wrist. She wished she had known her; perhaps the woman just needed a friend.

At the edge of the pool she pondered what might have been going through Astrid's mind. She couldn't comprehend how her life could have become so intolerable she would forsake her husband and her children. Laura shivered, not from the morning breeze.

Later, she joined Jack for a breakfast of papaya, pineapple, mango, and toast. As he sipped Sumatran coffee, she watched him, trying to decipher his mood, though it hardly mattered. She intended to talk to him in any event. "We need to move to another house," she said. "It's depressing here, plus the noise from the tofu operation is worse. And I still have this premonition."

Jack set his cup of coffee on the table. "I can't blame you for being depressed. I'm sorry." She knew he meant well, though she wished he would stop saying he was sorry all the time.

"I can't stop thinking about poor Astrid. But she's not the reason. It's something else. I felt the house was unlucky even before I knew about her." She paused and glanced away. "Something bad is going to happen."

Jack frowned. Throughout their marriage, he never felt comfortable with Laura's strange beliefs and superstitions.

"Since arriving in Indonesia, I've noticed my feelings more attuned, closer to the surface. And we should have had a chance to select our own place, not be forced to live in someone else's mistake. Talk to Tom back in New York. Get us out of here."

Jack about to object, said "I don't know if —" But then he nodded. "We shouldn't have to live where someone took their life." He rose from the table. "I'll phone Tom once I get to work."

***

At the office Jack called New York, and was told that Tom was on the other line. He listened to Muzak until Tom's voice boomed and echoed through his speaker box. "Jack, good morning, or whatever it is there. You and Laura settled in okay?"

"We're fine. Pak Wulundari had quite the welcoming reception for us. Most of Jakarta showed up. And I made some important business contacts."

"That's great, Jack. I knew you were the right guy for the job."

"Thanks for the confidence." Emboldened by the praise, Jack went straight to the topic. "You know the house the bank rented for us? Laura's not happy there. We need to find another place."

Silence followed. Jack pictured Tom leaning back in his chair, his feet propped up on the desk.

"It's important to keep the wives in good spirits," Tom eventually replied. "Look at what happened to poor Astrid. Course, she had problems before she got there. Laura's not like that. And didn't we already pay for the lease on that place? Have her give it more time. She's not acclimated yet, strange culture and all."

"Why didn't you tell me about Astrid before we came here?" Jack said, his tone no longer cordial.

"I thought you knew."

"I didn't. And it's not my problem the bank committed to a three-year lease. You can't expect us to live in a house where someone committed suicide."

"It happened in the house? I didn't realize that. No wonder Laura wants to move."

"And there's a mosque next door," Jack added. "The call to prayer wakes us early in the morning." Jack had been reluctant to use the xenophobic trump card, but he tossed it in anyway. Tom from Indiana was parochial in his thinking. Jack couldn't understand why he had been appointed to head up the international department.

"You're living next to a mosque?" Tom asked, his voice rising. "Why didn't you say so? Look what happened in Iran five years ago. Those crazies held Americans hostage for over four hundred

51

days, and jackass Carter screwed up getting 'em out. Fortunately, Reagan's in the White House now. He's a no-nonsense guy. But I still wouldn't want to take any chances. Do what you have to do."

Though Jack had gotten what he wanted, he suspected Tom had known about Astrid taking her life in the house and chosen not to say anything. He meant to ask Tom about the bad loan in Bandung and why he hadn't alerted him to the judge's request for money under the table. But Tom had already hung up.

Jack called Laura to share the good news.

"Honey, I got the okay. Find us another place to live."

"Wonderful! I may have to change my opinion of Tom. Maybe he's not just another coldhearted banker after all," she said with a laugh. "What did you tell him?"

"You mean did I tell him about my kooky wife and the tofu-maker? No way!"

***

Laura searched for Doreen's phone number, thinking she might have some idea as to how an expat went about finding a suitable place to live.

"Why, sugar, I was hopin' you'd call me. Billy and I had such a good time at y'alls reception," Doreen said. "I looked for you before we left. Someone told me you went home early. You okay?"

"I'm fine. I spilled shrimp sauce on my dress and had to go change."

"Well now, that's a shame. But hardly worth frettin' over."

My sentiments exactly.

"So, are you interested in goin' to the auxiliary and checkin' out classes? Might find somethin' you like."

"Thanks, but right now I need help locating a house. The one the bank rented isn't working out. Do you happen to know a real estate agent?"

"With expats, it's word of mouth. But I do know of a place that'll be available soon. Has a large garden, swimming pool, and tennis court," Doreen said. "You'll love it. Helen, the wife, is already back in Houston, but Hugh's still around. I can give him a call."

"Sounds expensive. I don't know how much of an allowance the bank gives us for housing. I'll have to ask Jack. But I'd like to see it — today if possible."

Jack came home early and joined Laura. Haroon drove them through narrow streets where red and purple bougainvillea cascaded over high walls. Eventually they stopped in front of a metal gate and an enclosure with jagged multicolored glass shards imbedded along the top. To Laura it resembled a penitentiary, hardly the image Doreen had portrayed. Haroon tooted the horn, and a small man in worn orange overalls, wet with perspiration, swung open the gate and they drove in. Laura glanced around, disappointed. The house looked simple, nothing special.

A grinning, heavyset fellow with an Australian accent came out and introduced himself as Hugh.

"Doreen told me you were American," Laura said. "Not that it matters."

"My wife's American. She's from Texas," Hugh replied. "Doreen lumps us English speakers together. To her we're all American. Come, let me show you around. This is a super place. I hate to leave it."

Hugh's job was being taken over by an Indonesian. That was the trend and to be expected, particularly in the oil services business. Once locals acquired the requisite skills from expats, they would be in charge.

Jack and Laura followed Hugh up the walkway and through an unimposing front door. The plain façade masked the scene inside. A rock-rimmed pond dominated the foyer. Gold and black koi swam lazily beneath lily pads and white lotus flowers. Across the back of the huge high-ceilinged room, sliding glass doors opened to a tropical garden. The cool green blended in as if it were a natural extension of the house. The architecture, quiet and serene, stunning in its simplicity, reminded Laura of a Frank Lloyd Wright design. She loved it already.

"The bedroom wing's over there," Hugh said. He pointed to stairs that led to the second level. "There are four bedrooms upstairs, a couple more below. Plenty of room for guests."

Laura looked around comparing the big house to their small apartment in New York.

"I'll show you the garden first." With a rolling gait Hugh led them across the room. "That's the best part." He had the laid back, gregarious manner, typical of many Australians. "How're you enjoying Jakarta?" he asked.

"We haven't been here that long," Jack said.

"It takes a while. In fact, my wife Helen never got used to it. She missed her friends and family back home."

Another homesick expat wife, Laura thought.

Helen, more distraught than most, had apparently threatened Hugh with divorce if he didn't take her home to Houston. Hugh said he didn't want to leave and had considered staying behind and trying to find a different job. He liked Indonesia and his work in the oil fields. He finally gave in, and now he said he was worried he might not adjust to his new job shuffling papers.

Vines hung from a banyan tree. Its thick canopy shaded a stone terrace and flowering orchid plants clung to the massive trunk. The air felt fresh and clean, and Laura inhaled a sweet fragrance she didn't recognize. Climbers formed a thick green mat across the garden wall, and palm trees laden with coconuts sheltered a thatched-roof cabana beside a large pool.

It's so beautiful, Laura thought. Nearby, a tethered owl glared from a perch. The bird swiveled its head and stared through luminous gold eyes. Hugh said that he and Helen bought him at the bird market. They thought the owl looked ill, and afraid he might die, they brought him home. Laura, tempted to stroke the bird's tawny feathers, remembered the parrot bite and decided otherwise.

"His name's Hantu, the Indonesian word for owl. It means ghost, perhaps because owls fly silently through the night. Like spirits, you don't see them, but you know they're there. When we first moved here, I didn't pay much attention to Indonesian superstitions, but now I respect them. After a while you will too."

"I already do," Laura said.

Hugh pointed to a small tree near the pool. Gnarled branches extended outward, and small white flowers grew at the tips.

"That's a white frangipani. Normally you only see them in graveyards. The gardener won't go near it."

"So why's it there?" Laura asked, puzzled.

"I have no idea, but I doubt if anyone's buried underneath," Hugh said with a chuckle. "Probably some expat planted it long ago, not realizing the implication. Anyway, I never observed anything weird."

Looking uneasy with talk of ghosts and spirits, Jack fidgeted. "I understand there's a tennis court?"

"Behind that row of banana plants." Hugh pointed to the far corner. "It's not exactly Wimbledon, but playable. I'll take you there in a minute, but first let me introduce you to Diablo and the servants." They walked out through a partially obscured side gate to a wire-enclosed pen. A large black dog bounded over, barked, and jumped up on the enclosure.

Though Laura loved animals, she backed off. "What kind of dog is he? Looks like a German shepherd — but all black."

"A Belgian shepherd. Looks ferocious but very loyal after he gets to know you. The servants bring him inside at night. He wanders the lower floor while we sleep upstairs. With him around we don't have to worry about intruders."

"I can see why," Laura said, reluctant to get near.

"Actually Diablo's partial to women. Come," Hugh said. He took Laura's arm and led her closer to the pen. His touch made her tingle.

Diablo's bark turned to a whimper and he wagged his tail.

"Our new place in Houston doesn't have a yard, so we need to find him a good home. I hope the new tenants will take him."

Laura sensed Hugh's fondness for Diablo. She couldn't imagine having to give away a beloved pet. She felt sorry for them both.

They wandered around the side of the house to servants' quarters with two cubicles and cots. Laura spotted a hole in the cement floor and footpads on either side, obviously the latrine.

"The cook and maid live here," Hugh said.

Though the conditions might seem primitive to a Westerner, they were better than the way poor Indonesians lived. In the main house there would be modern plumbing, though straddling a hole in the floor in Indonesia was not uncommon.

Hugh opened the screen door and led them into a large kitchen and the pungent aroma of spices.

"This is Kartini and her niece, Maya," Hugh said. He introduced the barefoot women in crisp white uniforms. Kartini, busy chopping green vegetables on a butcher-block counter, had a soft, kind face; her hair was streaked with gray. She set the knife aside and dried her hands on her apron. "Selamat siang, good afternoon," she said.

"Selamat siang," Laura replied, having gained confidence with the basics of the language.

Maya stood on the other side of the kitchen. She walked across the room to greet them, her moves exaggerated. Her long, dark hair gleamed and her black eyes shown like agate. She greeted them in a low voice.

Laura shook Maya's hand, thinking she didn't look or act like a servant.

"Kartini's the best cook in Jakarta," Hugh said. "Her specialty's lime chicken. She's worked for expats for over twenty years. Knows how to tone down spicy Indonesian food for the Western palate." Laura smiled, remembering Pua's spicy gado-gado and the shrimp sauce on the front of her dress.

They left the kitchen and walked back into the main part of the residence. "What will happen to the servants when you leave?" Laura asked.

"They're available. If you want the house, I encourage you to keep them. Maya does the cleaning and the laundry. She gets thirty dollars a month, and Kartini fifty-five. Helen says Maya's lazy. She had to keep after her. But the two are a pair, so Helen put up with her. And there's also the gardener, Suparno. He's a hardworking little guy."

"The man who opened the gate?" Laura asked.

"I call him the Zen-sweeper. He sweeps as if in a trance. Unfortunately, he's a mute. Can't talk."

"Poor guy. How do you communicate?"

"Don't need to. He knows what to do. He has a sixth sense. He's there before the leaves fall."

"And what about the jaga, the night guard?"

"Don't recommend him. Spends most of his time sleeping."

"Sounds familiar," Jack said. "And the rent?"

"Three thousand, two hundred dollars a month," Hugh said. He walked on ahead.

Jack pulled Laura aside. "Our housing allowance is three thousand. We can cover the difference," he whispered.

"When's it available?" Laura asked Hugh. Taken by his Australian accent, she liked to hear him speak.

"In about two weeks."

"Any chance of moving in sooner?" Laura inquired, desperate to leave the other place.

"Sounds like you're in a rush."

Laura told him about the house, Astrid, and her premonition.

"You're living in Astrid's house?" he asked, surprised. "That was a shock what happened to her. So sad. Life here isn't for everyone. I can understand why you want to move out of there. I'll do my best to wrap things up."

Laura watched Jack as he glanced around, clearly admiring the surroundings. She knew this was the lifestyle he had had in mind when he agreed to come to Indonesia. It was suitable for the president of a bank. His ambition was rooted in his childhood. His Southern ancestors had been wealthy cotton brokers until someone discovered polyester. The money vanished; pride remained.

Hugh walked with Jack to the tennis court while Laura settled into a rattan chair on the terrace. She thought how peaceful it would be living here. From out of the corner of her eye, she spotted Maya strolling along the pathway, Diablo at her side. The servant girl had changed from her white uniform into a bright-yellow dress. To Laura, she resembled a nymph.

Jack and Hugh returned and interrupted her thoughts.

"It's a deal," Jack said. "The house, the servants, the dog — all ours."

Chapter 7

Laura, having never felt comfortable in Astrid's house, had unpacked only a few things. She looked around at the woman's personal effects still there. She doubted Astrid's husband would want them. Too many awful memories. She pictured everything being consumed by the tropics: the harp rusting, mildew on the black dresses, mice chewing the musical scores. Laura shuddered. Astrid deserved better.

When the phone rang, Laura picked up. It was Hugh saying he was finished with the transition early and would be leaving for Houston in a few days. Overjoyed, Laura informed Jack as soon as he got home.

"But Wati, my secretary, set it up with the movers for next week."

"Jack, we need to get out of here." Laura knew she sounded desperate. Haunted by nightmares, she had been unable to sleep. Once she thought she heard Astrid at the harp, and on another occasion, cries for help resonated from the pool. That night, she got up and crept outside, but all she saw was the reflection of the moon on dark water.

"Okay, if you want to move sooner, call Wati. Just let me know when you're ready so I can meet you there with my toothbrush."

She wasn't in the mood for joking. "Fine, I'll call her in the morning."

"What about Pua? We have more servants at the new place than we know what to do with."

"Doreen found her a nanny job with a British family."

***

A few days later Jack and Laura sat in the vast dining room of their new home at a long table with ten empty chairs. Unopened cardboard boxes lay scattered about, most filled with books Laura brought from New York.

Jack, oblivious to the emptiness and the boxes, glanced around. "Beautiful!" he said. His arms outstretched, he directed his gaze toward the lush garden.

"I feel bad for Hugh. I could tell he didn't want to leave," Laura said. "He seemed so at home here. I hope things work out for him in Houston."

"The weather's the same, hot and humid. Why the concern about Hugh?"

"Must have been taken by his accent," she said, her smile mischievous.

"He's got a beer gut." Jack passed his hand over his own flat mid-section.

Laura laughed. "Don't tell me you're jealous."

"Why would I be jealous of an accent?"

"I wouldn't worry, you're still my love." Laura kissed him on the cheek and went out to the garden. She smiled as she walked around, reflecting on the light-hearted banter. With their careers and busy schedules there had been little time for that in New York. She picked a yellow hibiscus and put it behind her ear. "The room needed some color," she said as she walked back in. "And me too."

Maya entered balancing a large white porcelain platter of steaming food. Unfamiliar yet pleasant aromas wafted through the room. Maya set the dish on the table and Laura thanked her. The servant girl nodded, her sullen expression unchanged.

Laura spooned food onto a plate, picked up her fork, and took a bite. "Delicious. Try it, Jack. Must be Kartini's famous lime chicken." A cook in the kitchen was a new experience for Laura.

"Wonderful, I could eat this every day."

"I have a feeling Kartini has a repertoire of delicacies," Laura liked Kartini; she just wished her niece Maya wasn't so haughty — or pretty.

After dinner, they retired to the master bedroom upstairs. Laura climbed into bed, and Jack nestled beside her. He nuzzled her neck and caressed her face. She turned to him, kissed him lightly on the lips and said, "I'm bushed. Let's wait till tomorrow, okay?"

"How about a rehearsal?" he grinned. He ran his finger along her cheek.

She reached and took his hand. "I'm easy." She lifted her extra-large sleeping T-shirt with *I Luv NY* emblazoned across the front and tossed it onto the floor. She snuggled in close. His hand moved over her breast, and she kissed him, gently at first, then with passion. He pressed against her leg, and she could feel him. His fingers stroked her stomach, her hips, her thighs. She moaned. She so wanted this to be good for him too. She grasped his shoulders and pulled him to her. He raised his head. He grimaced and tensed. She cried out and held him tight, their bodies bathed in the sweet sweat of making love. Exhausted, yet fulfilled and happy, she wished they could lie together forever.

After a while, Jack rolled over and fell asleep. Laura spooned in beside him. She kissed him on the shoulder. This was the passionate lovemaking she yearned for when she gambled her career to follow him here. Perhaps things might work out after all.

Content, she drifted off.

***

She hadn't been asleep long when a loud sound awoke her, not by a call to prayer, but an explosion in the distance.

"What the hell?" Jack said. He sat up and rubbed his eyes.

"Probably fireworks." Laura's tone was more hopeful than convincing.

In the dark they lay still. When the house shook, rocked by an explosion louder than before, they jumped from the bed. Laura slipped on her robe and Jack grabbed his boxer shorts off the floor. They hurried out onto the balcony where flares traced through the night sky. Sirens wailed and an acrid smell of gunpowder filled the air. Lights in the garden flickered and the electricity failed, throwing the house and surrounding area into darkness, the only illumination a surreal glow across the horizon.

"Maybe it's a coup," Laura said, her hand at her throat.

"I doubt it. The president rules with an iron fist. Only the military would attempt a coup, and he's one of them. He rewards his generals for their loyalty."

Laura wasn't convinced. The coup and massacre that brought the president to power wasn't that long ago. Murderers, edged on by government special forces, had never been brought to trial for their atrocities. Many still roamed the country.

Jack picked up the phone. "Dead," he said. The lights blinked on, then off in a tease. "I don't suppose we have candles."

"We're better off in the dark," Laura whispered. She imagined frenzied servants mounting the stairs. Though they seemed polite and docile, they owed her no allegiance. She preferred to remain unnoticed in the shadows.

"I'm going downstairs," Jack said.

"Why?"

"I feel helpless sitting here doing nothing. I want to find out what's happening."

Laura followed.

They groped their way down the hall toward the stairwell. They saw Diablo below at the same instant Diablo saw them. The black dog lunged forward and charged the stairs. They fell back and quickly retraced their steps to the bedroom.

"The dog doesn't know us. He thinks we're burglars," Jack said. "We're trapped in our own house." Again he tried the phone. "Damn, still dead. But who would we call anyway? We don't know anyone."

Laura considered herself capable of handling anything, but she had never been tested in such strange and ominous surroundings.

"We can't just stay holed up here," Jack said.

He went out onto the balcony, lifted himself over the railing, and grabbed onto a tree branch and climbed down.

"Watch out for Diablo." Watching him, Laura tensed; she expected the dog to bolt out of the house.

"It's okay. I see him inside." Jack dropped to the ground and crept across the terrace. Laura spotted a figure moving in the shadows. About to shout a warning, she recognized Bambang, the night guard brought with them from the previous place.

"What going on?" Jack asked. He pointed up at the sky.

The jaga, his eyes big, spoke rapidly. Laura thought she heard the word *bomb* interspersed with his Bahasa. The two men walked around the side to the front of the house. When he returned, Jack climbed back onto the balcony.

"The street's deserted," he said.

"I thought I heard Bambang say something about a bomb."

"I didn't hear that." Jack sounded annoyed.

"Maybe we should go to the U.S, Embassy. We'll be safe there," Laura said. Her hand at her heart, she was convinced she'd heard the word "bomb."

As if someone threw a switch, the explosions ceased, and everything became eerily quiet.

"Odd," Jack said.

They returned to bed, though Laura dared not sleep. Certain there had been a coup she thought they should make their way to the airport when the sun came up. She retraced the route to the airport in her mind. She wondered if there might be roadblocks. Would they make it to safety?

***

The next morning Jack and Laura ventured down the hall. Though Laura still felt nervous and afraid, the sunlight made things seem less forbidding. They peered into the living room below.

"I don't see Diablo," Jack said. "The servants must have put him back in his pen."

Cautiously they descended the stairs. They didn't see Kartini or Maya either, yet the dining table had been set with hot coffee for Jack, tea for Laura, toast, butter and jam, and sliced pineapple, mango, and papaya. Strange, Laura thought. It's as if nothing happened. The *Jakarta Times*, the local English language newspaper, lay on a chair. She picked it up and scanned the pages.

"Nothing in here," she said then realized the explosions occurred too late to make the morning edition.

Jack ate quickly and got up.

"I'll see what I can find out at the office and give you a call. Hopefully the phones will be working by then."

"You can't leave me alone," Laura said realizing he intended to do just that. She still harbored thoughts of a coup and images of a bloodbath in the streets. She didn't know the servants well and doubted they would stick around to save her when whatever was out there stormed in.

"You're better off here. Besides you're not dressed. I need to go."

She stood up from the table. "It won't take me long."

"First let me go talk to Haroon. Maybe he knows what happened."

In a few minutes, Jack returned. "Haroon's excited. He wants us to come with him."

Laura rushed upstairs, grabbed a dress from the closet, and put on shoes. She wondered where Haroon wanted to take them. She couldn't imagine him excited about anything.

As they drove through a familiar area, Laura glimpsed burned-out hovels.

"Oh my God! What happened?" She realized they were close to where they used to live.

Haroon halted the car, rolled down the window, and conversed with a man at the side of the road.

"An ammunition depot not far away catch fire," Haroon said. "Last night bombs and rockets everywhere. Much damage. People killed."

"An ammunition depot in the middle of the city. How dumb is that?" Jack said.

As they drove on, Haroon occasionally stopped to drag debris to the side so they could pass. When he turned off onto the road leading to their old house, Laura gasped. Blackened stucco columns towered over broken red roof tiles. Chunks of concrete and smoldering wood lay amidst the debris.

Goose bumps covered Laura's arms. "We would have been killed." She stepped from the car and walked aimlessly through the rubble. The house always felt unlucky to her, yet the destruction exceeded anything she could have imagined. The harp lay on its side, its strings broken. She picked up a piece of gold-leaf frame and a canvas remnant of the knight on horseback. She walked to the pool and looked down into the muddied water, wondering if Astrid came back to wreak havoc on the site of her despair.

Jack stood beside the crumbled wall and looked out toward the village.

"Tofu operation's still there," he said.

Laura rushed over, concerned about the little girl she had seen sitting beside the pathway. To her relief, she saw no damage anywhere.

"Maybe it's crazy but it's almost seems like we were targeted," Jack said.

"Too much damage along the way for that. Besides, we just arrived. No one knows us."

"The police took Pak Hajji and some villagers to jail for questioning," Haroon said. "They think maybe they set fire to the ammo depot."

"Why would they suspect him? And why would he do that?" Laura asked. "He's head of the mosque."

"I do not know, nyonya. Police have their own reasons."

As Laura continued to walk around, she tripped. On glancing down, she cringed in horror. A human leg protruded from the rubble.

"Jack!" she yelled. She dropped to her knees and began to dig.

Jack and Haroon rushed over. They tossed rocks aside and uncovered the body of a young girl; her long braid caked with blood and mud. When Haroon lifted her, Laura cried out, "Pua!" She looked into lifeless eyes and took the limp form from Haroon while Jack checked the pulse. He shook his head. Laura cradled the servant to her chest and sobbed "Pua, Pua." Men from the village approached, took the body, and carried the nanny out the gate. Laura attempted to follow.

"You've done all you can do," Jack said his hand on her arm.

"Where are they taking her?" Laura expected an ambulance. Her face wet with tears, and her dress covered with dirt and blood, she watched the men and the dead girl disappear into the depths of the kampung. Feeling hopeless, she lowered her head. "Yesterday before we left, I checked the rooms. She wasn't in the house. Maybe she came back looking for us. Maybe she didn't want to go to the new job. Nobody asked her. We just assumed." Jack put his arm around her shoulders. "Don't go blaming yourself."

Haroon looked at Laura. "Maybe she return in middle of night to take Astrid's things. House without jaga available to everyone."

Distraught, Laura walked through the ruins as villagers began to wander in from the road. Shyly they reached out and touched Jack and Laura. Laura grasped their hands and smiled graciously. Jack deferred.

"Why are they touching us?" he asked Haroon.

"Because you are lucky. You moved out before bomb hit. They hope your luck rub off and they be lucky too."

Laura could understand how the villagers would attribute their timely move to luck and the supernatural. She too believed the unknown had intervened.

Jack looked uneasy with the villagers touching him. He headed toward the car while Laura stayed behind. Eventually she and Haroon followed.

"Can we just sit here for a minute?" she asked when Haroon inserted the key in the car's ignition.

"You're shaking," Jack said to her.

"Poor Pua. I never got to know her. I wonder if she has family. We should send flowers."

"She live far away," Haroon said. He started the car.

"She was just carted off like a sack of potatoes. I wish there were something we could do."

They rode in silence until Haroon spoke. "Tuan, you need to have a *selamatan*, a blessing of your new house. Maybe evil spirits follow you there."

"Haroon's right," Laura said. "Bad spirits could have followed us. We should have a selamatan."

Chapter 8

Contrary to Laura, Jack concluded that the bombing was a coincidence. He dared not think otherwise. But when his employees heard about what happened and how their boss and his wife had been saved, they insisted he have a selamatan and they wanted to participate. Reluctantly, he yielded to pressure.

"Don't worry, tuan," Haroon said. "I take care of everything. I talk to another imam, a holy man, for best time. Pak Hajji still in jail."

A week later the imam arrived. Attired in plain garb with a tan cloth wrapped about his waist, a long-sleeved beige shirt, and sandals, he fit the image. Elfin ears framed a gaunt face, and a white skullcap covered his baldhead. Bank employees carrying containers of special foods filed in behind him. Maya rolled an oriental carpet across the white tile floor, and the imam sat cross-legged at one end. The men took places along the edge of the carpet, the women behind. Jack joined the men; Laura sat among the other women.

The imam began to chant, his tone prolonged and mournful.

"He's chanting in formal Javanese. He's asking the good spirits to come and chase away evil, to bring harmony to your house," an Indonesian woman whispered to Laura.

Laura found herself fascinated by the blend of Islam with superstition and belief in the spirit world. She recalled studying the catechism in parochial school and believed in the powers of the Holy Ghost. Similar to those gathered here, she accepted a spirit without question.

The imam closed his eyes and clasped his hands, his face serene, tranquil, mystical. Laura glanced at Jack. She expected him to be checking his watch. To her surprise, like the other men, his eyes were shut, his palms outstretched. She wondered if he pretended or if he too had gotten caught up in the moment.

Her emotions heightened, Laura felt an urge to pray. She recited the Lord's Prayer to herself. And prayed to God to take Pua's soul to heaven. She went through a mental checklist and asked for more, a strong marriage, help for Jack at the bank, and to keep her from ending up like Astrid or boozing like Doreen.

As the chant slowed and faded, the imam reached into the small cloth sack beside him and took out an urn. He struck a match, held it over the brass bowl and a flame flickered. Wisps of white smoke drifted, and the pungent, sweet smell of incense floated through the air. The holy man circled the room sprinkling fragrant water from a long-necked silver decanter. He returned to the gathering and took his place on the carpet. He bowed his head as if to signal that the evil spirits had departed and all was safe. With the simple, elegant ceremony concluded, Laura brushed a tear from her eye.

The woman beside her rose, went to the kitchen, and returned with a large yellow rice cone on a platter. She placed it in the center of the carpet.

"It's nasi *tumpeng*," she said. "Traditional selamatan food. Rice is cooked with coconut milk and turmeric. Very tasty." She handed a knife to Jack and motioned for him to cut the cone.

After he had been so reluctant to have the house blessed, Laura thought it ironic that Jack should be the one to have the honor.

Several other women brought out steaming plates of fish, chicken, and beef; they spooned small portions of food onto fragments of banana leaves and passed them around. Eating with fingers, no one spoke.

The meal over, the imam gathered his things and prepared to depart. Jack followed him to the door and slipped a wad of rupiah into his hand.

***

When everyone left, Laura glanced at Jack. "Seemed to have gone well," he said.

"Such a beautiful ceremony, and your employees were happy to see you respect their customs."

"Was the right thing to do. Thanks for insisting." He put his arm around her shoulders.

"I hope the imam sprinkled a few drops of holy water on you," Laura said, her smile playful. Jack looked at her, questioning. "Isn't tomorrow the day you play golf with the evil judge?"

"Hardly funny."

"Wasn't meant to be funny."

"Come outside. I have something to show you."

In the driveway was a car, bright red, shaped like a shoebox. "Yours, a Kijang — made in Indonesia."

"Wow! Red hair, red car. They'll definitely see me coming." Haroon opened the rear door and she stretched to reach the high chassis. So much for tight skirts, she thought as she settled into the backseat.

"Nice and roomy." Laura waved from her perch. "Thank you." She blew Jack a kiss and dismounted.

"Now all you need is a driver."

Haroon hustled around the corner of the house and reappeared, followed by a teenage boy. The youth had shoulder-length hair and wore a rimless black hat — a *topi,* a symbol of nationalistic pride popularized by former Indonesian president, Sukarno. He had a confident stride and a cocky grin.

"Hi, I'm Mille," he said. "In your country Millie's a girl's name, but in Indonesia it's macho."

Laura shook his hand. "Did you study English in school?" she asked, impressed by how well he spoke.

"I learn English from Sylvester Stallone. I watch *Rocky* many times."

Laura laughed. She liked his spunk.

"Have Mille take you for a spin," Jack said. He headed toward his sedan. "I'm off to the office."

Laura glanced at Mille. He looked so young. She hoped he knew how to drive.

Chapter 9

Jack could not miss the judge, who wore a bright pink Arnold Palmer trademark shirt. Understated himself in conservative khakis and a white polo, Jack chuckled. He recalled his golfing buddies back home who resorted to the latest attire and gadgets, hoping it might improve their game.

"Should we warm up at the driving range?" Judge Hartono asked when he saw Jack coming.

"Sure. Been a while since I've played."

The men strolled along a gravel path. Jack was nervous. But he had no choice but to spend time with the judge. Larry White hadn't accomplished anything. And under pressure from his head office in New York to turn the bank around, and with his career on the line, Jack couldn't afford to write off a million-dollar loan. The borrower had other assets. If he could just get the judge to hear the case, the bank would get its money back.

Jack spotted an old woman on the practice putting green. She squatted on her haunches gripping blades of grass in her fingers. Her eyes were set in deep sockets, her face heavily creased. A large conical bamboo hat shaded her head and shoulders. "What's she doing?" he asked.

"Trimming the grass. She's more efficient than a mowing machine. We only use mowers on the fairways. The old women are better on the greens. They clip close so the ball rolls perfectly."

Jack walked toward her. Not wanting to be obvious, he halted some distance away. He needn't have worried. Absorbed in her work, she didn't look up. He watched as she snipped grass with scissors, a blade at a time. He could imagine Laura dropping to her knees to help.

"How much does she get paid?"

"About a dollar a day. She's grateful for the money. I know it's difficult for Westerners to understand. No one in your country would do what she does — too many better opportunities. But here, not yet."

Jack glanced at the judge. He felt uncomfortable beside someone with so little concern for the poor, clearly more intent on lining his own pocket.

The two men hit a bucket of balls before walking to the first tee. Perched on a hill, it looked out over an emerald green fairway carved from jungle still thick along the sides. Though Jack had played on many courses in the States, none could match such extraordinary natural beauty.

Jack's caddy, a young Indonesian boy, handed him a titanium driver, and Jack teed up. He thought through the steps, *head down, chin cocked, grip the club but not too hard, concentrate.* He rotated his shoulders and brought the club head back. *Slow and steady.* He paused at the top, swung down, and whipped the club through a wide arc.

When he heard the discordant thwack, his heart sank. He had expected the distinct ping of a ball well hit. He glanced up and saw a white speck rise and hook toward the jungle. The wind caught the ball, and Jack gritted his teeth. He watched it drop onto the fairway, bounce into a thicket, and disappear. "Son of a bitch," he muttered.

The judge teed up, swung, and hit the ball straight.

Jack wiped perspiration from his brow as he strode after his ball. He plunged into the brush at the spot where his ball disappeared.

"Don't go in too far," Judge Hartono said.

After several minutes and about to give up, Jack saw his caddy bring his finger to his lips and gesture. Just ahead, a snake slithered.

"Be careful! It's an *ular sendok,* a spitting cobra," the judge shouted.

Jack stepped back. He watched as the snake rose and spread its hood. Sunlight gleamed off a glossy underbelly. The cobra swayed from side to side; its forked tongue flitted.

"It can spit venom several feet. It aims for the eyes."

Jack moved further back. Snakes gave him nightmares. He reached down and touched the old scar at his ankle where as a young boy, a rattler got him.

"Cobras can be fatal. One struck a Dutchman a few weeks ago. He was foolish. He went into the rough to search for his ball. Poor fellow convulsed and died before they got him to the hospital."

The beads of sweat on Jack's forehead became more pronounced.

"Indonesia has more deadly snakes than any place in the world," the judge said with obvious pride. "They're not a problem unless you do something to make them mad."

His stomach doing somersaults, Jack returned to the fairway. He reminded himself he could keep his eyes open and avoid what slithered in the jungle; he was more concerned about the judge and the game they played.

Though reluctant to take a penalty for a lost ball so early in the match, Jack had no choice. He set another ball just inside the fairway at the spot where the other had disappeared. He hit it straight and eventually reached the green in four strokes. He felt confident until the judge sank a long putt to win the hole. Normally Jack would have been upset, but he reminded himself that he wanted the judge to win. It was part of his strategy.

They arrived at the second tee and sat on a bench to wait for the foursome in the middle of the fairway ahead to move on.

"That's Wibawa up there. He plays here every Thursday, sometimes with the president. They're golfing buddies."

"I met him at our reception. Wibawa, I mean," Jack said.

The judge took a pack of cigarettes from his pocket. "Care to try a *kretek*, an Indonesian cigarette? They're made from cloves."

"No thanks. I don't smoke. But please, go ahead."

The judge lit up and took a puff. The aroma of burnt clove reminded Jack of Easter ham.

"Kreteks are the poor man's cigarette. When Indonesians become wealthy, they don't smoke them anymore. They prefer expensive Western cigarettes. I smoke kreteks when I play golf.

Surrounded by jungle, I'm reminded of the village where I grew up."

Jack noted the judge's contemplative look and thought this might be the time to broach the subject of the money. But he didn't want to be the one to initiate. Instead, he reached for the towel attached to his golf bag, wiped moisture from his hands, and got ready to participate in the small talk. He wondered when the judge would bring up the bribe. He didn't have long to wait.

"Jack, about the twenty-five thousand dollars. I understand why you're reluctant to pay. You're American, but this is Indonesia. If you're going to succeed here, you need to play the game." The judge paused as if to gather his thoughts before proceeding. Jack looked at the man. With his half-lidded eyes and studied expression he had the wise look that comes with age and experience. "I love Americans," the judge continued. "Americans are open and friendly, but naive. You think you can impose your morality on the rest of the world. Someday perhaps you will, but not in my lifetime, nor in yours."

This was the conversation Jack had anticipated.

"Our president has done much for this country. He's a great man. He created a middle class and kicked out the Communists. But the poor are still poor, and he has turned a blind eye to the shenanigans of his family. They act like royalty. They think they're better than everyone else. They have a finger in practically every business. The president's wife formed these *yayasans*, charities to help the poor, but most of the money goes to her and her family. They have mansions all over the world, yachts, private jets, and billions stashed offshore. Mark my word, the president's family will be his downfall." He took a drag of his cigarette and ground it out on the bottom of his shoe.

Jack looked out at the thick jungle surprised the judge had been so blunt in his comments about the first family. He wondered if the judge had picked this isolated spot where he wouldn't be overheard. "You may wonder why I'm telling you all this," the judge said. "I wouldn't be so open with an Indonesian. I'm telling you so you can understand the culture you're dealing with."

"I appreciate that," Jack said.

The foursome ahead moved on, and the judge stood to tee off. He swung and though his ball sliced, it landed far out on the fairway. Jack wasn't so fortunate. His club head nicked the ground and the ball rolled a short distance.

"You're nervous, Jack. Relax."

"Still thinking about that snake."

Exasperated by the stalling of the conversation, Jack decided he needed to take the initiative and get the conversation back to the money, the court case, and a favorable resolution. "Judge, you're a professional. I'm sure you want to do the right thing. The company in Bandung that borrowed the million dollars from our bank defaulted," he said as they walked on. "Defaulting on a contract is against the law, not only here but in any country. They should be prosecuted. They even had the nerve to sell the bank's collateral." He paused and glanced at the judge. "Corruption undermines society. It's an added cost of doing business and inhibits growth. Why would an honorable man like you want to get involved in that sort of thing?"

"You don't seem to understand. Corruption starts at the top in Indonesia. Everyone sees the first family taking money on the side, so they do it too. It's self-preservation. The president and his wife and children have fostered a culture of greed, of permissiveness, of expectation."

Jack had not expected the judge to be so articulate. He understood, though he didn't agree with the older man's point of view.

"Our culture dates back thousands of years," Judge Hartono continued. "But Indonesia only became independent in 1945, some forty years ago. Compare that to America, which is more than two hundred years old. You have had time to sort out your problems. We haven't yet found our own version of Honest Abe or George and the cherry tree, but we will. In the meantime, we will do it our way." He looked at Jack. "The system only moves when greased."

"It's amazing what has been accomplished here, Judge. Governing seventeen thousand islands spread over three thousand miles is no easy feat. But past accomplishments are no excuse for corruption. And it's illegal in my country to pay bribes overseas or anywhere else. I couldn't give you the money even if I wanted to."

"Jack, let me put it to you another way." The judge spoke in a voice that sounded like a patient uncle. "I am the gatekeeper. Unless you give me twenty-five thousand dollars, your case will not be heard. It will be postponed indefinitely, and your bank will have to write off a million dollars." He paused for effect. "Your boss in New York will not be happy, and it will be bad for your career."

Jack wasn't surprised his moral suasion hadn't worked. He had resorted to it as a place to begin, a means to size up his opponent. Now he had to try a different tack.

"I can't give you twenty-five thousand dollars directly," Jack said. "But I can lend one of your relatives the money, and it doesn't have be paid back. I can write off a small amount like that, but the bank can't write off a million. You get your money, and you can hear the case." Though Jack knew that what he proposed wasn't completely ethical, he felt it was a clever solution.

"Jack, you're a smart man, but I don't want my family involved. I'm sure you can figure out a way to pay the money directly. Others have done it. But enough talk — let's play golf."

At the eighteenth hole, Jack and the judge tallied the score. Jack had played well, and he won. Initially he wanted the judge to win but changed his mind. His competitiveness took hold and he became determined to beat the judge at something.

The pair headed for the clubhouse and ordered Bir Bintang, the local beer. They discussed golf strategy and the difficulties of the toughest holes. After a while, Jack decided he had met his post-game social obligation and could leave.

The judge walked to the car with him. At the parking lot, he dropped his paternal demeanor and looked Jack in the eye, his voice steely. "Don't forget what I told you. This is not America."

Chapter 10

After Jack left for golf with the judge, Sarinah stopped by to take Laura to the Museum Tekstil.

"Awful thing that happened to your house," Sarinah said. "You are so lucky."

"Not so for poor Pua, the nanny."

"What happened to her?"

"Didn't you know? She was killed."

"I hadn't heard that part of the story. How awful."

The women settled into the backseat of the Kijang, and with Mille at the wheel, they headed out. Laura looked forward to the day at the textile museum. She hoped she might come up with a fashion idea that would keep her occupied. Yet she was preoccupied. She couldn't stop thinking about Jack with the judge.

"Do you know Judge Hartono? He was at our reception."

Sarinah shook her head. "Why do you ask?"

"Jack's playing golf with him."

"Harold probably knows him."

Laura dropped the matter. Though she had hoped Sarinah might allay her fears, she decided it would be better not to broach the delicate subject of corruption with an Indonesian whom she hardly knew.

Mille stopped the car at an open iron gate across from a shaded park. When Laura and Sarinah got out, hawkers peddling postcards, cold drinks, and slices of mango rushed over. Sarinah shook her head, and the vendors scurried off to the next car pulling up to the curb.

Inside the white colonial building, high ceilings offered a cool respite from the heat. A guide approached and introduced herself as Tatiana. Her pretty young face contrasted with her drab gray Muslim headscarf. Tatiana escorted them into a large room with glass cases filled with an assortment of old fabrics. "Javanese royalty in the palaces of Solo and Yogyakarta were the first to wear batik. That was over six hundred years ago," she said. She walked to a display case with a cloth called *larangan*.

In the dim light Laura squinted to make out the intricate geometric design.

"You see the triangle in the center?" Tatiana said. "The girl in the palace who wore that batik was concubine of the day." She put her hand to her mouth to mimic shyness.

"If I ever work with batiks, I'll have to remember not to use that design," Laura said with a laugh. "I wouldn't want Indonesian men to get the wrong idea."

"They don't need a triangle." Tatiana's eyes twinkled. Laura hadn't expected such humor and personality from a young woman wearing a religious head covering.

Tatiana showed them batik designed by Carolina Josephina von Franguemont, an Indo-European woman who started a successful business in 1840.

"It's vibrant, like the rainforest." Laura looked at the cloth of vivid greens. "Batik is like wearing art."

Tatiana pointed to another fabric she referred to as *petani*. "This was worn by women who worked in the rice paddies." The cloth pictured farmers and animals set against a background of lush, young, green rice stalks.

"Is a replica of that cloth available in the gift shop?" Laura asked.

"Sorry, we don't have that one. Not many people in Jakarta wear it."

Laura took a pen and notepaper from her purse and jotted down *petani*.

The tour ended, and the women exited the rear of the museum. They shielded their eyes from the sun and followed Tatiana across the terrace to a small building. Inside an old man sat on a cushion before a low table. A middle-aged Caucasian couple and their teenage boy sat hunched over squares of cloth beside him.

"Hamid can give you a demonstration on making batik," Tatiana said, gesturing to the aged man. The women thanked her and gave her a tip. "I hope you do good batik," said the young guide as she walked away.

"You do batik before?" Hamid asked.

"First time," Laura said. She glanced at the half-completed efforts of others' batiks lying on the table.

"It is easy."

"Are you American?" the middle-aged woman inquired as Laura took a seat next to her.

"From New York."

"Iowa," the woman said. She had plump rosy cheeks, plump arms, and stubby fingers. Beads of sweat lined her forehead. "And don't believe Hamid. It's not easy. I ask you, does this look like a sunflower?" She held up a cloth with the image of a large brown blossom.

"You're right, not too sunny," Laura said.

"You have to be careful with the dye." The woman sounded harried.

"My husband's doing a yellow-and-green cornfield, and my son a red sports car batik. Doesn't their work look nice? I never realized they were so artistic." The man and the boy glanced up, nodded, and returned to their work. "I'm thinking maybe I should just forget batik and stick to photography."

Laura suspected the woman sought affirmation her batik might not be so bad after all.

"We're visiting my brother," the woman continued. "He's the Kodak rep in Indonesia. We've been in Jakarta a week and we're running out of things to do. Joe dumped us here, said he'd be back in an hour."

Laura recognized the woman as a chatterer and wished she had chosen to sit further down the table.

"My sister-in-law didn't like Indonesia at all," the woman said. "After three months she went home. I felt sorry for Joe, so we came to visit. I thought he might enjoy the company." The woman leaned closer, her voice low. "Didn't take him long to find himself a girlfriend." She shook her head. "And Joe used to be so shy."

"Have you decided on a design?" Hamid handed Laura and Sarinah squares of white cloth.

"I'm thinking of trying a bird of paradise," Laura said.

"Are you sure you want to do that?" the woman from Iowa said. "So many colors to worry about. If you're not careful, your bird might end up looking dead like my sunflower."

"I'll be careful." Though not wanting to appear rude, Laura shifted her shoulders in the other direction, toward Sarinah.

Hamid looked at Sarinah. "A pattern of interlocking circles," she said.

"The cloth has been especially processed for batik. Feel how smooth."

Hamid handed the women a sample, and Laura rubbed it between her fingers. It felt like thin velvet.

"First you do a sketch, then apply wax resist with this canting tool." He held up a piece of bamboo the size of a pencil; it had a small cup with a pointed stem attached to one end.

Laura sketched a stylized bird.

"Fill the cup with the hot wax and pour so it covers your sketch.

Laura tried to follow Hamid's instructions.

"Next dip the cloth in dye, and then wash off the wax in hot water."

She lifted the cloth and lowered it into a vat with blue coloring.

"Good," Hamid said. Perhaps sensing her distress, he directed her through the rest of the application process.

This is so time-consuming, she thought.

"It can be done faster," Hamid said, as if picking up on her perception. He lifted a wooden block with a large handle. One side had a raised design in copper. "Wax is spread over the metal and stamped onto the cloth multiple times. Then it's dyed. It has almost the same effect as sketching by hand. And there are even machines that can reproduce the batik look in industrial quantities."

Laura heard a rap at the window. An overweight, white, balding man stood there, a wide grin across his face. A pretty, young Indonesian girl with large, dark eyes and long black hair had her arm wrapped in his.

"You folks finished?" he asked.

The woman from Iowa looked up and saw them. Her eyes narrowed. "Oh, hi, Hani, didn't know you'd be coming too."

"She quit her job," Joe said. He patted the girl's hand.

Laura bit her lip. Hani reminded her of Maya.

"He's making such a fool of himself," the woman whispered to Laura. "Okay, guys, grab your stuff. Let's get out of here." She struggled to maneuver her legs from under the low table.

The group walked away across the courtyard with Joe's arm around Hani's tiny waist. Laura remembered Doreen's comment about Western husbands going gaga.

Laura and Sarinah finished and held up their work. Pleased, the women thanked Hamid, and lifting the still-wet cloths by the edges, they departed. Laura wanted to show Jack her work.

As they drove away, Laura asked, "Does Islam forbid color?"

"Not at all," Sarinah replied. "Many mosques have beautiful colored tiles, and look at the carpets from Iran. Strict Islam prohibits the portrayal of living things, but colored geometric patterns are fine. Why?"

"Just thinking about Tatiana's gray head scarf. It would be simple to design something more fashionable, something with color."

"Really?" Sarina frowned and made no further comment.

They passed an old colonial canal where two naked brown-skinned boys frolicked in the fetid water, a woman washed clothes, and a man urinated. Fashion seemed to be the least of the country's problems. Laura wondered if making fashionable head coverings was a good idea. She didn't need to decide now. She'd give it further thought. She changed the subject. "What's happening with your literacy program?"

"It's so discouraging. I still haven't found a place."

"How many kids will you be tutoring?"

"Eight to start."

Mille pulled into the drive at Laura's house. "If you have a minute, I'd like to show you something." Laura led Sarinah around back to the garden.

79

Sarinah's eyes widened. "It's so beautiful," she said. "Most homes in Jakarta don't have such a big property. It's like a park."

"Would this work for your program?"

"You're kidding," Sarinah said her hand at her mouth. "It's perfect. The kids would love it."

"I'll check with Jack. I can't imagine he'll have a problem."

"I can use some help," Sarinah said. Hesitant, she glanced at Laura. "I know it wouldn't be as exciting as being a fashion designer."

Laura hoped Sarinah would ask her. Though she knew nothing about teaching children, she wanted to give it a try. She couldn't keep living her life through Jack. "I've never done anything like it before, so don't expect much from me."

"It's mostly patience. Don't worry. I'll show you what to do. Now I can start looking for more kids for the program. I wanted to wait until I found a place. I don't want to be too far from where they live."

"You might check the kampung near our old house. It's close, and Mille lives there. Maybe he can help."

"I'll speak to him on my way out," Sarinah said as they walked back to the front. "And call me after you speak to Jack."

"Sure." Laura couldn't imagine Jack would object.

Chapter 11

"So how bad was it?" Laura asked when Jack walked in that evening.

"I need a beer," Jack said. He tossed his cap on the couch and headed for the kitchen.

Laura followed. "What happened?"

Jack searched through the refrigerator, pulled out a frosted green bottle, and opened it. "The judge is tough." He walked back to the living room, plopped on the couch, and took a swig.

"I hope you didn't agree to pay him any money."

"Of course not."

"I still think Larry White should take care of it. He's the lawyer." Laura didn't want to nag, but she was worried about the situation and Jack's involvement.

Jack didn't say anything.

"I still don't see why you've made this your problem," Laura continued. "You told me Tom was the one who approved the loan to begin with then didn't tell you the company defaulted."

"I'm going to take a shower." Jack got up and headed for the stairs.

Laura picked up the book on batiks she purchased at the museum and flipped through the pages.

Jack came back downstairs in Bermuda shorts, sandals, and a faded blue shirt. He walked over and gave her a kiss. "Sorry you have to be in the middle of this mess. Tomorrow I'm going to call Tom, let him know what's going on."

"Good. He asked you to come here. Least he can do is help."

"The judge is very articulate. He tried to convince me that bribery is okay. That it's cultural."

Laura just glared at him.

"Dinner is ready." Maya had entered without a sound, and the suddenness of her voice startled them.

They sat down to a meal of stir-fry and rice. "I hope your day was better than mine," Jack said as he dished food onto his plate.

"I went to the museum with Sarinah. We had a great time. The old batiks are beautiful. I even tried my hand at making one. It's not easy."

"I'm sure," Jack said nodding his head.

"I have an idea," Laura said. She sounded excited. "I'm thinking of designing fashionable headscarves for Muslim women. Something in bright colors."

Jack set his fork down. "You accused me of wanting to change a culture and now you want to do the same. You're talking about tampering with garb that has religious connotations." Jack's voice rose. "That would be like switching nuns from the black habits they've worn for years into a Dior."

Laura slumped back in her chair. She knew he was right. And that probably explained Sarinah's look of disapproval when she mentioned colorful headscarves in the car. Tatiana appeared quite happy with the scarf she had on. It would be unkind to tempt her with something she didn't need and probably couldn't afford.

"I'm so desperate to do something I'm grasping at things best left alone."

Jack placed his hand on her arm. "Keep thinking. It'll happen."

"There's another possibility. Remember I told you about Sarinah's literacy program?" He nodded. "She asked me to help her."

"You'd be interested in something like that? I never thought of you as a teacher."

"And why not?" Laura replied, feeling resentful even though she agreed. She had never imagined herself as teacher either.

"I didn't think Sarinah had found a place."

"That's what I want to talk to you about. We have this big house and garden, and the cabana would be perfect for the classroom."

Jack set his fork down. "What about the liability? What if something happens? The bank's name is on the lease. One of the kids could fall, break their leg, and the parents sue the bank."

"That's ridiculous. This isn't the States. Indonesians aren't litigious. Most are too poor to hire a lawyer. Besides, the bank's support of a literacy program would be great publicity."

"What about the pool?"

"I'll be careful." Laura hadn't anticipated resistance. Her anger rose. "I agreed to come here and support you and your job. Least you can do is help me with something I want to do." She paused. "Or maybe you want me to sit around drinking like Doreen." About to mention Astrid, she bit her tongue.

Jack got up from the table. "I'll think about it. Right now I have to go to the office."

As he walked away, Laura raised her arms in victory. She knew she'd won.

***

Maya came in to clear the breakfast dishes from the table. To Laura, her every move conveyed insolence. In the short time they lived in the house, her discomfort with the servant girl had grown. She remembered Hugh mentioning that his wife thought Maya lazy. She agreed.

"Maya, there's a spider web hanging from the light fixture," Laura said. She pointed overhead. "It's been there a few days. Maybe you can brush it off with the feather duster when you clean in here."

"It too high for me."

"Isn't there a step stool in the kitchen?"

"There is." She walked from the room with a tray of dirty dishes.

This was similar to their conversation the day before when Laura showed Maya dust balls under the bed. Maya's look left no doubt she considered the task an imposition. At times Laura felt like a tyrant. And it had nothing to do with overlooked dust balls. It was Maya's attitude. Unlike many in the country, she had a job, yet she acted like an ingrate.

Laura changed into her swimsuit. Both she and Jack had established exercise routines. He joined the Kediri fitness center

83

and went there after work a few times a week. She did laps in the pool.

Laura walked across the lawn, and Diablo bounded over. Since the night he charged the stairs, she had spent time getting to know him, and they were buddies. She dislodged a slobbery tennis ball from his mouth and tossed it. He scampered out and caught it on the bounce. He plopped down in the shade, the ball between his paws. Laura set her towel and sunscreen aside. At the edge of the pool, she raised her arms, dove in, and swam several laps. Invigorated and breathing heavily, she hoisted herself out, dried off, and settled in a lounge chair.

Near the house Suparno swept leaves with a broom made of twigs. Hugh had been right about the small man's Zen-like focus. Diminutive, he was less than five feet tall and his skin stretched tight over his round head. Pointed teeth protruded from his mouth. He looked primordial, as if he had been the first human to stand erect. Laura wondered if he was born mute and if he had a family.

While Laura continued to speculate about Suparno, Maya came out and handed him a glass of water. The kind gesture took Laura by surprise. She hadn't expected that of the sultry servant. When Maya glanced toward the pool, Laura turned away. She hadn't gotten used to having servants underfoot and the lack of privacy. She felt restless and uncomfortable doing nothing. Kartini shopped, cooked, and planned the menus. Maya made the beds, did the laundry, and cleaned the rooms, though not very well. Suparno tended the garden and cleaned the pool. Mille drove. Laura's only job was to supervise Maya, who paid her little heed.

Laura thought about New York. She wondered if Grace had hired her replacement. She knew Grace would have enjoyed seeing the old batiks. And she would have been impressed hearing about Carolina Josephina von Franguemont starting a business in Indonesia over a hundred years ago. How difficult that must have been.

With the sun now beating down, Laura gathered her things to go inside. She had begun to have trepidations about the literacy program though unsure why.

***

Sarinah and Mille went to the kampung to meet with Pak Hajji, now out of jail. Sarinah wanted to make sure that as the head of the mosque he supported their efforts. She needn't have worried. He recognized the value of education and gave his support. He said he'd encourage parents to let their children participate.

When the first day arrived, Laura glanced at her watch as she waited in the driveway. She hoped everything went perfectly. Mille pulled into the driveway, and Laura counted eight kids in the Kijang — four girls and four boys — one of them the little girl she had seen sitting by the pathway. The children climbed from the car. Quiet and shy, they glanced about wide-eyed, unaccustomed to luxury. For an instant, Laura questioned if it was a good idea to bring the children here. She didn't want them to get the impression that all Americans were rich. Back home she and Jack wouldn't be living in a grand house with a cadre of servants. They would be just like everybody else. But when she and Sarinah led the group to the garden and she saw their faces light up, she dismissed her concern.

The children delighted in the birds. They pointed to Hantu, the owl with the huge yellow eyes, and Nuri, the colorful parrot. He bobbed up and down seeking attention. Laura once again felt thankful they brought him along to the new house before the explosion. Laura decided to put Diablo in his pen for the morning. She still remembered him charging up the stairs at them. Maybe he was not used to being around children.

"*Siapa nama*? What's your name?" Laura asked the shy girl from the pathway.

"Dewi," she replied, her voice barely audible.

The youngsters followed Laura and Sarinah to the cabana, now converted to a makeshift classroom with two tables, several small chairs, and basic books in English, as well a few in Bahasa.

"Sarinah, make sure the kids don't get close to the pool."

"No problem. Laura, why don't you work with Dewi, Eko, and Wayan?" Laura smiled, pleased to have Dewi in her group.

"This morning we will begin with letters of the alphabet," Sarinah said. She handed Laura a set of cards. Laura glanced through the stack. A large letter appeared on one side, with an identifying picture on the reverse. The three children fidgeted in anticipation.

"Okay," Laura said, "*A* is for *avocado*." She expected "*A* is for *apple*," and felt glad to see the learning tool was customized for Indonesia. She flipped through the cards, and the kids repeated the sounds, their English better than she expected. Partway through, Laura remembered one of her teachers years ago used music to teach.

"*S* is for *snake. S...s...s*," Laura sang. She writhed her arms. "*T* is for *tall. T...t...t*." She lifted her hand high. "Okay, sing with me." She started back at the beginning. "*A* is for *avocado. A...a...a*." The group worked their way through the alphabet and ended with, "*Z* is for *zebra. Z...z...z*." The children clapped. Laura wondered if there might be an Indonesian animal she could use for *z*.

"Excellent," she said having gotten caught up in the routine.

"Time for a break," Sarinah said after half an hour. Pleased by how well the day was going, Laura looked at the young students with a sense of pride.

One of the boys brought a soccer ball. The children ran about on the grass, kicking it and laughing.

"Exercise is good for them," Sarinah said. "It stimulates the brain, makes them more alert."

The ball rolled toward Laura, and she angled it off the side of her foot as she had seen in soccer played on TV. She had never played the game before but quickly caught on. Not being particularly well coordinated, Laura shunned team sports in school. Now she ran with abandon.

"Eko, don't let the ball go in the pool," Laura called as it rolled in that direction

"Okay, kids — and you too, Laura," Sarinah called. "Snack time."

Earlier, Suparno had shimmied up a palm tree and retrieved coconuts for Kartini to make macaroons. Now the cook came out and set a plate of freshly baked cookies and a pitcher of guava juice on the table.

Afterward the group returned to the cabana to practice phonics.

Sarinah handed Laura a different stack of cards. "Pronounce each syllable, then say the whole word. Have the kids repeat it."

"Wa-ter-mel-on, *watermelon*," Laura began.

"Wa-melon," Eko said shyly. He covered his face with his arm. Laura smiled at his effort.

"Wa-TER-mel-on," Wayan said. He elbowed Eko.

Laura marveled at the kids' curiosity, their eagerness to learn, and their progress. She could see why Sarinah chose teaching as a career. She couldn't think of anything more admirable. And the youngsters prompted her to think how wonderful it would be to have a family.

She knew she couldn't have children of her own, yet yearned for a child to love and care for. Once she considered adoption. With her career she questioned whether she would be able to devote her energies to both. She mentioned adopting a child to Jack, but he brushed aside the idea. He didn't think New York was the place to raise a family and said they were too busy. Though she agreed, it hadn't been the response she wanted to hear.

The session ended at noon, and Mille drove the children back to the kampung. Laura waved as they drove away. "They seemed to have enjoyed themselves," she said. She turned to Sarinah for affirmation. Sarinah, in a white blouse and dark skirt, looked composed. She always did. An expensive gold watch adorned her wrist. Laura noticed she wore it everywhere — even into the kampung.

"Everything was perfect." Sarinah put her hand on Laura's shoulder. "You are a natural. I would have thought you'd been around kids all your life."

"I can't have children," Laura said.

"I'm sorry, I didn't mean…" Sarinah's voice trailed off.

"It's okay," Laura said. She felt uncomfortable. This wasn't something she talked about, now felt compelled. "Growing up I loved to climb trees. One day I slipped and fell onto a spiked iron fence. I lost much blood and almost died. Scar tissue from multiple surgeries left me infertile."

Sarinah put her hand on her friend's arm.

"Thanks, Sarinah. I've gotten over it. I look forward to tomorrow."

***

The next morning Laura stood at the gate, waiting, when Mille pulled up and the kids piled out. Dewi, no longer shy, ran over. Laura bent down and gave her a hug. She felt a special relationship with the little girl. She would always remember her from that first visit to a kampung. Not wanting to show favoritism, she embraced the others too.

The group headed toward the cabana and settled into a routine similar to the day before's. Laura listened to Dewi, Eko, and Wayan blend syllables, surprised at how quickly they formed new words and grasped pronunciation.

At the break, Kartini came to the cabana with more cookies and juice. Preoccupied as she was helping to fill the kid's glasses, she was suddenly startled. "Where's Dewi?" Sarinah sounded frantic.

Laura quickly glanced around the room and didn't see the little girl anywhere. *Oh no, the pool!* As she ran for the door, she heard the ominous sound of a splash. At the far end, she saw a thin brown arm slide below the surface. Laura dove in, resurfaced, and swam for the spot where the arm had disappeared. Taking a deep breath, she plunged down. At the bottom, she saw Dewi, her arms and legs moving in slow motion, her dark hair floating about her head like the tentacles of an anemone.

Oh God, don't let Dewi die. She wrapped her arm around the girl's small waist and struggled to the top. At the surface, she floated Dewi horizontally while trying to keep the little girl's nose and mouth out of the water. Laura grasped the small chin with one hand and stroked with the other as she made her way to the edge of the pool. Years ago, Laura worked as a summer lifeguard and knew what to do; she just hoped she was in time.

Sarinah leaned over and lifted the waterlogged girl up over the side of the pool. "Dewi! Dewi!" she cried, but there were no signs of life.

Laura hurled herself out of the pool. She bent over and pried Dewi's mouth open. Out of the corner of her eye, she was grateful to see that Kartini had come out to distract the other children. She began resuscitation and the minutes passed. *Please, God, let her breathe.*

When Dewi's eyelids fluttered, Laura wanted to jump up and shout. But she continued mouth-to-mouth until the girl breathed on her own.

Sarinah wrapped a towel around Dewi, gathered her in her arms, and rocked her. Overcome by the magnitude of what had happened, Laura covered her face with her hands. Jack warned her about the pool, yet she'd been careless. And because of her, a little girl almost drowned.

Chapter 12

Her hands clasped in her lap, Laura waited in the living room to face Jack.

After she told him, he said, "She could have died!" He paced in front of her. "I hate to think what might have happened. I can see the papers now: 'Indonesian Child Drowns in Americans' Pool.'"

"Jack, stop it!" Laura shouted. She looked up at him. "It was an accident!" Though warranted, she couldn't take his accusations.

"We could have been kicked out of the country. My career ended."

"All you care about is that damn bank."

"I told you to be careful." His face reddened; his voice rose. "I can't believe it."

"You make it sound like I threw her in on purpose." Laura began to sob. Jack clenched his fists. A tear rolled down Laura's cheek. "I'm going back to New York."

Jack stiffened.

"I called Grace. My job is available."

Jack dropped down on one knee. He took her hand. "Honey, you're overreacting."

She looked at him through tears. "And you're not?"

"I'm sorry. It wasn't your fault. It was an accident. You shouldn't blame yourself."

"Do you realize how many times you've said you're sorry since we got here? Astrid, the bombing, the judge — this isn't the place for either of us."

"I'm not ready to leave. And I can't let you go either."

***

Before she left for New York, Laura wanted to apologize to Dewi's grandmother for her carelessness.

"I will miss you," Sarinah said as the two women walked along the path in the kampung. "But I can understand why you would want to return to a life of glamour."

"We'll keep in touch," Laura said. Immediately she regretted her comment. The overused phrase sounded lame and insincere.

At Dewi's grandmother's, Sarinah rapped on the door of a small house neater than the others. A woman came out, and for a moment Laura was confused. With few wrinkles or creases in her face, she hardly resembled a grandmother. But then Laura realized Indonesian girls started families at an early age.

The woman looked at them, puzzled. Sarinah introduced herself and Laura. The grandmother directed the youngsters who had gathered to pull a bench over for her visitors. Speaking Bahasa, she offered the women tea. Sarinah translated. Laura and Sarinah nodded, and the grandmother went inside, returning with three small cups on a tray. Though Laura understood the warning about drinking unbottled water, she took a sip. She didn't want to appear rude.

Laura leaned forward, her shoulders hunched. Her tall frame compacted she was eye level with Dewi's grandmother. She wrung her hands, struggling to find the words to convey her remorse. But she tried.

"No need to apologize," the grandmother said when Laura finished. "Dewi told me she fell in the water and you saved her."

As if on cue, Dewi came running up the path.

"Nyonya, nyonya," she cried. "I missed you. Can I come back? I want to see the birds. And read."

Laura hugged her. Now overcome with emotion, she couldn't bring herself to tell a little girl she had come to love that she planned to leave.

***

After dinner that evening, Laura told Jack about her visit to the kampung, the grandmother, and Dewi.

"Dewi said she wanted to come back to our house. She promised not to go near the pool. I got emotional and cried. You know I hardly ever cry. Now I seem to be crying all the time."

"Did you tell her you're leaving?"

"I couldn't bring myself to do that."

"You didn't have any problem telling me." Jack leaned back and ran his fingers though his hair.

Her feelings were conflicted; Laura rode an emotional rollercoaster. She was excited when she spoke to Grace about the latest fashion gossip and the upcoming shows. She visualized herself in her old office at the drafting table, her adrenaline pumping. Earlier at the kampung, surrounded by poverty, she expected to be elated by the thought of leaving all that behind, returning to a place she knew and where she felt comfortable. Instead, she saw herself as a failure. And she knew that if she went back, with or without Jack, her marriage would be over. Jack had little tolerance for failure. Even in his wife.

Jack tapped his fingers on the armrest of the chair.

Laura got up from the table.

"Where are you going?" he asked.

"Upstairs to unpack," she said.

"To what?"

"I'm staying, I doubt you'd be able to survive here on your own."

***

Sarinah and Laura decided to relocate the program far from the pool. Pak Hajji found a place in the kampung where the women could tutor. They headed there now. Mille lagged behind, struggling with a carton of books.

"Don't worry," Sarinah said in an attempt to reassure her friend. "Everything will go just fine." Laura hoped she was right.

Dewi ran out to greet them. Laura lifted the little girl off the ground, and her fears disappeared.

"The classroom will be over there," Mille said. He indicated a shaded spot with a table and several chairs. Sarinah divided the group as before, and Laura searched the box for her favorite story, *The Little Engine That Could.*

"Would you like to read about a train?" she asked her group. She held up the book and pointed to the picture of a locomotive on the cover.

Eyes wide, they nodded.

"As it went on, the little engine kept bravely puffing," Laura read.

"What *puffing*?" Eko asked.

Laura smiled at his question. "You see the stack," Laura said. "That's where the smoke from the engine comes out. It's puffing." About to compare the word to something familiar — like puffing a kretek cigarette — she decided to just continue. "As it went on, the little engine kept puffing faster and faster, 'I think I can, I think I can, I think I can.'" Laura stopped, making sure they were keeping up with her. "What does the story make you think about?"

Dewi squirmed. She glanced up at the sky. "I don't know."

"Sure you do. What's the little train saying as it tries to climb the hill?"

"That he thinks he can. And he's trying hard," she said, her face scrunched up.

"Let's see if he makes it," Laura said. "Up, up, up. Faster and faster and faster and faster the little engine climbed until at last it reached the top of the mountain.'"

The children clapped.

"The little train is like us. Sometimes things look difficult; then we try hard and it works. We surprise ourselves."

Proud of her young students, Laura thought again how wonderful it would be to have a child. Now, without a demanding career, she felt an emptiness she hadn't experienced in New York.

"Nyonya, can you bring your birds here?" Dewi asked.

Laura laughed. "Hantu's too big to carry, and Nuri bites." She held up her index finger to display the scar. "But I have an idea. Once I had a pair of lovebirds. They were small and perched on my hand. Maybe I can find birds like that."

The lesson finished, the women made their way to the car, and Mille drove them back to Laura's house.

"I'm relieved." Laura said. "Everything went well."

"I'm so glad you decided to not go back to New York," Sarinah said.

Laura nodded. She was too.

"You're such a good teacher," Sarinah said. "You work well with children. And I like your idea about getting some small birds."

"I grew up with a menagerie — a hamster, yellow lab, black cat, white rabbit, goldfish, bearded dragon, canary, and a parakeet. Once a baby robin fell out of its nest and was deserted by the parents. I put it in a shoebox and fed it with an eyedropper. After it developed flight feathers, I released it. When I moved to New York, my father gave me a pair of lovebirds. He said they were the perfect pets for the city. They didn't need to go out and pee in the snow."

Sarinah laughed. "My grandfather had songbirds. There's a Javanese saying. 'A man is not a real man until he has a house, a wife, a horse, a dagger, and a bird.' My grandfather had no room for the horse."

Laura smiled and asked, "So where can I find a pair of small birds?"

"*Pasar burung*, the bird market. They sell everything there," Sarinah said. Laura recalled Hugh mentioning that as the place where he and his wife had gotten Hantu. "But you'll be appalled at the conditions. You'll want to buy all the creatures and bring them home."

Laura said goodbye to Sarinah and went inside. On the bookshelf, she found the copy of *Birds of Southeast Asia* she had brought from New York. Sitting outside on the terrace she glanced through, admiring photographs of parrots, honeysuckers, and brilliant birds of paradise. How beautiful, she thought.

She fixated on a picture of a bird with snowy white feathers. An electric blue stripe highlighted its black eyes. Stunning, though was dismayed to read that the Bali starling, poached for the pet trade, verged on extinction. Only ten remained in the wild. She closed the book and went to find Mille.

"Let's go to the pasar burung," she said.

On driving through the streets of Jakarta, it was customary to encounter ubiquitous young entrepreneurs manning intersections, selling an array of items. They approached cars stopped at traffic signals and tapped on the windows or just stood there with a forlorn look. Laura attempted to ignore them, but to no avail.

While Mille waited at a red light, a boy approached with plastic bags of *krupuk* — shrimp crackers — strung on a bamboo pole. He pressed his sad face against the glass. Unable to resist, Laura pulled out a few rupiah, lowered the window, and took the krupuk. Once, after a drive across town, she ended up with a carved Dayak statue, a pair of mismatched socks, a baseball cap, a box of sweets, and an antique Dutch clock — things she wouldn't use and food she dared not eat.

The pasar burung, with many makeshift stalls, stretched for blocks along Pramuka Street, the name now synonymous with the place to buy birds and other creatures. The scene was a maze of cages. They hung from poles and rafters and sat atop empty crates. Soft tweets competed with loud squawks. Merchants held their birds aloft and called out to pedestrians.

Mille parked and then followed Laura. She passed stall after stall in her search for small birds. She stopped to peer at a caged mynah. Tufts of yellow on either side of its head contrasted with its wings and body of glossy black. Laura didn't notice a man approaching from behind.

"*Cockatua?*" he asked.

Startled, she jumped and turned around.

He pointed to the one-legged salmon-colored cockatoo on his fist.

"How beautiful!" Laura said. How sad, she thought. The bird raised its crest. Its eyes pleaded. "What happened to the bird's other leg?"

"I not know. He come like that. He from Maluku Islands."

"Can I pet him?"

"He like people."

She stroked the bird's head. Pleased by the attention, it bobbed up and down. She felt sorry for the poor creature. Tempted to buy him, she resisted. She tore herself away and walked on.

"What price you pay?" the man asked, following her.

She knew if she looked back she would no longer be able to resist.

At another stall she saw more mynahs crammed in a wire box. A dead one lay on the bottom. She rushed past.

She saw not just birds but other creatures too. Occasionally she stopped to peer. She pointed to an animal resembling an anteater, which was curled up in a crate.

"Pangolin," a man said.

Laura's face questioned.

"Chinese people like meat. Scales for medicine to help stomach." Laura put her hand over her own stomach and shuddered. She wondered if Westerners consumed things the Chinese might consider abhorrent. She couldn't think of any.

Nocturnal fruit bats hung upside down in an enclosure, their black leathery wings folded across small, pointed faces in an attempt to shield their sensitive eyes from the bright sunlight. Laura looked into a cage that held a furry kitten. Spotted like a leopard, it looked like it must be some kind of jungle cat. It arched its back and hissed. Too young to be without a mother. She wanted to leave the market but found herself pulled toward the bizarre like a magnet.

"Psst," a man beckoned from the shadows of a stall. She glanced behind her to make sure Mille followed. Inside the man picked up a cage and took off the cover. A beautiful, bright-lime-green parrot ruffled its feathers. "Special," he said.

Laura already knew the bird was special. She recognized the eclectus parrot from a picture in her book. It was classified as endangered.

The bird kept opening and closing its beak. "Do you have any water?" she asked. The man retrieved a plastic bottle and poured water into a paper cup. Laura opened the cage door, and disregarding her prior bird-bite episode, she held the container near. The bird dunked its beak and swirled its tongue.

The man held up another cage. "Oh my God," Laura said. Another parrot, this one its plumage red, the feathers on its breast and abdomen dark blue and purple. "The female, the mate," he said. For years ornithologists had been fooled by the starkly different coloration of the eclectus sexes, thinking them to be separate species. Laura looked at the pair, admiring their beauty. They could be hers. She struggled. She knew she shouldn't be buying endangered birds.

"How much for both?" she asked. She had let her emotions overcome her better judgment. She knew bargaining was cultural and expected, yet unfamiliar with the process, she was unsure where to begin or when to stop. Already she worried she had shown too much interest.

"Eighty thousand rupiah. Eighty dollars," he replied.

"Forty thousand."

The man shook his head. "Seventy-five thousand. Birds special."

"Sixty thousand, final price," Laura said, becoming more confident.

Again the man shook his head.

"*Terima kasih,* thank you," she said. She walked out of the stall.

The man followed. "Okay, okay," he called out.

Though not heartened by her victory, she gave him the money.

"What do they eat?"

"Mango and papaya good."

"Beautiful birds, nyonya," Mille said as he lifted the cages and headed toward the car.

"I'll be right back, Mille. I forgot something." She hurried off to find the man who approached her earlier. She returned to the car minutes later with the one-legged Mollucan cockatoo perched on her shoulder. "I couldn't leave him behind," she said in response to Mille's surprised face. As Sarinah warned, she wanted to buy everything.

"I thought you want small birds," Mille said. "These big."

Mille was right. She had come to buy birds for the children and ended up with birds for herself.

"We don't have room for more today. We'll have to come back." As she said that, she realized she never wanted to come here again.

Mille was about to drive away when a man rushed over and tapped on the window. He glanced nervously over his shoulder. "Baby monkey," he mouthed. "Special. Come see."

Laura hadn't seen monkeys at the market. When she visited the Bronx Zoo, however, she loved observing their antics. Curious, she got out.

"Wait here," she said to Mille. No longer afraid of going alone, she followed the man to his stall. She hadn't previously stopped there, as only bird and animal food were displayed: mice, crickets, worms, bananas, and seed packets.

He led her inside and out the back. Laura gasped, her hands clenched in front of her. A small, hairy creature sat shackled to a large crate. "Orang," the man said. Laura needed no explanation. She already knew what it was. Tufts of reddish hair stuck up on the back of the baby's otherwise bald, round head. Its large, sad eyes resembled black marbles. When the orangutan stretched out its long, thin arms toward her, Laura dropped to her knees. Dragging its chain, the baby rushed forward and wrapped its arms around her. It twirled her red locks in its fingers.

"We have the same color hair. He thinks I'm his mother," Laura said. "Where is she?"

The man shrugged.

When Laura unwound the baby's arms, it squealed. "You're selling him?" Laura asked in disbelief.

The man nodded.

"How much?"

"How much you pay?" he asked.

What would she do with an orangutan? Overwhelmed and emotional, she rushed out, the sound of the baby's cries resounding in her ears.

***

"So how was your day with the kids?" Jack asked when he got home from work.

"Everything went fine," Laura said. "After tutoring, I went to the bird market. Come see." She led him out to the garden.

The two brightly colored parrots perched in cages hanging from a tree. "Those colors are amazing," Jack said. He moved closer.

"I felt bad buying them. They were taken from the rainforest. But I can give them better care here."

"Don't you think the poachers will just go get two more? You can't buy them all," Jack said. He noticed another bird, the cockatoo. "What happened to that one's leg?"

"No one seemed to know." Then Laura told him about the baby orangutan.

"How cruel," he said.

"I wish there was something I could do."

Jack glowered. "The last thing we need is an orangutan."

"I know."

***

In the days that followed, all Laura could think about was the baby orangutan, alone, shackled to the crate. She remembered those small arms clutching her, and the heartbreaking cries when she fled. She swore she would never go back there; yet she had to see him. She wanted to bring the baby food: she just hoped he was still there. She purchased a book about primates to see what orangutans ate. She didn't want him getting sick or, even worse, dying because she had fed him the wrong thing. Seeing they ate mainly fruit, she filled a basket with mangos and papayas.

At the market, Mille dropped her off and went to park the car. With the basket under her arm, she glanced around. All the stalls looked alike. As she walked along, vendors approached with parrots on their arms. She ignored them. She continued searching and perked up when she recognized the man ahead. He sat on a wooden crate, a kretek in one hand, a fly whisk in the other.

He waved to her. "Selamat pagi," he called.

99

"I've come back to see the orang."

He shrugged. "Baby not here."

It was as if someone had punched her in the stomach. "Where is he?"

"Baby sold."

Laura didn't believe him, didn't want to believe him. She rushed inside and out the back. There the crate lay on its side, the chain and shackle nearby.

"General buy. Present for daughter birthday."

Laura remembered Sarinah telling her about orangutans being purchased by the wealthy and military generals as status symbols. At the time, she didn't believe her.

"If you want, I find another," the man said.

"I don't want." Laura's shoulders slumped. She wrung her hands as she thought of the poor infant at a birthday party, scared as children poked at him and screamed in delight.

"Why do you do this?" Laura asked. "What if someone killed your wife and took your baby? What would you think about that?" She knew he wouldn't understand that orangutans and humans shared 97 percent of their DNA, that they might have similar feelings of abandonment and despair.

"My wife no like me sell orang. She say better sell birds. But not much money selling birds. Family need money."

"Where do you get the orang babies?" Laura asked. She doubted he could afford to travel to Borneo.

"Government man bring to me."

Laura searched in her purse for rupiah. She handed them to him. "Who?"

The man shuffled the bills then stuck them in his pocket. He glanced over his shoulder and lowered his voice. "He work at forestry ministry."

Angry and breathing hard, Laura left the market. Determined to help the orangutan, she didn't yet know how she would do that.

Chapter 13

The scene outside the Hotel Kediri had become a familiar one. A line of chauffeur-driven sedans inched forward through the dark night toward the ballroom entrance. The doorman ran from car to car, opening doors for the elegantly attired attendees on their way to the reception. This evening's event honored the president of the Royal Bank of Canada on his visit to Indonesia.

Up ahead, Judge Hartono alighted from a dark sedan accompanied by another man. Laura caught her breath. She looked at Jack, relieved he hadn't noticed. A month had gone by and there had been no progress on the bank's lawsuit. She knew Jack was getting frustrated.

Laura lifted the hem of her turquoise silk dress and stepped out onto a red carpet lined with floral displays and wreaths welcoming the important visitor. The scene resembled the Academy Awards.

On Jack's arm, she strode into the ballroom with crystal chandeliers glittering overhead. A handsome young man at the head of the receiving line introduced himself as Harold Miller. He had a head of thick black wavy hair, and his broad smile displayed straight white teeth. Laura wore braces in middle school and was called "metal mouth." She noticed others' straight teeth and wondered if they too had endured torment.

"You're Sarinah's fiancé," she said.

"She told me about you," Harold replied. "You're the fashion designer. How impressive."

Laura smiled at his recognition of her profession. "With all the well-dressed women here tonight, I wonder if my skills are needed."

"There's always room for new ideas," he said. "Sarinah told me you've been a big help with the literacy program."

Laura was thankful he didn't mention the near disaster at the pool. She knew Sarinah must have told him.

Harold introduced them to the tall, silver-haired man in a navy-blue pinstriped suit who stood beside him. "This is Hamish Smith, president of the Royal Bank."

What a distinguished-looking man, Laura thought.

"I hear Bank AmerIndo is doing well here," Mr. Smith said to Jack. Laura, aware of the bank's problems, listened for Jack's response.

"I can't take credit for the success. I haven't been here that long."

Good answer. When they moved out into the crowd, Laura spotted Judge Hartono. She attempted to steer Jack in the opposite direction.

"A lot of the same faces," Jack said, looking around as Laura led them to the far side of the room. "Bankers, businessmen, government officials, They're all here."

Sarinah walked over and greeted them. She asked Laura about her trip to the bird market.

"You were right. I wish I hadn't gone. I wanted to buy all the poor creatures."

"I know. It's so sad."

"The saddest was this baby orangutan. It hugged me like I was its mother."

"That's what happens. The mothers end up being killed during logging operations in the rainforest. The babies are snatched and sold. It's illegal to sell an orangutan in Indonesia, but the law is rarely enforced. Owning an orangutan is special."

Tempted to ask Sarinah what could be done, Laura held back; she knew this was neither the time nor the place for that.

"Laura bought three birds. She's turning our place into a zoo," Jack said with a grin.

"But that's okay. They're to show the kids in the literacy program," Sarinah said.

"Not really. Too big," Laura said.

Harold came over and interrupted. "Sorry to drag you away," he said to Sarinah. "Need you to be in the photos with the big boss."

They left and Jack glanced around. "There's Judge Hartono."

"Jack, you said he's a son of a bitch. Stay away. You accomplished nothing playing golf with him. He's only going to upset you again."

"I despise the man, but I haven't given up." Jack headed to where the judge stood, and Laura followed. On the way she noticed Doreen chatting with several other women. Tempted to join them, she decided she didn't feel comfortable leaving Jack alone with a corrupt judge.

"Good to see you again," Jack said, feigning respect and extending his hand. "You remember my wife, Laura."

"Of course," Judge Hartono replied. "Jack told me about your premonition."

"We were lucky."

"You are an intuitive woman, Mrs. Harrison. Perhaps in another life you were Indonesian. We believe in superstition and the spirit world."

An Indonesian man attired in a bold red-and-blue batik shirt with stylized dragons and giant flowers stood beside the judge. Laura recognized Johnny, son of the president of Indonesia, from pictures she had seen in the newspaper. The judge introduced him.

"Johnny was just telling me about his logging project in Kalimantan, the Indonesian part of Borneo. There might be an opportunity for your bank," Judge Hartono said to Jack.

Jack visibly perked up. The first family served as gatekeepers for the most lucrative deals in the country. "How much money is involved?" he asked.

"Forty million dollars," Johnny replied.

"I'm interested." Jack handed Johnny a business card.

"I'll have my secretary call and set a date for lunch."

As Jack and Laura turned to leave, the judge stopped them. "Have you given any more thought to what we discussed on the golf course?" he asked Jack.

"So far I'm not persuaded," Jack said.

"That's unfortunate," the judge said. "Perhaps we should play golf again." He bowed slightly and walked off.

Jack and Laura headed toward the buffet table. Jack took a carrot and munched it. "Did you hear what Johnny said?" he asked, excitement in his voice. "Forty million dollars. That would be the biggest loan our bank has ever made in Southeast Asia." He pumped his fist. "Tom will piss in his pants, especially when he hears the president's son is involved."

Laura had held back as she listened to the men's conversation. She didn't think it her place to intrude. Now looking directly at her husband, she knew now was the time. "You know Kalimantan is where orangutans live. I can't believe you're considering financing a logging project there." Her jaw squared, her eyes narrowed.

Jack quickly curbed his enthusiasm. "It won't hurt to see what they're up to."

Laura, eager to continue, when Doreen with the ubiquitous drink in her hand joined them. Laura cooled her ire. "Doreen's from Texas," she said, introducing her to Jack. "Her husband's in the oil business. Works for CALCO."

"Doesn't stick around here much. Always off at regional meetings in Thailand," Doreen said. "Not sure why they go there. All the oil's in Indonesia."

Laura noticed Doreen slurring her drawl. "So how do you keep busy while he's away?" she asked.

"I take cooking classes at the American Women's Auxiliary — Chinese food. Though not sure when I'll use it. My Billy's a meat 'n' potatoes man."

"Jack used to be like that. Now he's more adventurous. Even eats spicy ethnic dishes." Though Laura struggled her mind still on the orangutan and Jack's logging project, she managed to keep her composure.

"No more burgers for me," Jack said with a grin.

"I'm also taking a class in decoupage," Doreen said. "Got a house full of my mistakes. You should come to the auxiliary with me sometime."

"Why thank you, Doreen. That's very kind." Laura appreciated Doreen's gesture, though she couldn't see herself doing decoupage.

When Doreen left to look for Billy, Jack and Laura wandered through the crowd, stopping periodically to chat with others. After a while, Jack glanced at his watch. "I have a big day tomorrow. We should be heading home."

Outside under the portico they encountered Wibawa and Ari.

"Hello, Jack," Ari said, her eyes flirting.

"Johnny said he spoke to you about our logging project in Borneo," Wibawa said, turning to Jack. Though Jack looked surprised, he shouldn't have been.

"I partner with Johnny and the first family on most deals," Wibawa said. "I hope your bank will be able to help us"

Laura looked at Jack, waiting to hear what he would say.

"I'll do my best."

Chapter 14

The following week, a newspaper article caught Laura's eye. "Southeast Asian Forestry Ministers Meet in Jakarta." The agenda included talks on illegal logging in the rainforest and the unhealthy haze of slash-and-burn land clearing drifting toward cities. The meeting was to be held the following Wednesday at ten in the morning at the Kediri. Laura set the paper aside. There was no mention of the orangutans.

She recalled demonstrations outside the United Nations in New York bringing world attention to diverse causes. She remembered the countrywide protests against the war in Vietnam that resulted in President Johnson's decision to forego a second term. Why not a protest in support of the orangutans? The press would be at the Kediri covering the minister's meeting. It would be the perfect opportunity to garner support.

But Laura knew she had to be careful. She couldn't risk embarrassing Jack's bank. And she couldn't risk getting tossed out of the country or thrown in jail, though she doubted either would happen. It seemed even larger infractions could be taken care of with a handful of rupiah. Still, she didn't want to test the system — she might encounter that one honest government official. Not wanting to go it alone, she thought of asking Sarinah; but she was Indonesian. This was her home, and Laura didn't want to get her in trouble

Later that evening at dinner Jack said, "You seem distracted. What are you thinking about?"

"Nothing, really." She dared not let on what she was up to.

The next morning she called Doreen to ask if she could stop by.

"Be there around three," Doreen said.

"I'll make us a pitcher of mojitos."

"Mo whats?"

"Mojitos, Hemingway's favorite drink. They're made with rum and lime. Very refreshing."

"Hemingway knew his booze. Sounds good to me."

Though Laura thought it too early for drinking and didn't want to support her friend's habit, she needed her cooperation and thought mojitos might help. She ventured to the kitchen to make sure there was enough rum.

Doreen, her blond curls coiffed, arrived on time. "I was at the Kediri beauty parlor," she said. "Though I'm not sure it's worth the money. Today it's hotter'n mice in a wool sock. My hair will be a wreck in no time."

"Looks nice," Laura said, chuckling at her friend's weather witticism.

"I bought you a present," Doreen said. She handed Laura a bottle of perfume. "Enjoli. It's the career woman's fragrance for the '80s. I saw it advertised on TV last time Billy and me were in Singapore. I love the jingle." Her face lit up and she began to sing, "I can bring home the bacon, fry it up in a pan. And never, never let you forget you're a man."

"Funny," Laura said, laughing. She removed the glass stopper, dabbed a drop on her wrist, and took a sniff. "Lovely." Actually she thought it overpowering, though she was appreciative of the gift and happy Doreen considered her a career woman. "There's a pitcher of mojitos in the refrigerator. I'll get it and join you in the garden."

Laura fetched the pitcher, went outside and poured the drinks.

"On the phone you sounded excited," Doreen said. "What's going on?"

Laura told her about the visit to the market and the baby orangutan snatched from its mother during a logging operation, then purchased by a general as a present for his daughter's birthday.

Doreen's eyes got big. "Why that's criminal," she said. "And so sad. But that's just the way it is here. Matter of fact, there's a grown orangutan lives next door to me. I can see him from the upstairs window. He sits in the yard all day chained to a palm tree eating bananas."

"You're kidding," Laura said. Doreen's story confirmed her worst suspicions. "We have to do something."

"Like what?" Doreen asked. "I'm not about to climb the wall and release it while you hum 'Born Free,' if that's what you mean."

Laura laughed. "I have a better idea. Next week, there's a forestry ministers meeting at the Kediri. We can hold a protest."

"We'd get arrested. I'm not keen on going to jail anywhere, and I'm sure not keen on getting tossed in the clink in Indonesia."

"We can make costumes out of red fleece and wear masks. No one will know who we are. We'll carry signs. The press will be there covering the meeting. We'll attract attention. Then we'll get out quick." Laura knew a two-woman protest sounded foolish, but she had to make do with just her and Doreen, and she hoped the press would carry the message.

"I'm not so sure. I've never protested before. It's usually quacks who do that stuff in Texas." She finished her drink and poured another.

"It's for a good cause." Laura noticed Doreen fidgeting. "I need your help. We can be the ones to make a difference. We can save a species."

"I do love animals. Growing up in Odessa, I was in 4H — the goat project leader. I won a blue ribbon. I really wanted to raise hogs, but when the county fairs over you have to sell 'em to a slaughterhouse. I couldn't do that."

"That same thing happens to the orang mothers during logging. They get slaughtered."

"There's a difference in not raising hogs as a silent protest in Texas, and waving a sign in front of the Kediri."

Laura noticed her friend's empty glass and refilled it.

Doreen glanced up at the sky. Her face serious, she recited a Bible verse. "And the wolf will dwell with the lamb, and the leopard will lie down with the kid, and the calf and the young lion and the fatling together; and a little boy will lead them." She paused and took a sip of her drink. "If Isaiah knew about orangutans, he'd have mentioned them too. I need to check Billy's schedule," Doreen said. "He'll probably be in Thailand as usual. If he's away the day of the meeting, I'll do it. This place needs some shakin' up."

Laura hugged her friend.

The next day the women went to the market and bought a portable Singer sewing machine. And after considerable searching, they found a bolt of red fleece fabric similar to that used for blankets and nightgowns. Though not meant for the tropics, it was the closest match to an orangutan's hairy hide.

"That machine was expensive," Laura said when they returned home with their bundles. "Everything here that's imported costs twice as much as at home. I can't imagine the poor are able to do much sewing."

Later Doreen brought over one of her caftans. She watched as Laura took measurements and created a pattern from newspaper. Laura had taken a sewing course at Parson's and knew what to do.

"When I first thought of going into fashion, I didn't have animal costumes in mind." Laura laughed, pinning the pattern to the fleece cloth and cutting around it. "I was twelve at the time and had seen *Breakfast at Tiffany's*. I wanted to wear glamorous clothes and be like Audrey Hepburn."

"I can't imagine Audrey in a monkey suit. She's much too elegant for that."

Laura smiled to herself. When she left New York she couldn't have imagined she would end up using her fashion skills to protest for animal rights in Indonesia. She wondered what Grace would say if she could see her designer protégé hunched over a portable sewing machine, stitching together pieces of red fleece. Laura finished the costume and handed it to Doreen to try on.

"So what do you think?" Doreen asked. She did a slow twirl in the middle of the room. "Look like an orang?"

"Perfect," Laura said, thinking she actually resembled a tomato. They hadn't been able to find the right shade of orang red. But Laura didn't care; it was close enough.

***

The day of the ministers' meeting, the women put on their homemade orangutan masks, and wearing their red-orange costumes, strolled out of the house. Beneath the mask eye sockets, Laura had painted a teardrop.

"Wowee," Mille said. He stepped back to get a better look. "So where do you two orangutans want to go today?"

Laura smiled inside her mask pleased he had correctly identified them.

"To the Kediri," the women replied in unison.

Shaking his head, Mille opened the door.

"Wait, we forgot the signs about not killing orangutans," Laura said. She struggled out of the car and rushed back inside. She reappeared with two placards. "*Tidak Mata* Orangs" proclaimed the bold lettering.

"I forgot something too," Doreen said. She hastened to her car and returned with a flask. "For my nerves."

Mille started the car and they drove off. Laura glanced at Doreen. Her costumed friend was tapping her fingers on her fleece-covered knees. Laura prayed she wouldn't change her mind or consume all the booze in the flask before they got to the Kediri.

"Mille, park on the street outside," Laura said. She didn't want to chance anyone at the hotel spotting her car. "But first drive slowly past the gate. I want to see what's going on." As she expected, TV cameras and news reporters had gathered at the entrance.

"There's more press than I hoped," Laura said, now nervous, her throat dry.

"Not good," Doreen said, her voice muffled. "And it's hot and itchy in this suit. Maybe we should go home." She lifted her mask and took a drink from her flask.

"Not much longer," Laura said. She hoped Doreen wouldn't refuse to get out.

Laura spotted two black Mercedes with tinted windows turn into the drive. "Okay, this is it," she said. "Remember, no English. We don't want them to know we're expats. And when I tap you on the shoulder, make a dash for the car."

The women climbed out and took up positions across from the hotel entry. They hoisted their signs. "U-u-hu-u-u-hu," came their high-pitched cries. The press ran down the steps and surrounded them. The whir of cameras interspersed with the women's orangutan grunts.

Laura couldn't see Doreen through the tiny eye slots of her mask, though she knew she was close by. Her friend's cries sounded like a woman on the verge of orgasm. Reporters snapped pictures and shouted in Bahasa. A hand reached for Laura's mask. She panicked, tapped Doreen on the shoulder and pointed to the gate. The two women, still waving their signs, scurried away.

Hyperventilating, Doreen struggled to get in. "Damn, my costume's caught on the door handle," she said, her voice frantic. Laura reached around and freed her. Both women tumbled into the backseat.

"Out of here, Mille," Laura shouted. As he sped off, she looked back and moaned. A reporter stood at the curb, pen in hand, jotting down the license number of her car.

Chapter 15

The next morning at breakfast, Laura perused the newspaper while Jack drank coffee. She flipped through to see if the protest had been reported and scowled when she didn't find anything. She stowed the costumes in a spare bedroom closet, not wanting Jack to see them. Though Laura didn't like to keep secrets from him, she knew he would explode if he found out. She hadn't slept much the previous night. And though proud of herself and Doreen, she worried about the reporter.

"So what are you up to today?" Jack asked as he speared a slice of papaya with his fork.

"Sarinah and I are going to the kampung to work with the kids."

"Glad the program's back on track," he said. He took a sip of coffee.

"Those kids are so bright. They continue to amaze me."

Maya came into the room and said, "Tuan, there's man at gate. He from newspaper."

Laura raised her napkin to her face, wishing the cloth were big enough to hide behind. She dabbed at the corners of her mouth.

"Tell him we already subscribe," Jack said.

"He say he come to talk about orangs."

Jack glanced at Laura. "You know anything about this?"

"Maya, tell him expats live here. We don't know what he's talking about," Laura said. She dared not look at Jack.

"What's going on?" he asked when Maya left.

She had no choice but to tell him.

"Have you gone crazy?" he yelled when she finished, his face red. "You're going to get us kicked out of the country." With his chest heaving, he leaned back in his chair.

"Newsman not go," Maya said when she returned.

Laura made a move to get up from her chair. Jack stretched out his arm. "I'll take care of this." He headed for the door.

Laura got up and went to the window. She cringed on recognizing the reporter who had written down her license plate number. She watched as Jack conversed with him. After a few minutes the reporter hopped on his motorbike and took off.

"He wants to interview the women dressed up like orangutans," Jack said when he came back inside. "I told them he had the wrong house. Doubt if he believed me. He'll be back." He glared at Laura. "I'm trying to run a bank, and you're flitting around Jakarta in a costume. You could end up in jail, and then what?" Laura understood his concern. She took a big risk. Her only regret was that she forgot to cover the license plate with a handful of mud.

"No one else cares what happens to the orangutans or the rainforest," she said. She knew her comment sounded lame but couldn't think of anything else to say.

Jack glanced at his watch. "I have a meeting at the office. We'll talk more when I get home. If I were you, I'd stay inside." He tossed his napkin on the table, grabbed his briefcase, and stormed out the front door.

Laura tapped her fingers together. He was right. She did come here to support him, not create problems. Though she didn't intend to forsake her quest, she would have to be more careful. She didn't think she and Doreen did anything wrong. She hoped that Jack dissuaded the reporter from continuing to follow her. She counted on the reporter not believing a foreigner would risk a cushy lifestyle by protesting. She finished her coffee, and despite Jack's warning to stay inside, she went to get ready to go to the kampung.

Later Laura opened the door a crack and peered toward the gate. Not seeing anyone there, she ventured out.

"Selemat pagi," she said to Mille, who as usual busied himself washing the car.

"I see you and other nyonya last night on TV," he said. "Everyone in my village watch. They think you funny."

"Oh no, you told them it was me?"

"I do something wrong?"

Laura noticed the hurt expression on his face. "Of course not." She doubted if the villagers would report her to the police. She was more concerned that they had missed the point of the protest. It seemed like they thought she and Doreen were a local version of *I Love Lucy.*

"Could you see the signs?" she asked, her tone hopeful.

"You and other nyonya jumping around. Hard to read."

"Damn," Laura muttered. She had managed to get press coverage, but the message had been lost.

When Sarinah arrived, Mille drove them to the kampung. He dropped them off and as the women walked along, Laura told Sarinah about the protest.

"I'm so proud of you," Sarinah said. She pulled down her sunglasses and looked at Laura over the tortoiseshell rims. "I wouldn't have had the nerve."

"It's interesting," Laura said. "I wonder if I would have done something like that in the States. Perhaps people tend to be more daring when there's no one around they know."

"I can tell how committed you are," Sarinah said. "I could hear it in your voice the day you came back from the market. You have the maternal instincts of a mother protecting her young."

She's right. Laura thought about that poor baby most of the time.

"You remember once I mentioned visiting Borobudur?" Sarinah said. "This might be a good time to go. You could use a break. And when we get back, the reporter should have given up, if he hasn't already."

Laura had read about the ancient Buddhist monument and wanted to visit. And it might give Jack time to cool down. "Great idea."

"We could go Tuesday and Wednesday of next week when we're not busy with the kids," Sarinah said.

"Doreen's husband goes to Thailand often, and she's home alone. Maybe she'd like to come along"

When Sarinah left, Laura checked her agenda. She grimaced. She would be gone on February 14 — Valentine's Day, the day she and Jack had gotten engaged eight years before. They celebrated that special day each year. Laura hesitated, and though tempted to call Sarinah to reschedule, she instead scribed *Borobudur* in her calendar. Busy at the bank, Jack probably wouldn't even remember. And he was so upset with her she couldn't imagine he would want to sit through the pretense of a romantic dinner.

***

"You're going off by yourself?" Jack said when Laura told him about the trip. "And on Valentine's Day to boot. You know we always do something special then. I already made a dinner reservation. "

"Jack, that's so sweet," she said, surprised. "We can celebrate when I get back."

"Our house gets bombed, and you go traipsing off around the country alone. Who knows what else might happen. And on top of it, you've got a reporter dogging your trail."

"I'm not going alone. And the house bombing was an isolated incident. You said so yourself. It could have happened anywhere, and I'm over it. The reporter is a good reason to leave. By the time I get back, Doreen and I will be stale news."

"You're probably planning to take your protest to Borobudur and really get us in trouble." He paused; his nostrils flared. "Fine, do what you have to do." In the days that followed, Jack and Laura spoke around and past each other, avoiding anything meaningful.

***

One morning following their quarrel, Laura couldn't find her hairbrush in the bathroom cabinet. And when she went to the closet, she noticed one of her sandals missing. Downstairs she confronted Maya.

"Maybe Diablo take sandal," Maya said.

"Diablo never goes upstairs. You know that."

"Maybe you leave by pool when you swim."

"Why would I come back to the house wearing one sandal?"

"I dunno."

"And I don't suppose you've seen my hairbrush either."

"Maybe spirit steal brush and sandal," Maya said, batting her eyes.

Since their argument, Jack turned in after Laura was already asleep. Now she lay back and pulled the sheet up under her arm. She moved her hand under the pillow felt something sharp, sharp like the quills of a porcupine. Screaming, she jumped from the bed, grabbed the pillow and tossed it onto the floor. *There was her hairbrush.* How had it gotten there? She never brushed her hair sitting on the bed. On a hunch, she rushed to the closet. The missing sandal was back in its place beside the other. Laura, jaw firm and her fists clinched in front of her, strode across the room and out onto the balcony. She took a deep breath and gripped the railing. It had to be Maya. Sensing the discord between her and Jack, she had taken advantage of the opportunity to taunt her

The next morning, amidst heavy tension in the house, Laura left for Borobudur

Chapter 16

Laura, Sarinah, and Doreen checked into the Hotel Indah in Yogyakarta, the city nearest Borobudur. Laura regretted leaving Jack without having talked through their argument. In her room she picked up the phone and called him, but was disappointed when she got no answer. She surmised he must be working late.

The women gathered for dinner in the dining room, a drab setting that evidenced age and neglect. Dark paintings hung on white walls now yellowed. And threadbare cloths covered round tables. Laura found the scene depressing. She wished they had gone somewhere else.

"Happy Valentine's Day," she said. Her voice feigned lightheartedness. The women clinked glasses.

"My Billy sent me a bouquet of flowers and a box of chocolates before he left for Thailand," Doreen said.

"Harold's traveling too. Valentine's isn't celebrated here, so I didn't expect anything, but he surprised me with a dozen red roses," Sarinah said.

The women looked at Laura.

"Jack and I had an argument," she said. "We got engaged on Valentine's eight years ago. He made a dinner reservation for this evening, but I came here instead."

"Oh, honey," Doreen said. She patted Laura on the arm. "You must feel terrible. But it's okay. You two can celebrate when you get back."

"And isn't Jack the romantic," Sarinah said. "Making a dinner reservation to surprise you. Laura, you're so fortunate."

In her kind, sweet way Sarinah had meant to be consoling, yet she only added to Laura's feeling of guilt.

"You're right, Doreen. We can have dinner when I get back." Laura sought to change the topic. "Where did you and Harold meet?" she asked Sarinah.

"On the tennis courts at the Kediri. Tennis is Jakarta's answer to a singles' bar," she said with a laugh. "It's difficult for Indonesian women to meet men, and even more difficult for someone like me who's tall and Western-educated. Sometimes I think Indonesian men are afraid of me. Once I got desperate and went to a pub in Jakarta where foreign guys hang out." She leaned forward, her tone conspiratorial. "As soon as I walked in, I knew I had made a mistake. Most of the women there were from the street, hustling drinks." She paused to swirl her martini. "I got up the courage to take a seat at the bar expecting Prince Charming to join me. When I ordered a cocktail, the bartender gave me a wink and asked if I was one of the 'new girls.' I felt ashamed. I was afraid my parents might find out I was there. I didn't want to bring dishonor to the family so I left."

"I can't picture you perched on a stool in some sleazy bar. You're so regal," Laura said. Sarinah's story reminded her of those occasions when she used to frequent a singles' bar near the United Nations. Trying to appear nonchalant, she hoped a tall, dark, and handsome diplomat from South America would wander over and chat, but the only men she ever met were from the Bronx.

"What do your parents think about you marrying Harold?"

"They would have preferred that I marry an Indonesian man. Now I think they're just happy I'm getting married at all. And they like Harold."

"No barstools for me," Doreen said. "Me and Billy were high school sweethearts. He was captain of the football team. All the popular girls were chasin' him. Then I got pregnant." Doreen tossed her blond curls and downed the last of her drink.

"I didn't know you had children," Laura said, surprised.

"Troy, our son, was a star football player like his dad. Then he got in with the wrong crowd and ended up on drugs."

"Oh, Doreen, I'm so sorry," Laura said.

"It gets worse. He robbed a 7-Eleven to pay for his habit and the police nabbed him. Now he's in the state penitentiary."

When a tear streaked Doreen's mascara, Laura reached in her purse for a tissue. "Billy's been my support through it all," she said. "I love that man so much."

The women ate in silence while Doreen regained her composure.

"What about you, Laura? Where did you and Jack meet?" Sarinah asked after a while.

"It wasn't so romantic. We met at Columbia University in the cafeteria. After I graduated from Parsons School of Design, I took some finance courses, thinking someday I might want to start my own business." Laura paused and glanced down. "There was a time I thought we shouldn't get married. That it wasn't meant to be."

Their eyebrows raised, Sarinah and Doreen stared at her.

"I was trying on a wedding dress at Saks Fifth Avenue. I bent over, threw my back out, and had to stay in bed. My mother came down from Connecticut to help. I couldn't do anything."

"How awful," Sarinah said. "I can't imagine."

"Two days before the wedding, there was a blackout in Manhattan, the worst ever. The entire city went dark."

"So what did you do?" Doreen asked, her tone incredulous.

"The ceremony was scheduled for Saturday afternoon. Friday there was still no electricity. The baker called to say he couldn't bake the cake. The florist called to say the flowers had wilted without refrigeration. I called the caterer. He said he couldn't prepare the food, and even if he could, the elevator wasn't working. He wouldn't be able to get up to the penthouse, the place for the reception."

"You must have been frantic," Sarinah said.

"Riots and looting broke out in several parts of the city. Guests saw it on TV. They were afraid to come."

"Can't say I blame them," Sarinah said.

"Saturday morning power was finally restored. And that afternoon Jack and I rode up Park Avenue in a horse-drawn carriage to the church. In spite of all that happened, we got married."

"That's quite the story," Sarinah said.

"Sometimes I wonder if it was an omen."

"What an awful thing to say. You two make a handsome couple," Doreen said.

"Maybe we should order dessert," Laura said. She glanced around for the waiter. "I want to try calling Jack again before it gets too late."

***

Back in her room, Laura dialed the house. No one answered. She thought he might still be at the office and called there. After many rings, Gunadi picked up.

"Oh, Gunadi, I'm so glad you answered. I'm calling to speak to my husband."

"He's not here, Mrs. Harrison. Today he left early."

Laura set the phone down. In New York, she wouldn't have given it a second thought, but in a country neither of them knew well, she found herself worried. She sat on the edge of the bed and twisted her hands. She blamed herself for coming on the trip.

Chapter 17

To Jack's chagrin, there hadn't been any movement on the court case. And when Wati told him Tom was on the line waiting to speak to him, he tensed. He suspected his boss wanted to know why nothing was happening.

He picked up and from the echo could tell Tom had him on speaker. He despised the speakerphone, which was Tom's preferred way of communicating. It made Tom sound imperious and made Jack uncomfortable, suspicious someone else might be sitting at the other end unannounced, listening.

"What's happening with that damn loan in Bandung? Have you taken care of it?" Tom's voice boomed and echoed. "I'm under a lot of pressure from the auditors. If this isn't cleared up soon the bank is going to have to take a hit."

Intending to tell his boss about the judge, Jack waited for an opening. But Tom continued unabated. "My neck is on the line. The board is expecting better results from the international operations this year. I don't want Indonesia dragging us down. The borrower has the means. He's just being difficult."

Jack didn't dare mention the judge's request for a bribe over a speakerphone. Bribery was a toxic subject among bankers, something rarely discussed even in private. "Tom, take me off the speaker for a minute."

Jack heard a click and the annoying echo disappeared. "The judge wants money to hear the case." The prolonged silence caused Jack to think they had been disconnected.

When Tom replied, his voice seethed in a whisper. "That's not something we should talk about. I don't want to have to write off that damn loan. Do what you have to do. You get my drift?"

Jack gulped. It wasn't the kind of reaction he expected. It sounded like Tom was giving him the green light to pay a bribe.

"Jack, you're a smart guy. That's why I sent you there. I'm sure you can figure it out. Do what you have to do," Tom said, his tone measured. "Look, I'm in a rush, already late for a meeting. Hope Laura's enjoying the new house. Give her my best." The phone went dead.

"Bastard." When the intercom sounded again, Jack pushed the button. He hoped Tom might have reconsidered his predicament and called back.

"It's Larry White," the secretary said.

Hoping for good news, Jack grabbed the receiver. "Larry, what's up?" he asked. His heart pounded.

"Things don't look good, Jack. Judge Hartono postponed the bank's case indefinitely. He wants the money."

"Son of a bitch."

"I know. It's tough, but he's in the driver's seat."

"Okay, Larry. Not sure what more I can do." He hung up.

Though not surprised at the judge, he had expected more of Tom. After all, he was a member of the credit committee that approved the transaction a year ago.

Jack got up and paced. He couldn't let the bank fail. Failure was not a part of his makeup, nor was it something tolerated in New York. He had to figure out a way. He decided to take a walk and ponder his predicament.

A fierce sun beat down as he weaved his way through cars parked askew. At the end of the block he turned into a back alley where vendors at stalls sold colorful tropical fish in small plastic bags filled with ocean water. Jack spotted a sinister looking eel with rows of sharp teeth. He grimaced. The creature reminded him of the judge. As he walked, the discomfort of the humidity added to his anguish. He felt isolated. He hadn't been in the country long enough to make friends he could consult, and Larry White was a waste of time. Jack's father died of cirrhosis when Jack was eight years old. And he never had a mentor. He became accustomed to working through problems on his own. But he had never faced such a crisis of morality.

Yet that wasn't the way bribery was perceived here. Money under the table was the way things got done in Indonesia. Everybody did it. New York must have known that when they decided to make an investment in the country. And hadn't Tom told him to "do what you have to do"? Reconciled to the inevitable, he began to devise a plan.

He returned to the office and picked up the phone. "Judge, this is Jack. Can we meet later today, five o'clock in the Barong Bar?"

***

Haroon edged the sedan out into traffic and headed for the Hotel Kediri. Jack sat in the back. He loosened his tie and undid the top button on his shirt. He leaned back and continued to rationalize. His job was to turn the bank around, not let it fail, though he knew his father-in-law, Richard, would take immense pleasure in his failure. It would be confirmation Jack was not worthy of his daughter. If the bank didn't succeed, it would be a setback for his career, and he wouldn't get the promised bonus.

At the entry to the Kediri, Jack stepped out of the car and mounted the steps. His skin felt clammy, and not just because of the weather. He had purposefully chosen the Barong Bar and this hour for the meeting. A gamelan band with five musicians in traditional Javanese costume sat on the tile floor amidst an array of gongs, small drums, and a xylophone. Most of the time gamelan, the traditional music of Java and Bali, sounded as soft and gentle as a wind chime. The band at the Barong was loud and discordant. The percussion resounded off the walls, making it difficult to hear or eavesdrop. High stools surrounded a circular bar, and small tables in the shadows provided a place for patrons who preferred to sit and drink unobserved.

Jack took a seat in the corner, his eyes focused on the entry. He did not have long to wait before Judge Hartono appeared silhouetted in the doorway. Jack sat still and watched the judge search for him.

"Jack, hello. I didn't see you over here in the dark."

Though hardly in the mood for an exchange of pleasantries, Jack needed the judge's cooperation. "Hello, Judge, what would you like to drink?"

"I'll have a Bir Bintang."

The hovering waitress nodded and glanced at Jack.

"Make that two."

Jack studied the judge's face. He pondered how a man with such a paternal façade could be so corrupt.

"Let me get right to the point," Jack said, aware that was an Asian breach of etiquette. Considering the judge's own prior bluntness, Jack didn't think he would be offended. "If I give you Rp. 25 million, what assurance do I have you will render a favorable judgment and that the bank will get its $1 million?" Even with the judge's ruling, Jack knew there was no guarantee the borrower would repay. Still, he looked for some certainty.

"Unfortunately you have none, but you have no alternative. You have to trust me." Judge Hartono paused when the waitress returned with tall frosted glasses of beer. "The man who owes you the money is wealthy. He can repay the loan, no problem, but with Americans he knows he can play games. With me, he can't. I may only be a civil servant, but I am Indonesian. And I am a judge. I can make his life miserable."

Jack hesitated, still not sure he could trust the judge and unconvinced the bank would get its money back. He took a sip of beer. Tempted to get up and walk away, he contemplated the man who sat across the table. "I'll give you the money, but I need your help. I need a supporting document."

The judge looked puzzled.

"It's the only way. You have to give me something with an official letterhead that looks authentic, something to justify the payment. Make up the name of a fictitious law firm and add 'Rp. 25 million for legal services. Payable in cash.'"

The judge leaned back in his chair. "But that's illegal."

Jack smiled. He thought the judge must be joking, but saw no humor on his face. "Look at it this way, Judge, you're providing a legal service aren't you? I can't get the bank's controller to just dish out money without an invoice, particularly for an amount that large."

"This is an unusual request, Jack. No one else ever asked me for something like that."

Jack took another swig of beer.

"You're a smart man," the judge said. Jack thought it ironic the judge and Tom had both chosen the same insincere phrase to flatter him. "But I don't want a paper trail leading to me. You'll have to do better than that."

The judge stood up and walked away, leaving his half-finished bottle of beer on the table.

***

The following week, Jack sat staring at the wall in his office. Restless, he got up and walked the room. He hadn't heard from the judge, and the silence had begun to grate. Despite the judge's negative reaction, Jack was counting on him being unable to resist so much money.

He strolled down the hall to the conference room to meet with the loan officers. Business was picking up since his arrival, and he thanked them for their hard work. The bank was turning the corner. Everything was on track — everything except for the bad loan in Bandung. Afterward, he left for lunch.

When he came back, Wati, his secretary, greeted him.

"A messenger left something for you. I put it on your desk."

Jack went in, picked up the envelope, and turned it over in his hands. No return address. He tore open the flap and a sheet of paper fell onto his desk — an invoice.

J. H. Legal Advisory
Rp. 25 million for legal services. Payable in cash.

Jack chuckled. *J. H.* as in *Judge Hartono.*

He now had the invoice he needed yet the most difficult step lay ahead. Gunadi was keeper of the cash, and his cooperation was essential. If they had worked together longer, Jack would have had a better sense as to how his controller would react. But he didn't know him well, and Indonesians were difficult to comprehend. He wasn't convinced Gunadi would just give him the money based on this single piece of paper. It was a risk. He counted on the controller being intimidated by his position as president of the bank. Tempted to take the invoice down the hall to Gunadi's office, he decided to treat it as he would any other. He scribbled *Approved for Payment* across the bottom, signed it, and dropped it in the out-box on his desk.

Jack busied himself in meetings and with phone calls, yet all he could think of was the invoice and the Rp. 25 million payment. With the day almost over, he considered going to the controller's office, but decided otherwise. He didn't want to draw attention to the unusual request for payment in cash.

The next morning when Jack arrived at the office, Gunadi stood in the hallway, the invoice in his hand. "I don't understand," he said.

"I had some legal work done on that loan in Bandung," Jack replied. "Larry White wasn't making much headway. J. H. Legal Advisory is a small firm. They only deal in cash. You can just give me the money, and I'll make sure they get it."

"Has the case been resolved?" Gunadi asked. "The bank is going to be repaid the $1 million?"

"Looks that way." Jack sounded confident.

"Approval of an expense of this amount requires two signatures, yours and mine," the controller said.

"I know."

"Better to give them a check." The tic in Gunadi's eye had begun to act up.

"Says they want cash. Better we do what they want We've been screwing around with this long enough. I'd rather pay the money than write off $1 million." He paused. "Wouldn't you?"

Gunadi headed back to his office and Jack gritted his teeth. *He's not convinced.*

***

Later that afternoon, Gunadi returned to Jack's office, an oversized briefcase in his hand. He set it on the corner of the desk and opened it. Jack's eyes widened. Inside he saw stacks of neatly bundled rupiah.

"The largest denomination printed is only ten thousand," the controller said. "So there are many."

Jack picked up a bundle. He flipped through the bills like a deck of cards.

"I need you to sign a receipt," the controller said. He handed Jack a pen and pointed to a place at the bottom.

"All very efficient," Jack said.

After Gunadi left, he made a phone call.

"Hello. Judge. Barong Bar, same time?"

Jack despised the place. Nothing good ever happened at the Barong Bar. He headed for the same table in the corner and the waitress came over. She welcomed him back and asked if his friend would be joining him. Though displeased at her perception of his relationship with the judge, he nodded.

"Should I bring two Bir Bintangs?"

"Sure."

Once she left, he sat there and congratulated himself on having devised such a clever scheme. He was surprised at how calm he felt; he expected otherwise. Being corrupt in a culture of corruption, he didn't feel corrupt at all.

The judge walked in, followed by the waitress. She set beers on the table and left.

"Jack, you're looking well. More relaxed than the last time we met."

"I got the invoice. Thanks."

"You Americans are a lot of trouble. It's much easier working with Europeans. If I knew about the requirement for an invoice, I would have asked for more money," the judge said, his smile tight-lipped.

The major hurdle overcome, Jack had developed an odd fondness for the judge. He was articulate, smart, and had a dry sense of humor. Jack reached for the briefcase at his feet and hoisted it onto the table. He opened it enough for the judge to get a glimpse of the bundles inside. "Twenty-five million rupiah."

The judge looked at Jack and nodded his head "You're a smart man."

The expression started to grate. When the judge extended his hand across the table, Jack hesitated but then clasped it to conclude the deal.

"We're partners now," the judge said.

The men finished their beers in silence. After a while the judge got up, briefcase in hand, and walked out past the gongs of the gamelan. Jack sat in the shadows and drank alone.

Chapter 18

Jack left the Barong Bar and headed home. The emptiness and quiet of the house depressed him. He changed clothes and wandered the rooms. On other occasions, being alone wouldn't bother him, but now he dealt with pangs of guilt and fear of recrimination. He doubted he would have told Laura what he had done, but he wished she were here. And he wanted to apologize for their argument; he was unfair.

In New York, he could have gone outside and walked the busy streets, distracted by the energy of a crowd. But in Jakarta, walking at night was not an option. Dark, narrow roads made it unsafe for pedestrians. Back home he could have watched television, but the stations here broadcast only local programs in Bahasa. Though his car was in the garage, Haroon was gone for the day and foreigners rarely drove. He heard the story of an expatriate who struck an Indonesian walking on the side of the road. When he got out of the car, a crowd gathered and stoned him. Jack questioned the veracity of the story, but he didn't want to take the chance.

He walked into the kitchen, where Maya sat on a stool in the corner. She smiled at him, and Jack nodded. He made himself a gin and tonic and returned to the living room.

His gaze fixed across the room, Jack drank. He picked up a magazine from a nearby table, scanned a few articles, and set it down. He returned to the kitchen several times for drinks, and on each occasion Maya came over with a tray of ice cubes and offered to help.

To break the deafening silence, he selected a CD from the stack and inserted the disc in the machine in the living room. The distinctive wail of Willie Nelson singing a song about heartbreak filled the room. The lyrics and languid melody of "Always On My Mind" depressed Jack even more. Distracted and withdrawn, he didn't hear Maya enter. She asked if he wanted another drink. He looked at her. He saw no trace of the insolence Laura found so irritating.

"Sure," he said, though he knew he shouldn't drink another. He handed her his empty glass.

When she returned, Jack's eyes tracked her. She set the glass on the table and left. He watched her bare feet glide across the floor. He tried to divert his mind to something calming, yet thoughts of the judge and the money intruded.

He reflected on the day's events, surprised Gunadi had been so complacent. Maybe after the controller gave it more thought, he would question Jack and try to pin him down. He might inquire about the fictitious J. H. Legal Advisory invoice. How would he respond? Or maybe the judge would attempt to blackmail him and demand even more money. Where would he get it?

As the alcohol took effect, the unpleasantness of the day began to fade into the recesses of his drunken mind.

"Dinner's ready, tuan," Maya said.

Jack got up from the couch and headed for the dining room. He felt conspicuous in the vast space, like being the first to arrive at a restaurant. Though he loved the grandeur of the big house, it now seemed impersonal.

He sat at the head of the table, lifted his fork, and mechanically began to eat the salad sitting in front of him. Maya entered with a platter. In the soft light from above, her dark hair shone like the luster of black satin.

"Looks delicious," Jack said. She set the food on the table.

"I hope you like. It *ikan pedas*, fish," she said. "Not too spicy."

"Are you from Jakarta?" he asked. He already knew she wasn't.

"I am from Sukabumi, two or three hour from here."

"Your family's still there?" He looked at her as he ate. He enjoyed her presence and the sound of her voice.

"I have cousins." She stood beside him, poised and mature for a girl so young.

"Your parents?"

"My mother die when I born." Her eyes reflected sadness.

"I'm sorry," Jack said. He wondered about her father but decided not to ask.

"How old are you?"

"Nineteen."

She turned and walked from the room. He did not attempt to stop her, though he discerned from her slow gait she would have preferred to stay.

Jack finished dessert and went out to the veranda, the country-western music now accompanied by the chirp of tree frogs and the nocturnal sound of insects. He sat in a rattan chair and thought about Laura.

Though satiated from the meal, he got a beer and took a swig, upset with Laura for leaving him alone. It was her fault he sat by himself on Valentine's Day. His thoughts returned to Maya. He remembered once he walked past the servant quarters at the back of the house and had seen her sitting in her cubicle on a cot. It had been her day off, but she was there. Where would she go? She had little money and apparently no friends or acquaintances nearby. She too was trapped and alone.

Maya quietly reappeared. "Can I get you anything else, tuan?"

He reached to take her hand. "You're beautiful."

"My aunt asleep." She stepped closer. "We must be quiet."

Jack drew her down onto his lap and ran his fingers through her silky hair. He kissed the soft skin of her neck and moved his hand over her breast. Suddenly, out of the corner of his eye, he glimpsed a face peering from around the banyan tree. He startled. Suparno? But when he looked straight on, he didn't see anyone. Besides, what did it matter what Suparno saw? He was a mute.

Chapter 19

At dawn, the three women gathered outside the hotel for the trip to Borobudur. Doreen, wearing a bright-yellow print dress, hoop earrings, and much blue eyeliner, climbed into the van and took a seat beside Laura.

"Did you get in touch with Jack?" she asked.

"No one answered."

"Honey, he's a grown man. He can take care of himself," Doreen said. She squeezed Laura's hand. "You just relax and have yourself a good time."

Perhaps Doreen is right. I've only been gone a day.

With Sarinah in front beside the driver, the women bounced along on the road to Borobudur while Doreen attempted to take a sip of coffee from the Styrofoam cup that jiggled in her hand.

As they left the outskirts of Yogyakarta behind, they passed rice paddies and then slowed as they drove through small villages.

"Look," Doreen said. "A dentist's office." She pointed out the window to a sign with a picture of a large molar. Underneath the tooth it read, "*Dokter Gigi.*"

"Gigi is my favorite Bahasa word. Sounds French. And nicer than *tooth.*"

"I believe it's pronounced 'ghee-ghee,'" Laura said.

"Whatever, I never was good at languages." Doreen went back to looking out the window.

"It'll take about another forty-five minutes to get to the monument," Sarinah said. "This is the best time to go, before the crowds, and before it gets too hot."

"This is the earliest I've ever been up in my life," Doreen said.

"Borobudur is worth getting up early for. It's the largest Buddhist monument in the world. People come from all over to see it."

"Me and Billy once attended a gospel meetin' in a tent outside Odessa," Doreen said. "Sittin' on those wooden benches, singin' 'n' clappin.' I never been so hot. I wished I'd worn somethin' cooler. But it was worth it to hear Sister Sharon, the famous faith healer. She even performed a miracle. At first I couldn't believe it. She called out for sinners wantin' to be healed, so Mary Lou went on up. Mary Lou and I went to grammar school together. She wasn't a big-time sinner." Doreen chuckled. "But she did need healin.' All her life she'd been cross-eyed. Sister Sharon put her hand on Mary Lou's head and prayed. We all prayed. She spun Mary Lou around and around till she fell on the ground. When she got up all covered in sawdust, her eyes were straight as an arrow. It was a miracle. Everybody threw up their hands and shouted, 'Halleluiah!' Crying tears of joy, I ran over and hugged her. I've never been so happy for somebody else."

Laura stifled a laugh. She pictured Doreen with her mascara and false lashes sitting on a bench in a hot tent.

"I haven't heard of miracles at Borobudur," Sarinah said graciously. "But then, Buddhists tend to be more discreet."

"Doubt if I would make a good Buddhist," Doreen replied. "I like my religion loud."

The driver pulled into the parking area and stopped. The monument rose majestically over a fertile valley of vibrant green rice paddies and tall coconut palms. Elaborate and intricately carved stone terraces, galleries, and stairways extended skyward. A soft morning mist hovered just above the ground. Large blocks chiseled from lava formed the massive structure, their golden patina mellow in the sun's early rays.

The women got out of the car and stood transfixed, overwhelmed by the setting and the edifice that loomed before them. They moved forward toward the statues of lions that flanked the stairs. At the bottom, a gaunt Buddhist monk sat seeking alms, a black lacquer bowl in his outstretched hand. His head was shaven, and he wore a tan cloth draped over one shoulder. The sun had darkened his skin.

Laura reached into her purse, pulled out a handful of rupiah notes, and handed them to him. His smile reminded her of those occasions when she'd given money to the beggar on the subway grate outside her office in New York. Though one was a monk and the other a homeless man, their look of gratitude was the same.

"You would make a good Buddhist," Sarinah said. "Compassion is one of the steps on the path to Nirvana."

"Don't tell Jack." She was trying not to think of him. "He says I'm too generous, that if I quit giving people money they would get a job."

"This *is* his job. He's keeping the world safe for the rest of us."

Statues of Buddha stretched along the balustrade overhead. Cross-legged, hands palm up in their laps, they gazed across the plains.

"Best place to start is at the corner of the monument," Sarinah said. "Unfortunately, most tourists miss what's there."

Sarinah led the women to four carved stone reliefs she referred to as the Wall of Good and Evil. She told them, "Centuries ago, pilgrims couldn't read. Scenes depicted moral lessons to remind them that they could escape the sorrows of their daily existence by leading a good life and achieving Nirvana."

Sarinah stepped closer to the wall. "You see the figures on the right, the ones with the bodies of men and heads of monkeys? They did something bad and have been punished with ugly faces."

"It's like the Ten Commandments," Doreen said. "Except the commandments don't show what happens if you disobey."

"An ugly face *is* hell," Laura said. Reflexively she touched her cheek.

"In the next panel, you see a man forgiving his enemy. He's being rewarded with wealth and the happy family that surrounds him."

Laura wondered if there were carvings with lessons about marriage.

"There are more panels with life lessons, but they're buried," Sarinah said.

"Why is that?" Laura asked.

"I'm not sure. In 1890 they were uncovered, photographed, and buried again. During World War II and the occupation, the Japanese dug up these four, then stopped digging."

"That's strange. I wonder why they didn't uncover 'em all," Doreen said.

"Maybe after stumbling onto lessons about good and evil, the Japanese felt guilty," Laura said. She experienced a twinge of guilt herself and looked away. She wished she and Jack could have resolved their differences before she left on her trip.

"I remember a photograph I saw of one of the buried panels. You'd find it interesting," Sarinah said. She glanced at Laura. "It depicts the eight hells of Buddhist mythology. One punishes those who kill animals for pleasure. The perpetrators are forced to walk through the Sword Tree Forest, where leaves fall like daggers."

"It should be uncovered and displayed," Laura said.

The women left the Wall of Good and Evil and returned to the steep stone steps. They began their climb. "Pilgrims pray as they walk. For them, this is a spiritual journey. If you go all the way around the monument to the top, it's about three miles."

"This place is hotter'n a honeymoon hotel," Doreen said. "I may not make it." She wiped her brow.

Laura stopped and traced her fingers across a woman's stone face with eyes shaped like almonds, brows arched, nose chiseled, and mouth sensual. Her hair resembled a beehive, and an elaborate necklace rested just above her breasts. Laura wondered about the artisan who had carved the image fifteen hundred years ago. What was he thinking as he chiseled? Was the woman real to him or just a fantasy?

Ahead a family stared at Doreen and Laura as they spoke among themselves.

"They are villagers. They have probably never seen a real-life blond or redhead. They want to take your picture."

"Don't tell them my hair color came out of a bottle or they might not be interested," Doreen said.

Laura and Doreen posed in front of a Buddha and the cameras clicked.

"We'll probably end up in their family album, and the grandkids will wonder how we're related."

The family waved and wandered off.

"You two are the highlight of their visit to Borobudur," Sarinah said. "They will go home and tell others in their village about the women with the Technicolor hair."

The trio walked along observing the walls.

"Do Buddhists believe in God?" Doreen asked.

"Buddhists believe God is within each of us. They believe Nirvana, or happiness, can be attained here on earth. They don't dwell on the past or fret about the future. They live for the present. It's called *awareness.*"

"Sounds complicated."

"Not really, just difficult to explain."

"Buddhists meditate and concentrate on the rhythm of their breath," Sarinah continued. "It helps focus the mind, so eventually one reaches a state of mindfulness, where there's nothing there at all."

"I can't imagine people in Texas meditatin'," Doreen said. "They like to keep their eyes open, lookin' around. Buddhism sounds like a lot of hocus-pocus."

"Doreen," Laura said sharply. "Buddhism is one of the world's great religions. You need to be more open-minded."

"I mean, look at all these false idols," Doreen said. With a sweep of her arm she incorporated all the Buddha statues in her comment.

Laura clenched her fists. "Buddhists don't worship the statues. They follow the teachings of the Buddha, a holy man. Like you follow the teachings of Jesus Christ."

Doreen scowled, her hands on her hips. "Don't you dare go comparing Buddha to Jesus."

"Ladies, please," Sarinah said, her voice a loud whisper. "This is neither the time nor the place to argue about this."

Fuming, Laura followed Sarinah as she walked on ahead. Minutes later they were startled by the strains of a song. They turned and saw Doreen in the middle of the passageway, singing, her hands at her bosom, her eyes closed singing an old gospel hymn. She raised her arms to the heavens, and her voice resonated off the old walls. Two monks rounded the corner, their hands clasped in prayer. Laura caught her breath, concerned at the impending clash of cultures. But the men passed on either side of the singing woman, their solemnity uninterrupted. Doreen continued the rest of the song, not missing a beat.

On the final note and in the manner of a diva, Doreen bowed. "I just felt I needed to sing about Jesus."

"You should learn to be more respectful." Laura felt her face flush.

"It's okay," Sarinah said. "Buddhists are tolerant. Unlike other religions, there has never been a war fought over Buddhism."

Doreen leaned against the wall to catch her breath.

"Are you okay?" Sarinah asked.

"My feet are killin' me." She removed her open-toed shoe and kneaded her foot. "I'm goin' to go back, get myself a cool drink, and sit by the van." She wedged her shoe back on, waved, and wandered off.

"That was rude," Laura said, her mouth firm.

Sarinah placed her hand on Laura's arm. "You shouldn't let Doreen upset you. She's well-meaning. She has a good heart."

"Don't keep defending her. You're always so nice. You're so, so saccharine. Can't you show some emotion once in a while?"

Sarinah did show emotion — shock, then distress.

Laura put her face in her hands. She had hurt her friend. "I'm so sorry."

"Nothing to be sorry for," Sarinah said, embracing her. "You seem preoccupied. You've been distracted most of the day."

Laura dropped her gaze and walked on.

For the next forty-five minutes the two women continued around the monument until they finally reached the top. A breeze blew across Laura's face, and she breathed deeply. She looked up at the cloudless blue sky and out over the plains to volcanic peaks far in the distance. Below, farmers plowing their fields resembled Lilliputians. By comparison, giant Buddhas loomed beside her. As she stood in the presence of the stately statues, she experienced a sense of peace. Jack and their argument vanished from her mind.

"I knew very little about Buddhism before I came here. Now I'm intrigued, though I think it would be difficult to live in the present and stay calm even when things go wrong."

"That is the hardest part. Most of us don't like to think bad things will happen. It sounds pessimistic. Unfortunately, all of us will encounter suffering at some stage. Buddhism prepares followers for when that happens. It doesn't mean they don't feel the pain — they do. But they accept it as a part of life. The calmness attained through meditation allows them to cope."

"I'd like to learn more. Perhaps you can teach me."

"I wouldn't be the best teacher. I'll introduce you to my friend. She's Buddhist."

"Oh, but I thought you were Buddhist. You know so much."

"I'm Muslim. When I first visited Borobudur the beauty of the art and stone carvings impressed me. I wanted to learn more about the religion behind it."

Laura glanced at her watch for the first time since they left the hotel. "Perhaps we should go back to the van. It's been a wonderful day. But now it's hot."

They proceeded down the stone steps to the bottom. Laura stopped and looked back. She wanted to remember the monument and her special moment of peace at the top. She reflected on what Sarinah said about enjoying the present. She lived most of her life in the past or the future, pondering what might have been or fretted over what might happen. Her mind occasionally flitted back to New York and the career she left behind. She contemplated what might have been had she not followed Jack to Indonesia, or even if they had not met at Columbia and she had married someone else. She worried about her marriage. She suspected most people lived like her, fantasizing about the path not taken and uncertain as to the future.

She vowed to come back to Borobudur. Next time she would bring Jack. And though she knew this was not his kind of place, she hoped he might find peace here too. Originally eager to get away from Jakarta, she was now ready to return. She wanted to see Jack and make amends for their argument.

Chapter 20

Laura entered the house and looked around, expecting to see the servants. She trudged up the stairs with her suitcase while thinking the house unusually quiet. In the bedroom, Jack's clothes lay strewn about the floor, and the bed was still unmade. Not bothering to unpack, she headed down to find Maya. She crossed the living room and spotted Suparno on the veranda, a harried look on his face. She went out to speak to him.

"Suparno, are you all right?" From behind his back he pulled a colorful bouquet.

"How beautiful!" She sniffed them and thought how kind it was of him to welcome her home with freshly cut flowers. The silent man shifted from side to side, looking as if he might speak. But with a look of frustration, he picked up his broom and wandered off to the far corner of the garden.

Puzzled by his behavior, Laura entered the empty kitchen and set the bouquet on the counter. *Something odd's going on.* In the servant's quarters she found Maya sitting on a yellow bundle that was tied at the top. Beside her Kartini stood with a beat-up brown suitcase at her feet. "We want pay for work up to yesterday. We leaving," the cook said.

"Why? What's wrong?"

Kartini looked down and didn't respond.

"Is my husband here? Does he know about this?"

"He at work."

Laura rushed back into the house, picked up the phone, and dialed.

"Wati, may I speak with Jack please?"

"He went to a meeting outside Jakarta. He should return about four o'clock. Want me to have him call you, Mrs. Harrison?"

"Please." She hurried back to where the servants waited.

"Kartini, do you have another job? Is that why you're leaving?" Laura glanced at Maya; the young girl averted her gaze.

"We go to Sukabumi, to our kampung," Kartini said.

Laura noticed Maya look at her aunt and frown as if she didn't want to go. Laura was even more troubled by Kartini's response. She doubted an Indonesian would leave a paying job to return to their village, but she went upstairs to the stash of rupiah in the closet. She gave the pair their wages and watched as they strolled out the gate and then stood at the edge of the road talking with Pak Hajji. Laura was surprised to see him there. Occasionally the trio glanced back at the house. Eventually, the women piled into a *becak* and arranged their belongings, and the driver pedaled away.

"What happened?" Laura asked Mille, who had been washing the car and saw the women depart.

"I don't know, but don't worry, nyonya. I help find someone else. Plenty people looking for work."

Back inside she walked through the house and searched randomly, though not knowing what she expected to find. Wanting to talk to someone, she called Doreen. Neither had mentioned their argument on the monument again. She knew each thought the other wrong, and each thought the other should apologize. Despite their differences, however, the friendship continued. In the small isolated community of expats, the women needed each other.

"The servants quit," Laura said.

"Really? You go away for one night and they walk out. That's odd. But don't go blamin' yourself. Servants are unreliable. Maybe some new expat who doesn't know the rules offered them more money."

"They said they were going back to their village."

"Don't believe it. Besides, I thought you didn't like the younger one."

"That's the strange thing," Laura said. "Maya wasn't insolent or haughty at all. She seemed reluctant to leave. It was Kartini who was upset."

"What's Jack say about all this? He was there while you were away."

"He's out of the office at a meeting. I left him a message. Even Suparno, the gardener, is acting strange."

"I'm sure there's a good reason. Jack will put your mind at ease."

Laura hung up.

***

Jack didn't get home until eight o'clock. Laura sat in the living room, waiting. He took off his jacket and walked across the room, his arms outstretched, prepared to give her a hug.

"Why didn't you call? I left a message earlier," she said.

"I was in Bandung all day. I didn't get any message. What's wrong?"

"You tell me. The servants quit."

"You're kidding." He averted his eyes.

"What happened while I was away?"

"Nothing."

"When I left, everything was fine. Servants don't just walk out without a reason."

"I had an argument with Kartini. That's probably what happened."

"Argument about what?"

"I asked her to make lime chicken for dinner. This morning she gave me receipts so I could reimburse her." Laura listened. She scrutinized his face. "But there was no receipt for the chicken. She told me it cost Rp. 1,500. She said she bought it from a roadside vendor and didn't have a receipt."

"So. What's the point?"

"That's the place where you see those plucked chickens hanging in the sun covered with flies. I got mad and yelled at her. Told her I could get sick, to never buy there again. But I could tell she didn't think eating chicken covered with flies was such a big deal."

Laura pondered the explanation. The story sounded plausible, but she couldn't be sure.

"Maya seemed odd, and even Suparno's acting weird."

"He always acts weird."

"Where were you? I called several times and no one answered."

142

"I was working late."

"Gunadi told me you left early."

"Hey, enough! While you were off having fun, I had to deal with Judge Hartono and that messy situation in Bandung."

Laura gasped. "I hope you didn't do something stupid."

"Of course not."

Later that night Laura lay in bed. Beside her Jack snored, though it wasn't his snoring that kept her awake. She had never questioned Jack's truthfulness before. But now she wondered. She sensed the marriage she had come to save, slipping away, though she knew not why.

Chapter 21

Laura had fallen into an expat lifestyle that revolved around a house full of help. She felt compelled to replace Kartini and Maya and so she called Doreen again.

"Perfect timing," Doreen said. "Tomorrow's Servant Exchange Day at the American Women's Auxiliary." The demeaning term bothered Laura. It made servants sound like barter. Still she agreed to go.

"At times servants can be annoying," Doreen said the next day as they bounced along in the Kijang. "You know YaYa, works for me. She's always telling me about her family and asking for money. She knows I'm a softie. And course I give it to her. And my friend Mildred — her husband works at CALCO with Billy — she says things go missing around the house. Even a lamp in the living room disappeared."

Doreen rambled on while Laura half-listened. She was still trying to understand why Kartini and Maya had left.

"But what would we do without our maids, houseboys, cooks, and gardeners?" Doreen said in conclusion.

Though Doreen hadn't included "drivers" in her litany, Laura worried Mille might have heard her and be offended. She frowned at her friend and nodded toward the front seat. Embarrassed, Doreen put her hand over her face.

Mille pulled into the parking lot of the Auxiliary. Indonesian women squatted, their belongings in bundles on the ground beside them. The men stood in the shade. Wisps of kretek smoke encircled their heads. Laura felt uncomfortable; she sensed desperate, hopeful eyes following her.

"Big crowd today," Doreen said. "You should be able to find somebody good."

Inside the small white building, a bulletin board displayed notices, categorized by skill, placed there by those seeking work. Laura perused the listings for cooks and maids. *Worked for*

European and American families...gud English...no spizzy food...wash hands...happy. Laura jotted down names of prospects.

"Y'all ready?" the gray-haired woman in charge asked, her Southern accent thick as gravy.

Laura handed her a slip of notepaper. "Ati Rapar," the woman called out the door.

Laura and Doreen took seats on folding metal chairs in the corner, and a pretty young woman joined them. Slim and of medium height, she had black eyes that sparkled as if to confirm the "happy" comment on the bulletin board.

Laura leaned forward to ask a question, but Doreen spoke first. "Hi, I'm Doreen. I'm here to help my friend Laura. She needs a cook. The cook she had quit. Just walked out."

Laura glared. Doreen had made her sound like a tyrant.

"Who was your last employer?" Laura asked.

"I work for American family for two year. I like them very much. Then they go home. Before I work for Australian family. And before, French. They all go home."

"What kind of meals did you prepare for the Americans?"

"I make hot dogs and grilled cheese for kids. The nyonya like casseroles."

"Honey, were there problems with any of the families?" Doreen asked. She touched the woman's arm as if to entice her to reveal titillating information.

"Maybe French. Their English no too good. Sometime I make mistake."

Doreen whispered to Laura. "She's perfect, don't you think?"

Laura ignored her. "Thank you, Ati Rapar. I will let you know."

"What was wrong with her? She seemed nice," Doreen said when the woman left.

"Too pretty," Laura said.

"Honey, you're not worried about Jack, are you?"

Laura wished Doreen wasn't with her.

"That may be a problem," Doreen said. "They're all pretty."

145

Ready for the next candidate, Laura signaled to the woman at the door.

"Nissam," the woman with the Southern accent shouted.

A young man in a faded blue batik sarong and with handsome features entered. The woman pointed him to where Laura and Doreen sat. Poised, he approached.

"I'm Nissam," he said.

"Oh, we thought you were going to be a woman," Doreen said.

"Not a problem," Laura said. "Have a seat."

He brushed off the already clean chair.

"The notice on the bulletin board says you are a cook and a seamstress."

"I love to sew. My mother teach me. At my last job, I make silk dresses for the nyonya. She give me a cotton dress she bring from America and I copy it. And I make pillow covers and drapes," he said with obvious pride.

Doreen and Laura exchanged glances.

Nissam handed Laura a folder bulging with papers. "Letters of reference. All the nyonyas like me. And copies of my favorite recipes. I cook American, European, Chinese, and Indonesian."

Laura looked through the correspondence. He was right. All the women had high praise for him. They mentioned he was polite and a wonderful cook. His recipes included boeuf bourguignon, pasta primavera, chocolate mousse, and Mandarin and Indonesian dishes.

"What happened with your previous job?" Laura asked.

"Family go home."

Doreen leaned over and whispered to Laura. "He seems nice, but my Billy wouldn't be comfortable having someone like *that* in the house. I've never met one, but I think he's gay."

Laura turned quickly to Doreen. She tried to keep her voice low. "I thought you were Christian."

Laura turned back to Nissam and proceeded to discuss pay, days off, and other responsibilities. "When can you start?" she asked.

"My things outside."

"Wonderful," Laura replied. "Please wait by the red car in the parking lot, the Kijang. We'll be out there in a few minutes."

"Jack's not going to be happy," Doreen said.

"He'll get over it."

"Okay, so now you need a maid," Doreen said. She ignored Laura's disparaging glances, obviously enjoying the interview process and eager for the next prospect.

"I know." Laura glanced down her list. "But most of the others seem to be nannies doubling as maids." The thought of a nanny reminded her of poor Pua. She decided she'd had enough for one day.

"Let's come back next week," she said. She gathered her papers. "There's only Jack and me to clean up after. It's not that big a deal."

Outside Nissam stood beside the car. He held a portable sewing machine. "Yours?" Laura asked, surprised. It looked new. She remembered how much she'd paid for the one she bought to make the orangutan costumes.

"One of the nyonyas give to me when she leave."

Nissam put it and a small suitcase decorated with flower stickers into the car. *Perhaps he can do flower arranging too. He's like an Indonesian renaissance guy.* Laura liked Nissam already, though she suspected Doreen was right about Jack. She doubted he'd be happy.

"Nyonya, what about a maid?" Mille asked. "You didn't find anyone?"

"I didn't, Mille."

"*Tidak apa apa,*" he replied.

Laura smiled. The saying meant "never mind" or "don't worry." Indonesians used it about everything.

At the house, Mille took Nissam to the servants' quarters and Doreen left with her own driver.

"Excuse me, nyonya," Mille said when he returned. "I know houseboy looking for work. He live in my kampung. Can do laundry too."

A houseboy! How perfect, Laura thought. No more sultry temptresses.

***

"Come out to the kitchen and meet the new servants," Laura said when Jack got home. She had hired Budi, the houseboy recommended by Mille, and he and Nissam waited in the kitchen. She introduced the two young men to Jack and watched his face to gauge his reaction.

Jack shook hands and walked from the room. "Can we speak a minute?" he asked.

She followed him and spoke first, not giving him an opportunity to say anything. "Let me guess. You don't like Nissam because he's different."

"It's not that," he said, though Laura knew it was. "Most people have women servants."

"Jack, grow up. Don't be so chauvinistic. Both men have excellent references. And you've assumed Nissam's gay. Who knows, and what difference does it make? Or perhaps there are other reasons you want a house full of women? If you recall, the last women we had quit."

"Okay, I'm going to take a swim."

***

Jack dove into the pool and swam several laps. Breathing heavily he hoisted himself out and sat on the edge while dangling his feet in the water. He stared off in the distance, thinking about Laura. He was still annoyed about her foolish protest at the Kediri. And now she'd gone off and hired servants he didn't think fit in. When did she become so secretive? She didn't used to be that way.

He got up, dried off, and went inside to get ready for dinner.

Chapter 22

Punctually at seven thirty the next morning, in what had become a ritual, Jack strolled out the front door, briefcase in hand. Haroon, in a starched light-blue shirt and pressed dark trousers, usually stood beside the shiny sedan with the rear door open, ready to drive him to the office. Today Haroon rubbed his elbow, a grimace on his face.

"What's the matter?" Jack asked.

"My arm," he said. "It is not working. When I wake today, it have no feeling; it numb." The driver opened his hand and moved his fingers stiffly to demonstrate the difficulty. Jack looked at him, concerned that perhaps he had suffered a stroke.

"You can't drive like that. You need to see a doctor."

But now Jack had his own problem. He needed to get to the office and had no driver. "Haroon, see if Mille is around back." Shortly, Haroon returned with a smiling Mille.

"Mille, something's wrong with Haroon's arm. I need you to drive me. I'll go tell nyonya you are taking me to work."

Jack went inside and found Laura reading *In the Shadow of Man*, a book by Jane Goodall. He told Laura about Haroon and that Mille would have to drive him to work.

"Poor Haroon," Laura said, setting her book aside.

"Unfortunately he'll probably go see one of those quack *dukuns.*" Jack thought dukuns were charlatans who preyed on poor villagers with little or no money to see a real physician.

"They're not all quacks. And they're the only source of medical care for most Indonesians. They heal by using homeopathic remedies and the power of the mind."

"I wouldn't call curses, rattling bones, and talking to spirits 'homeopathic.'"

"From what I've heard, some are quite good."

"We'll see," Jack said. He went back out to where Mille stood, still beaming.

He thought Mille's cheerfulness odd; he expected him to show more sympathy for poor Haroon. They drove away, leaving Haroon rubbing his arm, looking forlorn.

***

That evening when Jack got home, Laura asked him about Haroon. "Mille says someone may have put a curse on him. Isn't that ridiculous?"

To his surprise, Laura laughed. "Doesn't surprise me. Makes sense."

Puzzled, Jack looked at her. "I'm not following."

"One of the most prestigious jobs for a driver is to drive a tuan. It takes many years to get to that level. The least desirable job is to drive the expat wife. Mille's an ambitious kid. He didn't want to wait. He probably had a dukun put a curse on Haroon, and now he gets to drive you."

Jack gave her an incredulous look. "You've been in the tropics too long. Time to head back to New York."

Laura laughed.

"So now what?" Jack asked. "We can't keep sharing Mille."

"I have no idea. We'll have to wait and see. Fortunately it's the weekend, so it's not a problem for now. Anyway, how about a barbeque on Sunday? I'll call Doreen and see if she and Billy can come. We've never met him. I know Sarinah and Harold play tennis. Not sure about Billy."

"Great," Jack replied. He looked forward to a couple of days of relaxation. And it would be good for Laura too.

***

On Sunday Doreen appeared in a bright-yellow caftan. A mass of golden curls topped her head. Laura, thinking she resembled Big Bird holding a baking dish, scolded herself for being catty. Doreen was her friend.

"I made some bourbon bread pudding," Doreen said, her blue eyes twinkling. "My mama's recipe. I added extra bourbon."

Billy, lean, fit, and tanned, with a crew cut and boyish grin, stood next to her. He had the honest, eager look of a Little League coach. Taken aback, Laura realized she expected Doreen and Billy to resemble each other.

When Harold and Sarinah arrived, Jack got beers for the men and glasses of sangria for the women. Laura took Sarinah and Doreen upstairs to show them a batik fabric she had bought.

***

"So Billy, you're in the oil business?" Jack asked as the men settled in the shade.

"My company does drilling work for Pertamina. Good business, but tough." He scowled and shook his head.

"How's that?"

"Corruption."

"That's the problem here. Indonesia's got a lot going for it," Harold said. "But it's difficult for foreign firms to operate. Everybody's got a hand out."

"Y'all ever have any dealings with Judge Hartono?" Billy asked.

Jack startled at the mention of the judge. He cleared his throat and shifted in his chair.

"You're not mixed up with him, I hope," Harold said "He's an expat's worst nightmare."

Billy said, "We're in a contract dispute. He wants a bribe. I told him to shove it."

Harold nodded his approval. "Good for you. Somebody needs to take a stand. Just be careful."

"Don't worry, I may be from Texas, but I'm not dumb. The judge probably hasn't heard of the Alamo. Texans stand their ground. We don't put up with a lot of crap."

"Jack, what about you?" Billy asked. "Ever run into Hartono?"

"Met him at our reception."

"Rumor has it an expat paid him $25,000 to get a case heard."

"Where did you hear that?" Jack asked.

"Scuttlebutt at the Barong Bar. You know how expats gather there Friday after work. You should join us sometime."

Jack gulped. He worried they suspected he was the one who paid the bribe. And he pondered where the talk might have come from. He couldn't imagine the judge bragging about taking a bribe. He could get in trouble too. Or maybe not.

"Wouldn't surprise me that someone gave in to the judge," Harold said. "You know how it is here. Everybody does it."

Jack stood up. "I need a beer. Anyone else?" Harold and Billy shook their heads.

When Jack came back, Billy was saying "Now, Thailand, that's the place. You guys should try to get a business trip there. There's this nightclub called Fish Bowl. Unreal."

"I've heard about it," Harold said.

"There's a glass enclosure full of pretty girls." As Billy related the story, he beamed like a kid on Christmas morning. "Wearing pink evening dresses and holding paddles with numbers, they're all smiles. They look like debutantes. You pick a girl's number, and the bartender calls her out. The lovely thing takes you upstairs for a bubble bath and the works. For a couple hundred dollars, you can even have a virgin."

"You're joking," Harold said.

"Why would anyone want a virgin?" Jack asked, happy the conversation had drifted away from him.

"Evidently old Japanese guys go for virgins," Billy said, clearly enjoying regaling the men with his firsthand knowledge of the trade. "Not sure why. Maybe they think it'll make 'em young and virile."

Jack spotted Laura and the other women coming down the stairs. He signaled to Billy to cut off his talk.

"Anyone up for a game of tennis?" Jack rose from his chair.

Laura approached him, her eyes narrowed. "Jack, can you help me in the kitchen?"

He grabbed his beer and followed.

"I heard you guys talking about Thailand and whores. Fortunately, Doreen was in the bathroom, and Sarinah pretended not to hear."

"I couldn't shut Billy up."

"Poor Doreen, she doesn't suspect a thing. She thinks Billy's a saint. I feel sorry for her."

"Yeah."

"I hope you've never been to those places." She stared at him.

"Of course not. You know I've never been to Thailand."

***

Already regretting his flip comment about Thailand, Jack walked away. It was a trite thing to say and implied he frequented whores in other places. That happened, but only once.

When he was sixteen, he and a few of his buddies drove to Savannah to lose their virginity. In a whorehouse downtown he climbed the stairs and walked along the narrow dimly lit hallway looking for the name "Savannah." The door was ajar and he walked in. A naked, aging woman with sagging breasts and lanky hair lay on a crumpled bed. He had expected someone young and pretty.

Still he took off his clothes and sat on the edge of her bed. She pulled him closer and attempted to kiss him on the mouth. He moved his head aside. She tried to arouse him, but her crude attempt failed. He got up, put his clothes on, paid her, and left. On the ride home, he regaled his friends with lurid tales of his sexual prowess with the beautiful Savannah from Savannah.

***

The group headed for the tennis court. "How about Billy and me against Sarinah and Harold?" Jack suggested.

"Take it easy," Sarinah laughed. "It's been a while since I've played."

Doreen and Laura sat in the shade to sip their drinks and watch.

"Billy can't play football anymore, so now he plays tennis," Doreen said. "We didn't have many tennis courts in Odessa. He learned in Saudi Arabia. But you can't play there in the summer. Asphalt's so hot you could fry an egg. My Billy's a natural. He learns quickly."

"Jack's not a natural; he's persistent. He just wears people down."

They watched their husbands playing tennis in silence for a while. Laura tried to focus on the game, but her mind kept wandering to Doreen and Billy. "Remember when you warned me about husbands going gaga over Asian women?" she asked.

"Worried about Jack?" Doreen asked.

"Not at all," Laura said a bit too quickly.

"My Billy's a good man. Back home he was the pillar of the community. He's not one to get in trouble."

Poor Doreen. She hasn't a clue. Looking out at her husband, she wondered if she might be clueless too.

On the court, Jack and Billy were ahead in the sets two to zero. They switched to the other side, and now with the sun in their eyes, they were at a disadvantage. Harold served.

"Come on, Billy!" Doreen shouted.

Harold botched his serve and Billy easily lobbed the ball back over Sarinah's head into the far corner to win the point.

With the score love to fifteen, Harold put a spin on the ball. Obviously determined not to lose, Jack sprinted forward. As he stretched, he tripped and fell and landed on his shoulder.

"Jack!" Laura cried. She jumped up and ran over. Jack sat up, grimaced, and tried to rotate his arm. "Are you okay?" A scrape on his elbow oozed blood.

"I'm fine." He got up and brushed himself off. "Nothing's broken. I can't understand what happened. My legs turned to spaghetti. Odd." He wobbled off the court.

"Maybe you should see one of those dukuns." Doreen chuckled. "They'll fix you up good."

Laura smiled. "Jack doesn't believe in that."

"I don't believe in that stuff either. Billy and I, we're dyed-in-the-wool evangelicals."

***

154

Monday morning, Jack left to go to work with his arm in a sling. He expected Mille to be outside, waiting to drive him to the office. Instead, Haroon stood there with the car door open.

"Haroon, you're back!" Jack said with surprise. "Your arm's okay?"

"Numbness disappear yesterday." He stretched his arm to show he could move it unimpeded.

"You saw the doctor?"

"I went to a dukun. He say someone put a curse on me."

Jack went back inside and found Laura arranging brightly colored flowers in a vase in the kitchen. "Haroon's back. He's okay. I won't need Mille to drive me."

"What was the matter with him? Did he say?"

"Someone put a curse on him."

"That explains everything. Remember when you fell yesterday and you couldn't understand what happened? The way someone gets rid of a curse is to pass it on."

"Laura, come on. You're being foolish," Jack said, frowning. Her self-appointed role as cultural expert was starting to annoy him.

"I'm not — Sarinah told me. It's even the same arm. It makes sense. Mille put a curse on Haroon so he could drive the tuan and now you have it. And maybe that's why Suparno can't talk. Maybe a dukun put a curse on him too. Strange things happen here."

"That's ridiculous. Suparno can't talk because he was born that way."

"Who knows? The only way for Haroon to get better was to have the dukun transfer the curse to someone else. Haroon picked you."

"You don't really believe that do you?"

"Why not? Remember, at the reception Judge Hartono said that in another life I could have been Indonesian." She gave him a wry smile and went back to arranging flowers in the vase.

155

Chapter 23

At noon, Jack walked into the bustling Hotel Kediri dining room. When a waiter passed with a tray piled high, Jack smelled the now-familiar pungent aroma of Indonesian spices. Nervous about having lunch with the son of the president, he adjusted his tie and glanced at his watch. Then Jack spotted Johnny at a table in the corner and headed over.

He had every reason to be nervous. Johnny had a reputation as being ruthless. Once a judge had the temerity to convict him of embezzlement. From his jail cell, Johnny allegedly arranged for a contract on the judge's life. A hit man killed the judge, and Johnny went free.

"What happened to you?" Johnny asked. He glanced at Jack's arm in a sling.

"A dukun put a curse on me." After making the comment, Jack felt foolish. He sounded like Laura.

Johnny laughed. "Oh, so you know about those things. First time I heard of it happening to a Westerner."

"Actually I tripped playing tennis."

"That's why I play golf. It's safer."

After the men looked over the menu and ordered, Johnny told Jack about the logging and plywood operation in Kalimantan, on the east coast of Borneo. He said that the factory produced ninety thousand cubic meters of plywood a year. He planned to double capacity. Now most logs cut in Indonesia were exported to Japan, but the government planned to institute a ban on sending logs abroad. Then logs would be made into plywood in Indonesia, providing more jobs and added profit from exports. Countries like Japan would have to cut back.

"What about illegal logging? I hear there's a lot of that going on," Jack said. "Can't those logs be shipped directly to the Japanese at a lower price?"

"Good question. You're a smart man, Jack, thinking of all the angles. Forget banking and join us. We'll make you rich." Like his father the president, Johnny was a charmer. "And don't worry about illegal loggers. We take care of them."

Though unsure what Johnny had in mind, Jack didn't inquire.

"And we're planning to bring Judge Hartono in as a silent partner. Sometimes the indigenous people make trouble when outsiders get too close. The judge might be useful."

This time Jack knew what he meant. The judge would likely give Johnny's business a favorable ruling no matter the issue — and without the need for a bribe. He'd have to consider the ramifications of Judge Hartono's involvement. "Who provided financing for your projects in the past?"

"The state-owned banks. They're the easiest to deal with, but now we want to broaden our sources to include foreign banks, particularly American. We would like to open new markets for plywood in your country. Your bank can help us with that. But I should caution you. We have approached others in the past without success."

"Why's that?" Jack asked, though he had heard some banks were skeptical about the long-term viability of the government.

"They are afraid to do business with the president's family. They think there might be a coup and they will be left holding the bag. That's rubbish, of course."

Jack's bank wasn't worried. President Reagan backed the Indonesian president. Reagan provided support for him and other dictators who offered opportunities for US businesses and presented a bulwark against Communism. Jack knew his bank wouldn't be concerned about political disruption. He suspected they would be more than eager to lend $40 million for a logging and plywood project that furthered their interests in Southeast Asia.

"Why don't you visit our operations in Kalimantan?" Johnny suggested. "Wibawa and I will be going there next week. You can see the business firsthand."

To his surprise, Jack was finding Johnny quite pleasant; he detected no sign of ruthlessness. He agreed to make the trip.

"Unfortunately my yacht is in Australia," Johnny said. "We'll take the Learjet. Not as nice, but faster."

Traveling in luxury appealed, but Jack suffered from claustrophobia and didn't relish being cooped up in a small plane. He always took sedatives before flying but didn't want to be sedated around Johnny and Wibawa. He had to land the deal — he'd rough it.

When Jack raised his hand for the check, Johnny waved the attempt aside. They got up to leave, and the unctuous staff rushed over. With nervous smiles, they bowed. Jack suspected the president's son could eat gratis wherever he wanted.

***

"You're headed for trouble," Laura said as Jack packed. "Those men are up to no good."

"They need $40 million. I'm doing due diligence by checking out the project. And don't worry; if I see orangutans, I'm out of there."

"I'd like to see the rainforest, even if it meant I had to endure a couple of crooks."

"We'll go another time," he said. He gave her a kiss.

***

Haroon pulled up in front of the deserted terminal. Jack looked around, hoping to spot Johnny and Wibawa, when a black Mercedes sped through the parking lot, scattering gravel, leaving a dust storm in its wake. Abruptly the sedan stopped at the curb. Ari stepped out of the back, fashionably dressed in a jade-green dress and high heels. Gold dangled from her neck and wrists. Jack had told Laura it was a business trip. She wouldn't be happy to hear Ari tagged along.

"Sorry we're late," Wibawa said. "Traffic in Jakarta gets worse every day."

Johnny walked past them, headed for the glass doors that led to the tarmac. "The pilot's ready whenever we are."

Outside a small silver jet waited, glistening in the sun. Just looking at it, Jack broke out in a sweat, and his heartbeat sped up; he was still hoping to keep his claustrophobia under control without medication. Crouching, he moved through the narrow cabin toward a plush leather window seat. He glanced around to locate the exits.

Once they were airborne, he looked out at white clouds and the sea far below. He thought how much better this mode of travel was than his commute in New York. Wedged in a subway car with faulty air conditioning and the summer reek of sweaty bodies, he got claustrophobia then too. Perhaps luxury might mitigate his discomfort. He leaned back in his chair.

After a two-hour flight, Jack awoke when they landed at Balikpapan, Kalimantan. To his surprise, he had managed to doze for most of the flight.

A van waited outside the terminal to take the group to Samarinda, the port on the Mahakam River, a three-hour drive over the mountain. Trucks and other vehicles crowded the narrow, treacherous highway as they made their way. The driver, seemingly oblivious to danger, floored the accelerator and zipped past a slow-moving truck on a blind curve. Cars jostled in and out, pressing to gain an advantage. Jack hunkered down, every muscle tensed.

Shanties in faded colors and rows of tall, broad-leafed banana plants lined the road. Motorcycles pulled into small stalls to fill up with petrol from plastic containers capped with rags.

"How much longer until we get there?" Ari inquired.

"About an hour," Wibawa answered.

"I'm bored."

"You didn't have to come," Wibawa replied. He gave her a disapproving look. "Take a nap."

They crested the mountain and coasted down the winding road into Samarinda, a dusty, bustling port situated on the banks of the muddy Mahakam River.

Foreign flags fluttered from the masts of ships that steamed up and down the waterway. An air of mystery and intrigue hung over the bustling seaport. They drove along a boulevard paralleling the riverbank and pulled up in front of a four-story hotel; its aged façade loomed, looking like a sanctuary for wayfarers seeking solitude.

"Best there is," Johnny said with a shrug. "We'll check in and meet in about an hour for dinner."

While Johnny and Wibawa conversed outside, Jack walked in to the lobby and headed for the registration desk. Ari followed.

"After you," Jack said, about to check in.

"I'll wait for my husband."

"Here's your key," the clerk said after Jack filled out the card. "Room 388."

"Eight's a lucky number," Ari said. "And you have two of them. See you at dinner."

She walked away, leaving Jack to contemplate her words.

***

In the hotel dining room the group ate and discussed the business of logging, plywood and pulp. Ari, in a chair next to Jack, actively participated. The intoxicating scent of her perfume surrounded him as he observed the delicate way she dabbed at the corners of her mouth with her napkin. When she smiled at him, her black eyes flashing, he sensed toughness within. He was reminded of the Southern term "steel magnolia" and wondered if there was an equivalent phrase in Asia. She made him nervous.

After dinner Jack hurried across the lobby, only to find himself in the elevator with Wibawa and Ari.

"Floor?" Wibawa asked. He had already pushed button number three.

"The same," Jack said.

When the doors opened, the couple walked off in the opposite direction.

He heard Ari call out, "Good night."

Jack lay in bed and thought about Ari. At dinner he was impressed by her intelligence and her business savvy. And he was smitten by her beauty. Still he didn't look forward to spending a day on a boat with her.

He had just dozed off when he heard a rap at the door. He burrowed his head in the pillow, but the sound became sharper, louder, and more insistent; he couldn't ignore it. Annoyed, he tossed back the covers and groped his way over. He squinted through the peephole and saw a woman, her face distorted by the glass. *Ari.*

Shit. He considered not opening the door. She knocked again.

"Just a minute." He flicked on the overhead light and grabbed his trousers off the chair, then unfastened the chain.

"Sorry to wake you," Ari said. "I couldn't sleep. Can I join you for a drink?" She walked in.

"I'll get dressed. We can go downstairs to the bar."

"It's closed. There should be liquor in the minibar."

Jack shut the door and stood there, his arms crossed. He felt awkward with her in his room.

"I'll have Scotch and a little water," she said.

He opened the cabinet below the sink and checked labels on the miniature bottles.

Still half asleep, he stirred the whiskey and opened a beer for himself. Ari sat on the edge of the bed, her legs crossed, her skirt hiked just above the knee. Jack took a seat across from her.

"Wibawa's asleep, in case you were wondering."

Jack was wondering.

"Mind if I smoke?" She pulled a pack of cigarettes from her purse and, without waiting for a reply, lit up and blew smoke into the air. "Wibawa doesn't like the smell."

"Not a good idea for you to be here," Jack said. He took a swig of beer.

"I told you the bar's closed. Wibawa's asleep. I needed a drink." She tossed her hair and took a puff.

"I'm surprised you came on the trip," Jack said.

"I've never been to Kalimantan. I wanted to see it, and I get lonely in Jakarta."

"That's odd. You're married to one of the most powerful men in the country. I would think you'd have many friends."

"I'm Chinese, not Indonesian. My Chinese name is Li-ying. It means *beautiful flower*. When I married Wibawa, I changed my name to Ari. Indonesians don't speak to me because I'm Chinese, and Chinese women call me a whore."

Fascinated, he watched her. Her facial expressions alternated between flirtatious and vulnerable as she told him she was born in a village in southern China and that her parents were peasant farmers. They sent her to live in Hong Kong with a cousin when she was thirteen. Her mother told her she was blessed with beauty, that she should use it, get a good job, and send money home. The cousin found her work as a maid with a wealthy Chinese family. They treated her like trash. The fat husband leered and made filthy remarks. She left to wash dishes in a restaurant.

"I can't imagine you washing dishes." Jack began to feel sorry for her.

She smiled and continued to tell him more about her life. How she studied English so she could get a job as a hostess in a nightclub and make decent money. The Red Lotus Lounge, Hong Kong's most exclusive men's club, hired her.

"That's where you met Wibawa?"

"He was a regular, younger then. Now he's an old man. As your Negro people say, he's lost his mojo."

Though uncomfortable, Jack chuckled at her use of American slang.

"We are alike, you and I," she said. "I could tell the first time we met by the way you looked at me."

Ari stubbed out her cigarette in an ashtray, stood, reached back, unzipped her dress, and let it fall in a crumpled heap at her feet. Jack did a double take. He had suspected she hadn't come to his room for a drink and yet was unprepared for her suddenly disrobing. Naked, she reached out to him. He looked at her hairless mound, her high small breasts and slender hips. She pulled him toward her, and together they fell across the bed. She moved her hand across his bare chest and unbuckled his trousers, pulled them off along with his boxer shorts and tossed them aside.

Aroused, Jack put his arms around her. His hand moved to her thighs. She opened her legs to his touch. Her fingers grasped his head. She pulled his face toward her and kissed him hard on the mouth. He rolled over on top of her. In their frenzied passion, Jack's elbow hit the bedside table and knocked the clock onto the floor. The alarm buzzed.

"Damn!" He reached down and snatched the clock from the floor. His fingers fumbled as he tried to locate the switch. The annoying alarm continued. Frustrated, he yanked the cord from the wall socket and tossed the black plastic box against the wall.

He sat up and slumped forward, his head in his hands. He thought of Laura. And he thought of Wibawa down the hall. Perhaps this was a trap, a setup.

"What's wrong?" Ari asked. Her hands stroked.

"Not a good idea," he said, turning toward her.

She pulled him down on top of her, grasped his head, and kissed him. With her arms around his shoulders, she pressed her breasts against him.

He moved away.

"What's the matter? I'm not good enough for you?" Her black eyes flashed in anger. Jack picked up her dress from the floor and handed it to her. She put it on and zipped it. She smoothed the wrinkled fabric across her abdomen and ran her fingers through her rumpled hair. She stepped closer and slapped him hard across the face. "You bastard! You'll regret this."

She raised her hand to strike again. Though stunned by her fury, Jack caught her wrist. She managed to struggle free, grab a vase from the table, and hurl it at him. He ducked as the heavy object flew past and smashed into the mirror above the dresser. Cracks spread across the reflective surface, momentarily suspended like threads in a spider's web. Then the pieces fell to the floor in a resounding crash. Shards of glass shot across the room.

Ari shoved Jack aside, grabbed her purse and rushed out. She slammed the door behind her.

Dazed, Jack sat on the edge of bed. He stared at the debris on the carpet and fingered his cheek, still stinging from the slap. Mentally and physically drained, he rested his head in his hands.

He had angered a vindictive woman, and now he shuddered to think what she might do.

Chapter 24

Groggy after a night of little sleep, Jack stepped into the shower, turned on the tap, and shivered when a stream of cold water pounded his chest. He washed quickly, got out, dried off, and glanced in the mirror, relieved to see no evidence of Ari's slap. Yet, unshaven and puffy-eyed, he looked like hell.

He walked from the bathroom and stooped to pick up slivers of glass, worried he might cut his foot. He dreaded going downstairs for breakfast and instead called room service. After dressing, he stood at the window. The lingering sight of Ari dropping her dress and standing there naked haunted him. He pictured her hurling the vase and the fury in her eyes. He couldn't imagine what she might say or do now. And he wondered if Wibawa might have awakened, discovered her absence, and confronted her when she returned.

The busboy arrived, and Jack took the tray at the door. He sat, drank the strong coffee, and munched on toast.

Unable to put it off any longer, he grabbed his overnight bag and opened the door. He glanced up and down the hall. Finding it deserted, he stepped out and headed down the corridor for the elevator. He hoped a door along the way didn't open and leave him face-to-face with Ari or Wibawa. He arrived at the elevator bank without incident, pushed the down button, and watched the round indicator lights slowly blink through a floor at a time. He considered taking the stairs and looked around for the exit sign. He didn't see one and didn't want to wander the floor, searching. When the elevator stopped, he got in and braced himself for that moment when the doors would open again and he would be exposed to the lobby and whoever might be there.

To his surprise he didn't see anyone. But then Wibawa stepped from behind a potted palm. It was if he had been waiting. "Good morning, Jack. Sleep well?"

"I did," Jack replied. He studied the old man's face for an indication as to what he might know.

"Ari won't be joining us," he said.

"Oh?"

"She has a headache."

"That's too bad," Jack said. He hoped he sounded sincere.

Though Wibawa's comment seemed innocuous, Jack took the old man's unflinching gaze as an indication that he knew what happened. Perhaps he awoke when Ari returned, and in trying to save herself, she implicated Jack. But Wibawa's demeanor remained calm and paternal, and Jack decided he must not know.

Johnny walked up. "The van's waiting. We should go." The three men headed across the lobby and through the revolving glass doors.

"Excuse me. I forgot something," Jack said. He rushed back into the hotel and headed for the registration desk.

"There was an accident in my room," he said to the clerk. "A mirror got broken. Whatever the costs are to repair it, just put them on my credit card."

Though the clerk looked at him quizzically, he took the card without comment.

Jack glanced out the large glass front lobby at Wibawa and Johnny, waiting in the van. The clerk took an imprint and handed it to him for signature. About to sign, Jack noticed he had given the clerk the bank's card by mistake; he meant to use his personal card. He didn't want to have to explain such an unusual expense, but there wasn't time to make the change. He would sort it out later.

"Find what you were looking for?" Wibawa asked when Jack rejoined them.

"Everything's fine," Jack replied, relieved he had had the foresight to pay for the damages; otherwise the hotel might have sent a bill to Wibawa.

The van wound through narrow, dusty streets that reminded him of Jakarta's prior to the rainy season. At the waterfront, a large speedboat languished alongside a pier, its mooring lines hanging limply in the muddy water. A man wearing a seafaring hat, his skin weathered, stood in the stern.

"Welcome, I'm the captain," he said as he helped Jack into the boat. Jack looked around and chuckled. There was no one else; the man was also the crew.

"We could have driven up, but I prefer being out on the water," Wibawa said. "The fresh air helps me think."

The captain started the engine and steered the boat out and away from the dock. As they gained speed, he headed for the open water. A large wake formed behind them. Jack and Johnny sat under the canvas canopy while Wibawa stood and peered ahead, his gray hair swept by the wind.

The Mahakam spread out before them. Empty ships rode high, headed upriver. The broad expanse of the waterway reminded Jack of the Mississippi. As a young boy, on vacation with his mother and sister, he stood atop a levee outside New Orleans. Mesmerized, he watched barges loaded with grain being towed from the Midwest to the Gulf of Mexico and the world beyond.

On that same trip, he remembered when he stopped at an open door on Bourbon Street and got a glimpse of a naked woman dancing on a stage. His mother grabbed him and hurried him along. "You're too young." "She must be cold," he said. His mother laughed. "The last thing she is, is cold." Jack hadn't thought of that incident in years. He suspected Ari had something to do with the recollection.

"The plywood factory's about an hour upriver," Johnny said.

Villages lined the banks, and an occasional factory smokestack belched soot into a cloudless sky. The Mahakam served as both laundry and latrine. Outhouses perched precariously on stakes over the river. Women washed clothes and draped them across rocks to dry in the sun, while small boys struggled up the steep banks, dragging colorful plastic buckets with water sloshing over the sides. A powerful tug moved past them, towing barges stacked high with large, freshly cut logs. The wake of the tug tossed the speedboat high into the air. Jack, caught off guard, gripped the gunwale. The hull rose and came down, whacking the water with a resounding thud.

The river narrowed and Wibawa pointed toward the shore. "Up there," he shouted. He motioned to the captain to cut the engine. Jack squinted. He heard shrieks. "In the trees above the mangroves. Proboscis monkeys," Wibawa said.

Jack spotted the creatures — about ten of them swung through the branches. Their honking sound reminded him of a flock of passing geese. The males, with large bulbous noses and protruding abdomens, had to be among the most unattractive creatures he had ever seen. He watched the troop disappear into a thicket. Laura would be jealous of him seeing the wildlife. Thinking about his wife made him tense up. Though nothing had happened, he hoped she never found out about the incident in the hotel room with Ari.

Wibawa put on a cap, and with it his sunglasses. He looked younger than his years — though the prominent veins and dark spots on the hand that gripped the canopy pole confirmed his age. He seemed deep in thought, and Jack wondered what the old man might be contemplating.

"That's our plywood factory," Johnny said. "Over there." He nudged Jack and pointed to a large corrugated-steel building with rusting smokestacks. "We will continue upriver to the logging site, then come back."

The boat's bow cut through islands of floating hyacinths. On either side of the river, the jungle loomed.

"We're close to Dayak country," Johnny said. "A century ago, Dayaks were headhunters and cannibals. They'd tie enemies to a tree and dance around. They would work themselves into frenzy, and eat the captives alive."

Jack cringed.

"Don't worry, they're Catholic now."

Given the atrocities committed in the name of Catholicism during the Crusades, Jack took little comfort in the statement.

The boat drifted along the bank and passed a lush green wall, where fronds of tall ferns spread like giant lace umbrellas. Mottled tree trunks rose high toward sunlight filtering through the canopy. They rounded a bend and headed toward stacks of freshly cut logs lining the bank. An army of trucks and yellow earthmoving equipment shuttled about like insects in a frantic search for food. Red dust billowed, casting a dingy film everywhere. As the boat closed in on the shore, the captain hopped out and secured a line to a log.

Jack, Johnny, and Wibawa climbed into a waiting truck. The driver made his way along a road scored by the metal tracks of heavy equipment. "Wouldn't be able to drive here during the monsoon," Johnny said. "Place turns into a quagmire."

Further up they stopped and watched a man with a chainsaw cutting into a tree. The blade's teeth cut through the thick trunk. They heard a sharp crack and the grating sound of the saw ceased. The man stepped back and glanced up. The giant tree quivered, tilted, and then quickly gained momentum. Branches cut a swath through the surrounding foliage, and the giant hit the ground with a booming crash. Silence followed. The man with the chainsaw took off his hat and wiped his face.

Jack, his emotions conflicted, stared at the scene. As a boy he would take off through the woods, seeking relief from the bitter quarrels of his parents. He would hike to an old oak, his favorite spot of solitude, lay in the shade of the branches, and read for hours. Those moments were some of the happiest of his youth.

"What kind of tree is that?" he asked.

"Meranti, mahogany, like those logs we saw on the barge headed to Japan," Wibawa said.

"How old was it?"

"Over two hundred years," Johnny said.

Further on a front-end loader pushed against a tree trunk. The tree uprooted and fell.

"Using heavy equipment is much faster," Johnny said. "But sometimes it's not possible to get a big machine into the thicker growth."

They passed a clearing, where wisps of smoke rose from blackened stumps. In the distance, a wall of green contrasted with the eerie, desolate landscape.

"Seen enough?" Wibawa asked.

Hot and sweating profusely, Jack nodded. They headed back, Jack feeling thankful they hadn't seen any orangutans. He knew Laura would ask him.

When they climbed into the boat, Wibawa pointed to a wormlike creature crawling across the deck. "A bloodsucking leech," he said. The captain scooped it up and tossed it in the water. "Don't fall overboard, Jack — that leech might crawl up your pants leg and bite your balls."

Jack flinched.

***

They headed back downriver toward the plywood factory. As they approached the site, the captain cut the engine and they eased alongside a pier of narrow planks. The high-water mark, visible on pilings pocked with green algae and mollusks, evidenced the pronounced tidal drop.

Johnny tossed a line to a man in a white hard hat who stood at the end of the dock. He caught it and secured the rope to the cleat beside his foot.

"This is Awat, the assistant manager," Johnny said as they climbed from the boat. "Ian, the manager, is on home leave in Australia. Awat has worked with us for over ten years. He knows what he's doing."

"My pleasure to show you around today," Awat said, his smile broad and infectious. He and Jack walked from the pier, followed by Johnny and Wibawa.

"How was the hotel? Sleep well?" Awat asked.

Jack cringed. *Why does everyone keep asking that?* He ignored the question. "Are you from Samarinda?" he asked instead.

"I'm from Sumatra," Awat said. "I have a degree in forestry from Bogor University." He made the comment with pride in his voice. Jack took an instant liking to Awat.

"Your family came with you to Indonesia?" Awat asked.

"My wife's in Jakarta," Jack said.

"Children?"

"Belum, not yet," Jack responded, prepared with the term he had heard Laura use. She didn't like it, nor did he.

"I have two wives and six children," Awat said with the same pride he demonstrated when he mentioned his college degree.

"How do you manage two wives?" Jack asked. He had never met anyone with more than one at a time.

"Very carefully," came the reply. The men laughed. He's the jolliest Muslim I ever met, Jack thought, contrasting Awat with the stoic Pak Hajji.

They left Johnny and Wibawa conversing and walked to the riverbank, where a pallet of logs, bound together with metal straps, sloshed in the water. A shirtless, barefoot boy about sixteen years old teetered atop the raft-like platform. He swung an axe while struggling to balance on the slick, uneven surface.

"What's he doing?" Jack asked.

"Breaking the straps that bind the logs. He never falls," Awat added as if to reassure.

From the river they walked toward a building that resembled an aircraft hangar. Impressed, Jack realized he had expected something on a smaller scale.

The two men stopped beside a stack of large sawn timbers. Awat ran his hand along the rough bark. He said there were two kinds of plywood — hardwood and softwood. "In Indonesia, it's all hardwood. Softwood comes from trees like the Douglas fir that grow in America. Indonesian plywood is used for high-quality interior finishes."

The side of the building facing the river was open to the elements. Inside, a conveyer belt moved logs toward two spinning stainless-steel rotor blades set eight feet apart. When the conveyer belt stopped, giant blades spun down and sliced the tree trunks like a knife through a stick of butter. Then the conveyor moved the eight-foot sections further along to the stripping machine where the bark was removed.

Further in, the men stopped beside a high, metal box structure. "This is the steamer. Careful, it can be hot," Awat said. "Cut logs are steamed to soften them. Afterward they go to the horizontal peeler." The men climbed up a catwalk, and Jack peered down. A high-speed machine spun a standing log like a roll of paper towels. A sharp blade peeled away a continuous layer of veneer. In less than a minute, the giant log resembled a broomstick.

"The veneer is put in the kiln, where it is dried, then cut into sections," Awat continued. "After that, adhesive is applied to hold the layers together." Women wearing rubber gloves and white gauze masks pulled sheets of the thin veneer from the glue machine. His senses assaulted by the pungent smell of glue, Jack covered his nose.

"Mainly women working here," Jack said. He hadn't expected that.

"They're more reliable and better at detail. They're especially good at quality control. Women are better at spotting flaws." Awat laughed at his little joke.

The men dodged yellow forklifts shuttling back and forth like bees in a hive.

"Very efficient," Jack said, surprised at the speed of the process. "Can Johnny and Wibawa's logging concession support the planned expansion?"

"If the concession gets depleted, they just ask for another one," he said. Jack detected a fleeting frown. "I'm not against logging. The world needs lumber, and my people need jobs, but there is a better way to do this."

"How's that?" Jack asked as they walked on.

"The same way illegal loggers cut trees. They can't afford heavy machinery, so they cut down the trees and then attach cables to them and drag them out. Does less damage and the young trees grow to replace those that are cut."

"So why isn't that done?

"Takes more workers and more time," Awat said. "Many people here need work, but that's not so important to the concession owners. They want their money fast and easy."

Jack suspected that having been raised in Sumatra, Awat resented the wealthy and well connected who came from Jakarta, destroyed the forest, and took the money with them. He already respected Awat. He wished he could lend *him* the $40 million.

But it was Wibawa and Johnny who had the concession, and their logging technique was no different from that used in Oregon and Washington. They just happened to be operating in the rainforest, home to most hardwoods.

When Johnny joined them, he asked Jack, "So what do you think of our operation?"

"Very impressive. You're fortunate to have such a good man working for you," Jack said. He nodded toward Awat.

"We own the surrounding property around here, so there's plenty of room for expansion," Johnny said, ignoring Jack's praise of the assistant manager.

"We're counting on you," Wibawa said. Jack winced. The old man's tone and the comment sound like a threat. He wished Awat would be returning with them; he considered him an ally. But when the boat shoved off, Awat remained on the pier.

On the return trip, Wibawa grasped the rail and stared straight ahead. Jack found the old man's demeanor, and his silence, unnerving.

Chapter 25

As the boat approached the dock in Samarinda, Jack spotted the waiting van and furrowed his brow. As they were going directly to the airport, he had expected Ari to be there too. Though he didn't look forward to seeing her, he thought her absence odd. He considered inquiring about her but decided against it. Wibawa might think it strange. Instead he sat in silence while they drove to the terminal.

As they checked in, Johnny said, "There's a storm passing through the Jakarta area." Jack must have looked worried, because he added, "But the pilot thinks it'll be okay to take off. He said it will pass before we get there, though it will be bumpy en route."

Jack's stomach flipped. He imagined being tossed around in a small plane in bad weather. His claustrophobia began to kick in. "Maybe we should wait for the weather to clear."

"I have business to tend to in Jakarta. Don't worry; the pilot knows what he's doing."

Jack trailed them across the tarmac and mounted the steps of the Learjet. He stiffened when he saw Ari seated in the front row next to the window. A wide-brimmed floppy hat and large sunglasses obscured her face. She had on the same blue dress she wore when she came to his room.

"Hello," he said.

Ari looked away. When he moved past, he saw a red welt on her arm. Beneath the dark glasses, he glimpsed her cheek, bruised and swollen. *Wibawa knows!* Jack settled into a seat in the next row. His heart pounded like a jackhammer. Wibawa and Johnny took seats across the aisle from Ari.

Wibawa glanced back over his shoulder. "You okay, Jack?"

"I'm fine. Just not comfortable in small planes."

"You should move up next to Ari. She'll keep you company."

"That's all right. I'll stay here. Nerves can be contagious." The plane lifted off, and they headed for Jakarta.

Jack expected his claustrophobia to flare up big-time in the turbulence. Still, he resisted taking a sedative. He needed to stay alert. Wibawa must have been awake when Ari returned, gotten angry, and struck her. Jack wondered what she had said to him. He didn't expect Ari to tell her husband the truth. Though Jack considered himself blameless, he knew he had made a big mistake letting Ari into his room.

An hour out the plane hit an air pocket. The cabin shook. The aircraft pitched forward and plunged. In a panic, Jack clutched the armrests of his seat. *I'm going to die.* Then the plane leveled. He grabbed the barf bag from the seat pocket in case he needed it.

It was hard to believe Jack once wanted to be a Navy pilot. He attended college on an NROTC scholarship, and on graduation signed up for the flight program in Pensacola. It was there he discovered his propensity for claustrophobia. It happened in the Dilbert Dunker, the apparatus used to teach pilots how to escape should their planes crash into the sea.

"Here's your parachute," the instructor said. He handed Jack a dark-green canvas pack. Jack hoisted it onto his back and cinched the metal clip at his waist. The instructor pointed toward a high ladder that led to a platform over a large pool. There a simulated cockpit teetered on a ramp leading into the water below. Jack climbed the ladder and strapped himself into the cockpit's tight confines. He dreaded what was to come. When he heard the click of the release, he took a deep breath and held it. The cockpit accelerated down the ramp, hit the water, and flipped over. It submerged in a mass of bubbles.

Disoriented, Jack had found himself upside down in a watery prison. Though in a panic, he managed to locate the buckle at his waist and free himself. Though his instincts told him to swim upward, he had been trained to go down, then out and away from the submerging cockpit. He tried to kick, but his waterlogged boots anchored him. With scant air left, he broke through the surface. He flailed, gasped, coughed, and spurted water. Defeated by his claustrophobia, the following day he resigned from the flight program. The Navy reassigned him to a desk job in a small windowless room in the Pentagon.

Jack dug his fingers into his palms as the Learjet shook again. He pictured the plane slamming into the water and flipping over. He rehearsed the Dilbert Dunker drill. *Get out quickly, swim down, swim away.* Unable to take it anymore, he reached into his briefcase for the bottle of sleeping pills. He popped one in his mouth and gulped. With his heart pumping adrenaline, the medication spread quickly, and he fell asleep. He dreamed of sharks circling Learjet wreckage.

He didn't know how long he had been asleep when he felt someone shaking him.

"Jack, wake up — we're about to land."

He recognized Wibawa's voice and bolted upright.

"You were talking in your sleep," the old man said. "Something about sharks."

The plane began a controlled but bumpy descent. Jack's ears popped and he swallowed in an effort to keep them open. Through the window streaked with rain, he discerned buildings below. The plane wobbled, and just above the runway a gust lifted the right wing. The aircraft hit at an angle. The left wheel struck the asphalt hard and items crashed to the cabin floor. The slick tarmac rushed past the window. Jack thought the plane was out of control, and he held on tight. Then he felt the deceleration, and they began to slow. He leaned back; his chest heaved. As the pilot guided the nose of the plane toward the terminal, Jack swore he would never fly again.

Three men with umbrellas stood in the downpour at the bottom of the steps. Without enough cover for everyone onboard, Jack made a run for it. Inside he stomped his feet to shake off the water. Ari followed, promptly escorted through the glass doors to the black Mercedes at the curb.

"I hope you found the trip useful," Wibawa said to Jack.

"I did. I learned a lot."

Wibawa took Jack by the elbow and steered him aside away from the others. The old man glared.

"Ari told me you pulled her into your room as she walked down the hall. She said you tried to rape her." His voice threatened.

Incredulous, Jack stepped back. "She came to my room on her own. Nothing happened," he said, flustered.

"I know she went to your room and you didn't rape her. But you don't expect me to believe nothing happened."

"But it's true," Jack said. His mind whirled at the mention of rape.

"You're a young man. Why would you reject the advances of a beautiful woman?"

"Because she's your wife." Angry, he emphasized his words. He considered telling Wibawa everything. How Ari attempted to seduce him, how he rejected her, and how she hurled a vase and broke a mirror. Instead he repeated, "Nothing happened."

"I don't believe you," Wibawa said. He turned and walked out to join Ari, who waited in the car.

Chapter 26

Concerned about Jack flying in foul weather, Laura sat, stood, paced, and stared out the window. The storm raged, the monsoon rains fell, and thunder rattled the house. Bolts of lightning illuminated the pool, where water flowed over the edge, turning the garden into a bog.

The door opened and caught her by surprise.

"Jack, thank God you're back." She ran to greet him. Despite his wet rain gear, she gave him a hug.

"Long trip," he said.

"You look tired."

"Exhausted. I'm going upstairs to change."

"Have dinner first. Nissam kept things warm for you." He must have suffered a bad bout of claustrophobia, she surmised, looking at his haggard face.

They went and sat in the dining room, and Nissam brought out food. "So how did things go?" she asked.

"It was okay."

"Are you doing the deal?" She felt more concern than curiosity.

"I need to convince New York, but I'm sure they'll go along."

Laura pressed her lips together and narrowed her eyes. She wanted the project to fail. "Aren't you concerned about doing business with Johnny?" She knew the story about him being in prison and having a contract taken out on a judge's life.

"There are many stories about Johnny. Who knows what's true."

"If I were you, I'd assume they're all true. And I wouldn't trust Wibawa either. Why take the risk?"

Jack shrugged.

"Did you see any orangutans?" She leaned forward.

"None."

"Probably afraid to show their faces. Or maybe they're all dead."

"The rainforest is a big place. They're not everywhere."

Laura ignored his comment. "Because of people like you and Johnny and Wibawa, there will be no rainforest left. Orangutans and all the other endangered species will be gone."

"Wait a minute. The government owns the rainforest and granted a concession. There are plenty of trees there. I saw them. And the world needs paper and lumber, in case you haven't noticed."

"Maybe the government granted too many concessions. And they haven't done anything about illegal logging. Orangutans disperse seeds that regenerate the rainforest. If we save them, we save all the other plants and animals." Laura paused, gathering her thoughts. "The jungles haven't been fully explored. There's an incredible diversity of life there. Maybe the cure for cancer lies in the jungles of Indonesia. How great would that be?"

Looking taken aback by her intensity, Jack said, "Since when did you become such an authority?"

"I went to the bookstore and bought some books."

"Glad you're reading up, but that doesn't make you an expert." He looked uncomfortable. "And besides, a single project can't be that destructive.

"That's what everyone says. Single projects add up."

Gaining confidence and with more emotion, she continued. She told him what she had been thinking about, that the government should allocate parts of the rainforest for parks similar to Yosemite or Yellowstone. Tourists from all over the world would come to marvel at paradise. Illegal loggers would have long-term worthwhile jobs as guides.

"Do you know what pulp is used for?" she asked.

"Sure, making paper."

"Tissue and toilet paper. The world blows its nose and wipes its butt on the rainforest."

"No need to get gross," Jack said, his brow furrowed.

"Okay, you get the point."

"Maybe we should talk about something else. You're getting upset."

But Laura hadn't finished. "You would be upset too, if you looked into the sad eyes of that baby orangutan at the market. The protest at the Kediri didn't generate any interest. And unfortunately I haven't yet figured out what else I can do. But you can do something. You can convince your bank to be more responsible and not finance projects that wreak havoc on the planet's limited resources." Her eyes blazed.

Jack leaned toward her. "Look, if our bank doesn't lend Johnny and Wibawa the money, others will."

"Here's your chance to make a difference." Her voice rose. "Isn't that what you told Judge Hartono on the golf course — that he could make a difference, that he could be the one to take a stand and change a culture of corruption?"

"I — "

Nissam rushed in. "Sorry, nyonya, big problem in living room."

Jack and Laura jumped up from the table and rushed to the other room, where water flooded in beneath the glass doors.

"Oh no! It's overflow from the pool," Laura said. "Jack, we need to move the furniture. Nissam, get some towels."

Jack took off his shoes and socks and rolled up his pants legs. He grabbed a chair and carried it down the hall. Laura followed with another. They moved tables, more chairs, and the sofa.

Nissam wedged a towel into the crack through which water poured. "Nissam, you look like the little Dutch boy with his finger in the dike." Despite the calamity, Laura laughed. Nissam looked puzzled.

Outside, winds whipped the trees. Branches beat against the side of the house. A loud crash followed a clap of thunder. A limb fell onto the terrace, struck the door, and smashed the glass pane. Muddy water rolled across the room.

"Jack!" Laura screamed. She pointed to a slithering snake.

"Stay back. Looks like a cobra," Jack yelled. "I saw one on the golf course."

From out of nowhere, Suparno appeared like Superman in miniature. A branch in his hand, he crept toward the snake. As he got close, he raised the limb, bringing it down hard on the reptile's head. Mud and blood splattered across the walls and Laura's skirt. The gardener picked up the limp creature and flung it out the front door.

Jack waded over and put his arm around Laura's shoulder. "You okay?"

"Better a soiled skirt than a snakebite. I thought my premonition was about the other house. I hope it's not ongoing." Water sloshed around her ankles.

"The floors are tile, so no damage done. Tomorrow we'll shovel out the mud."

***

The following day the sun was out when Laura and Jack sat eating breakfast. The scene reminded Laura of the morning after the bombing — calm and quiet as if nothing had happened.

"I can't believe the servants already cleaned up the mess," Laura said.

"I'm impressed. I should hire them to work at the bank. Make 'em loan officers."

"Oh, no you don't," Laura said, laughing. "Find your own people."

When he finished, he got up from the table. "I'm off to the office. I need to call Tom." He leaned over and kissed Laura on the forehead. "I feel bad about all you've been through." She thought it was sweet that he tried to calm her fears while he himself looked worried, though perhaps for different reasons.

"Look, I know you don't like me making a loan for a project that could potentially be harmful to the environment. I'm not thrilled about it either. But logging and oil are the main opportunities here, and the oil companies don't need our money. They have plenty of cash."

Laura listened and understood, yet questioned his sincerity. "Seems odd. The fourth most populous country in the world, and logging is the only banking business."

"Odd but true."

***

As Haroon drove him through the crowded streets, Jack reflected on Laura's words. He had never seen her so determined, and she did have valid concerns. Though he didn't share her rainforest passion, he didn't relish doing business with Wibawa and Johnny. But he had a job to do, a bank to run.

With an eleven-hour time difference between the US and Indonesia, Jack called Tom at his home in White Plains, thankful not to have to endure the annoyance of an office speakerphone.

"Jack, how the hell are you?" Tom said.

"Doing well, thanks. There may be some progress on that Bandung situation. I met with the judge a few days ago. Looks like he's going to hear the case."

"Terrific. I knew you'd think of an angle."

Jack didn't mention that the "angle" included a briefcase full of money. "Actually, I'm calling about something else. There's an interesting opportunity I want to run by you, see what you think. You might recognize the name Wibawa — very powerful. He and the president golf together. I met Wibawa at our welcoming reception."

"Wibawa, sure, worth billions. Jack, you've gotten right to the top."

Jack briefed Tom on his trip to Kalimantan with Johnny and Wibawa and their logging and plywood project.

"Sounds good." Tom sounded excited.

"There's an opportunity for our bank to finance the project."

"How much?"

"Forty million."

"Good hustling, Jack. I like it. I'll talk to the credit guys about our exposure to Indonesia and appetite for a deal this size. We'll probably have to syndicate it, sell a portion to banks in Hong Kong, but that's okay. Fee income from syndications is good business."

Jack relaxed. He had Tom's attention.

"Only stickler might be doing business with the president's family," Tom said. "Everybody knows they're corrupt, but they're the only game in town. Some say the president's days are numbered, but they've been saying that for years."

Jack leaned back and let Tom ruminate.

"Good thing is the U.S. tends to stand by its dictators. It's the old 'devil you know' scenario," Tom said.

When the conversation concluded, Jack hung up. He pondered his boss's comment about supporting dictators. Tom had conveniently neglected to mention the Shah of Iran deposed in a bloody revolution despite long-term U.S. support. Given time, dictatorships seemed to implode. But Jack doubted if Tom worried about that. He would be thinking short-term. He would be thinking of his bonus.

Though encouraged by his boss's enthusiasm, Jack knew much work had to be done to get the deal approved in New York. As a start, he called the bank's syndication team in Hong Kong. Based on the proposed pricing and structure of the deal, they sounded optimistic. The syndication team there worked closely with other banks in Asia and knew which were hungry for new business. Banks with recently opened Asian regional offices needed to book business to cover costs and justify their existence while their loan officers struggled to uncover deals of their own. In the meantime they gravitated toward the larger, more established banks for opportunities to participate.

Jack contacted the bank's forestry-products group in New York for an industry opinion. They raised concerns about the possibility of plywood overcapacity should Indonesia issue too many licenses for new plants and send the price of plywood plummeting. With reduced cash flow, borrowers might not be able to repay their loans. But data as to how many licenses the Indonesian government planned to issue didn't exist, or at least were not made available to the public. Overcapacity was a risk. As part of his due diligence, Jack noted that in his write-up, though it didn't worry him. No loan was risk-free.

He asked Imee, head of the credit department, to work up five-year financial projections for the project, with assumptions for best- and worst-case scenarios. She showed little enthusiasm. "Too bad the president's family has to be involved in all the deals." She shook her head and jabbed her finger in the air. "They're all crooks."

"Did you look 'em in the eye to see if they winced?" Jack asked, remembering her quip.

"I wouldn't dare get that close," she said, her voice emphatic. "We should be doing microcredit financing like they do in Pakistan."

"You mean lending to the poor? How can they possibly repay?"

"The loans are for small amounts like forty or fifty dollars. The money is used to help start businesses — a food cart, a hair salon, or buying chickens. It gives the poor a shot at getting off the bottom rung. Women are the best borrowers. They rarely default."

"What about the paperwork? We'd have to hire a warehouse full of clerks."

"Maybe not. I read where a young fellow in California named Jobs demonstrated a desktop computer called Macintosh. It can process faster than people."

"Doubt if it'll be viable in my time. And it'll probably cost a bundle."

He looked through the projections Imee left on his desk. Even under the worst case, the numbers showed sufficient cash to repay the $40 million loan. He expected the credit committee to require the personal guarantees of Johnny and Wibawa, a common practice for loans to family-owned businesses in the States. In Asia he suspected that might be an affront. With so much money involved, he intended to ask anyway.

Jack reread the thirty-page proposal. Pleased, he sent it off to New York. And then he braced himself for the confrontation with Laura.

Chapter 27

Laura was headed upstairs to get ready for her day when the phone rang. She ran to the bedroom to answer it.

"Laura?" It was Doreen.

"Doreen. I haven't heard from you in a while. How are you?"

"Billy and I are goin' home. Back to Texas. Back to dustin' and cleanin' my own toilet,"

"What happened?" Laura was concerned. Doreen didn't sound like her usual ebullient self, and she knew Billy had a year left on his contract.

"You remember those trips Billy's been making to Thailand? It wasn't oil business. He was hangin' out with prostitutes. I cried and cried when I found out. It hurt me so bad. But I've forgiven him. Livin' outside the States is different. Too many temptations. When you don't know anybody and don't think anyone's looking, you do things you wouldn't if you thought you'd get caught. It's like the Devil temptin' you every day with an apple. You take bites when at home you wouldn't."

"I hadn't thought of it like that." Laura wondered if she should have told her friend about Billy in preparation for what was to come.

"Me and Billy strayed from the path of righteousness, so we're returning to Texas and the Lord. No more skirt-chasin' for Billy, and I'm quitting drinkin' — 'cept for weddings and things."

Laura suggested a get-together before they left, and Doreen agreed. Laura said she would invite Sarinah and Harold.

She hung up and thought about Doreen and how she never suspected what her husband was doing. She wondered if Jack might be up to the same sort of thing. She sat down, her hands in her lap. She still suspected something happened while she was in Borobudur. The servants left so abruptly and without reason. And she remembered that while Kartini looked upset, Maya seemed like she wanted to stay.

***

They gathered at The Palms, a colonial mansion, now a restaurant. Built in the twenties by a Dutch man with vast holdings in coffee and tea, prominent Indonesians, tourists, and expats regularly dined there.

Inside the entry a gamelan trio played, the men in traditional batik costumes. Their mallets striking an array of gongs produced a deep, rich tone unfamiliar to Western ears. Laura stopped to listen.

The maître d' came out and escorted the group to a table in the main parlor. Maroon velvet curtains framed tall, corniced windows, and chandeliers sparkled overhead. The large room with high ceilings, dark teak wood beams, and floors of black-and-white marble retained the grandeur of an era long gone.

"How elegant," Laura said to Jack as they looked around. Doreen and Billy and Sarinah and Harold came in behind them.

Laura startled when she spotted Wibawa and Ari seated at a nearby table with several other couples. Their presence shouldn't have come as a surprise. More than six million people lived in Jakarta, yet few upscale restaurants existed outside those at the hotels. Laura glanced at Jack, noticing that he looked unsettled. He must have seen them too. Laura looked back at Ari, who faced in the other direction. The diamond clasp at the nape of her neck shone like a beacon. Wibawa spotted them and nodded in acknowledgment.

Laura noted The Palms menu included *rijsttafel* — a medley of island foods concocted by the Dutch, served by twelve sarong-clad attractive young women, each carrying a different dish. Laura hoped Jack wouldn't order it, though she suspected he would. He enjoyed the spectacle.

"Good evening, Jack, Mrs. Harrison," Wibawa said. He had approached quietly and now stood behind Jack's chair. Jack made an effort to stand; Laura noticed the strange expression on his face and was puzzled. "Please, don't get up," Wibawa said. "And greetings, Sarinah, Harold. It's good to see you."

"Wibawa, these are our friends, Billy and Doreen," Jack said. "They're leaving Indonesia to go back to Texas. This is their farewell dinner."

"I hope you enjoyed your stay here," Wibawa said graciously.

"We have," Doreen said, her smile sweet.

"And I hope you will come back to visit," Wibawa added.

"We will," Doreen said, her smile still sweet.

"That's the unfortunate thing about expats. They leave before you get to know them." Wibawa turned to Laura. "Too bad you couldn't join us on the trip to Kalimantan."

Laura looked at Jack. "I thought it was a business trip. I didn't realize wives were invited," she said, annoyed her husband hadn't been honest with her.

"Ari decided to come along at the last minute, though she didn't go with us upriver." Wibawa gripped the back of Jack's chair. "Any progress on the financing, Jack?"

"I'm working on it."

"We're counting on you. If you will excuse me, ladies."

"Very courtly," Doreen said as he walked away.

"So, Jack, how's that deal going with Wibawa and Johnny? Forty million dollars. That would be a real coup for you," Harold said.

Jack looked at Laura. She watched and waited for his reply.

"I sent the proposal to New York for approval."

Under the table, Laura clenched her fist; she was not pleased to hear the deal had moved on to New York. And why Jack didn't mention that Ari was on the trip?

"I wish you luck," Harold said. "Often a head office can be more a hindrance than a help. They're thousands of miles away and don't understand what it's like doing business here. Sometimes they seem to go out of their way to turn deals down. They're afraid they'll get the blame if it goes bad. It's easier to say no. Then guys like us in the field get in trouble for not booking business and making money."

Laura took comfort in Harold's comments. She hoped the credit committee said no to Jack's deal.

"That's not going to happen. Our bank is keen to do business here." Jack perused the wine list and then, when the waiter arrived, ordered with confidence.

"Pineapple juice for me," Doreen said. She sat with her arm entwined around Billy's. They looked like newlyweds. Amazed at how readily Doreen forgave Billy, Laura thought she wouldn't be so forgiving if Jack betrayed her.

A group of singers, different from those in the gamelan trio, strolled the room. Attired in colorful garb, they strummed guitars and belted out songs.

"They're Batak, from Sumatra," Sarinah said. "That's their traditional music."

"Sounds like mariachi," Doreen said as she swayed to the rhythm.

The trio came over to their table and belted out a happy song no one recognized. They draped a long multicolored embroidered cloth over the shoulders of the three couples and a photographer snapped a picture — touristy but fun.

Jack ordered the rijsttafel. So then, while waiters served the others, twelve pretty girls carrying large platters paraded in and lined up behind Jack's chair. One at a time they stepped forward and smiled at him as they dished food onto his plate. An aroma of pungent spices wafted over the table. Like a horse with blinders, Billy avoided eye contact with the women, while Jack returned their smiles.

A short, mustached man in a tuxedo stepped onto the small, spotlighted stage. He began to sing, "It's a Wonderful World," one of Laura's favorite songs. She got goose bumps listening to the familiar lyrics and beautiful melody. Laura dabbed at her eyes with her napkin and looked around the restaurant.

At the other table, Ari fixated on her compact as she reapplied lipstick. It didn't seem she cared about the wonderful world. The women's eyes met in the round mirror. Ari snapped the compact shut. Laura gripped the napkin in her lap.

After dinner, the couples gathered outside on the portico to say goodbye. Teary eyed, Laura and Doreen hugged. They promised to keep in touch.

***

"Ari was uncharacteristically quiet this evening," Laura said as they drove home. "I was surprised she didn't wander over and flaunt her jewels." Wanting to say more, she bit her lip. She was still upset that Jack didn't tell her Ari was along on the trip to Kalimantan.

Jack turned his head and looked out the window.

"You're going to just sit there?" Laura asked, her voice rising. "Aren't you going to say anything? Why didn't you tell me Ari went along on the trip?"

"I forgot. And I didn't think it was important."

"You're so damn secretive. It's like you're hiding something. You didn't used to be that way."

He shrugged.

"And quit shrugging. You're making me angry."

Haroon turned onto the narrow lane leading to their house and they spotted a becak parked outside the gate. A woman with a mane of dark hair, wearing a red dress, high heels, and layers of makeup, conversed with the driver. Startled by the car's headlights, she glanced up and then jumped in, and the driver pedaled off into the night.

"Who was that?" Laura asked.

"Nissam," Haroon said. "He a *banchee*, a he-she man."

"Oh my," Laura sighed, her hand at her throat. The unexpected scene caught her by surprise.

"Looks more 'she' than 'he.' He's a combo. A cross-dressing cook. Laura, you sure can pick 'em." He couldn't stop laughing.

At a loss for words, Laura didn't know how to react.

"I'd say it's time for Nissam to move on," Jack said.

Grated by the comment, Laura pondered what to do. "I'll speak to him."

Chapter 28

The next morning, Jack left for work and Laura sat alone sipping tea. Budi the houseboy, entered. "More tea for the nyonya?" he asked holding a teapot.

"Please," she said. "Is Nissam in the kitchen?"

"Nissam not come back last night," Budi said.

"Where is he?" Laura asked. She glanced up.

Budi showed no sign of concern. "I not know."

Different scenarios played in her mind. Maybe he's been in an accident. Maybe he met with foul play.

Later Laura went to the kitchen. Unwashed dishes were in the sink, and greasy pans sat on the stove. Nissam was neat and tidy. He must not have returned.

She called Sarinah. "Nissam didn't come home last night. He's missing."

"That happens. He'll be back."

"We saw him leaving the house in a red dress."

Sarinah laughed. "Oh, he's one of those. Probably went to the graveyard. That's where they gather. No one will hassle them there."

"I should call the police."

"Don't bother. They're not going to waste time looking for a servant. When he runs out of money, he'll be back." Laura expected Sarinah to be more concerned, though she suspected Sarinah was right about the police not caring. But she also took umbrage at her friend's comment about Nissam. He wasn't the type to just take off and fritter away his payday money.

Late that afternoon Laura heard sounds emanating from the kitchen. She hurried in, expecting Nissam. Budi stood at the stove with a wooden spoon, stirring sauce in a pan. Intent on what he was doing, he didn't look up.

"Where do you think Nissam is?" Laura asked, unable to keep the concern out of her voice.

"Not know, nyonya. His things still here."

Laura walked out back to the servant quarters. She had not been there since the tour with Hugh. She had no reason to go; she thought it an intrusion.

A poster of a sequined, feathered Cher decorated the wall of Nissam's cubicle. A small electric fan and a framed photograph of a woman cradling an infant sat on the table beside his cot.

Laura picked up the picture and took it to the kitchen. "Do you know the woman in the photo?" Laura asked Budi.

"It his mother and baby Nissam."

"Where does she live? Maybe that's where he is."

"She live in Purwakarta, but he not be there."

***

Jack came home, and they sat down for dinner. Laura didn't intend to tell him about the cook's disappearance. She doubted he would notice Nissam had vanished, and if he did, he would probably just say, "Good riddance."

Jack scooped vegetables cooked in coconut sauce onto his plate. He took a bite and choked.

"What the hell?" he spluttered. "Nissam must be trying to poison us."

"Budi's doing the cooking. Nissam vanished."

"Did they leave a ransom note?" Jack asked, his voice sarcastic.

"Jack, stop it. You're not amusing. I'm worried sick."

Jack rested his hand on her arm. "I'm sorry. But you shouldn't let yourself get so worked up. When he runs out of money, he'll be back."

Laura looked at him, her face taut. "Why does everyone keep saying that? Nissam's responsible." She was annoyed.

"Okay," Jack said. He picked up his fork, pushed the vegetables aside, and began to eat plain rice.

***

The next morning Nissam still had not returned. Laura wrung her hands. She imagined him floating in a rice paddy, or on a slab at the morgue. She went outside to talk to Mille. She knew he would be in front washing the car.

"Mille, Nissam hasn't come back. I want to speak to the *polisi.*" She had thought of calling them herself, but didn't know how to do that. "Can you see if you can find a policeman driving around and bring him here?"

Mille put down the hose and turned off the water. "Nyonya, Nissam come home. Don't you worry."

Laura had heard enough of that. "I want to talk to the polisi." Her tone left no doubt she was serious.

Mille put the sponge in the bucket and dried his hands. He looked at her, his eyes unsure.

Laura put her hands on her hips. "You don't need to be afraid of the police. You haven't done anything wrong. We need their help." Mille shook his head and got in the car. He pulled out of the driveway while Laura stood, looking after him.

Soon he returned, followed by a white car, a green insignia on the side.

"Selamat pagi," the officer said, climbing out. A notepad in his hand, he walked up to greet Laura. "Your driver tells me someone in your family is missing."

"He's not exactly family. He's one of the servants."

The policeman scowled at Mille, who looked sheepish. "I see," the officer said. "How long has he been gone?"

"Two nights now."

"Was it after payday? That happens."

"It wasn't."

"Can I see where he lives?"

Laura led him around back. The policeman walked into Nissam's cubicle, glanced around, and ogled the poster of Cher. Laura doubted he realized she was on display as an ardent supporter of the gay community.

"I'll take down the information, and we'll keep an eye out for him."

Laura could tell from his tone that Sarinah was right.

She considered asking Jack if the bank could help but decided to give it more time. That morning she planned to accompany Sarinah to the publishers to pick up books for the literacy program, but she didn't want to leave the house should there be news.

About to call Sarinah and cancel, she heard a car in the drive.

"I'm early," Sarinah said when Laura opened the door. "I can hang out by the pool with Diablo if you're not ready."

"I was just about to call you. It would be better if I didn't go."

"Nissam?"

Laura nodded.

"There's nothing you can do," Sarinah said, sounding exasperated. "And I need your help."

Laura knew Sarinah didn't need help, but she reluctantly got her bag and followed Sarinah out the door.

When she returned a few hours later, Budi was busy dusting

"Still no Nissam?" she asked.

"Nissam back."

"Back," she said, startled. "Why didn't you tell me? Where is he?"

"You out. I could not tell. And Nissam say not tell you. He asleep."

"Is he okay?"

"He tired."

Nissam slept for a day and a half while Laura fretted again. Perhaps he was sick. She asked Budi to check regularly. She didn't want to venture back there herself, unsure of what she might find.

As time went by, her annoyance flared. He disappears, comes back and sleeps. How inconsiderate. Maybe Jack's right. Maybe I should fire him.

***

The next afternoon, she sat reading in the living room when an aroma of boeuf bourguignon drifted through the room. She set her book aside and hurried to the kitchen. Nissam stood at the sink, his back to her.

"Nissam!"

"Nyonya, I sorry," he said. He didn't turn around.

"Where were you? I was worried." She walked over and glimpsed a bruised and swollen face; his eye was black and purple.

"Oh my God! Are you all right?" She moved closer. "What happened?"

The cook hesitated.

"Nissam, I need to know."

"I at a party. Soldiers come. I run out the back door, but they catch me. They beat me with club. My friend Susi, he run too. He jump in canal. But not swim good. He drown." Nissam stopped talking and sobbed.

"You poor boy." Laura wrapped ice in a towel and pressed it to the side of his face. "Hold it here. I'm going upstairs to get aspirin."

"I okay," he said. "I sorry I cause problem. I need to cook. Tuan come home soon."

"Don't worry about him. You need to see a doctor."

"No doctor," he said in a panic. Laura understood immediately. A doctor might make him report the incident to the police — the very people he feared.

Laura returned and gave him two tablets. "Keep the bottle. Take two more in four hours."

"Terima kasih, nynoya. Thank you. "

"Nissam, how long have you been wearing dresses?" she asked, her voice kind.

"Since I move to Jakarta, but first time since I work here. I not do it again, nyonya. I promise. Please don't fire me. I need money send my mother in Purwakarta." As he pleaded, tears rolled down his discolored face. Laura grabbed two Kleenex from the box on the counter and gave one to Nissam. She wiped away her own tears with the other.

"Don't worry; I'm not going to fire you."

"You kind, nyonya. May God bless you." He walked to the stove. "Now I make dinner."

Laura wasn't about to get rid of Nissam, particularly after what happened to him. Jack would have to learn to live with a transvestite in the kitchen.

***

Days followed, and Laura couldn't get Nissam out of her mind. One afternoon she walked to the kitchen to talk to him. He stood at the butcher block counter, busy preparing their next meal.

"Nissam, you know the red dress you were wearing — you made it yourself?"

"Like it?" he asked. He stopped slicing onions and beamed through a face still discolored.

"I did. You're a good seamster." Laura thought the rarely used term odd. She had first heard it at Parsons.

"My mother, she better than me. Many women in Purwakarta sew."

"I have an idea. We could make casualwear using Indonesian batiks. I'll do some sketches and send them to a friend in New York who works in the garment district. She'd let us know if they might sell. If we get an order, you and your mother and other women in your village can start a co-op to make the garments."

"New York!" Nissam said. "Maybe I go there. Maybe I meet Cher."

Laura laughed. "One never knows."

She didn't want to get Nissam's hopes up, yet found it difficult to suppress her own, particularly as she had something else in mind. She planned to design batik with scenes of colorful tropical birds, orangutans, and exotic flora. She got excited thinking of women strutting down Madison Avenue, the Champs-Élysées, and boulevards all over the world in attire that brought attention to the plight of the rainforest. She envisioned a cosmetics line with orang orange lipstick hues and eye makeup in vivid plumage colors. And Nissam gave her another idea. *Cher!* Perhaps Cher might support the cause. She could appear on stage in Vegas in sequined rainforest batik. How much more effective all this would be than protesting at the Kediri.

Upstairs she retrieved her sketchpad and hurried out to work by the pool. Her mind focused, she began to draw.

***

In a few days, Laura finished several sketches, and she sent them to her friend in Manhattan's garment district.

Later that evening, when Jack came home, she told him as soon as he walked through the door.

"Really?" he said, his tone lacking in enthusiasm. "Good for you. That's great." He went upstairs. Disheartened, Laura stared after him in disbelief.

Chapter 29

"How long does it take to drive to Purwakarta?" Laura asked as she and Sarinah walked back to the car after their literacy session.

"One and a half hours, depending on traffic. It's over the mountain on the same road to Bandung," she replied. "Why? You want to go there?"

"Maybe. Remember when I considered designing fashionable Islamic head coverings?"

"Of course. Now you're actually going to do it?" Sarinah's eyes narrowed.

"Not really. I have a different idea." She told Sarinah about her plan and that she had sent sketches to New York. "I already heard back. They requested a quote for two hundred sundresses. And if those sell, they'll place a bigger order."

Sarinah stopped midstride. "You're kidding! You didn't tell me about all this. How wonderful! But you sound concerned. I'd be ecstatic."

"I'm a designer. I don't know anything about production or pricing. I may have gotten ahead of myself." Laura hadn't expected New York to respond so quickly, if at all. Nor had she thought they would want to place such a big order.

"You told me you took finance courses at Columbia, thinking you might want to start your own business. Here's your chance. And what about Carolina Josephina? Remember her? She successfully started a business over a hundred years ago. You can do the same."

"You're right. And I need to do this not just for me. There's so much more at stake. The village women would have decent jobs. And the garments with special batik designs might help save the rainforest." Laura knew it sounded idealistic, but she had to try. "Maybe you could help me," she said, trying to keep a hint of desperation out of her voice. "Between the two of us, I'm sure we could figure it out." She didn't want to go it alone. And she trusted Sarinah's judgment.

Sarinah shook her head. "Thanks for the confidence, but I know nothing about fashion or making garments."

"And I didn't know anything about working with children, but you showed me what to do. Now I love it."

"Not the same. But nice try."

They arrived at the car and climbed in.

"Nissam's from Purwakarta," Laura told Sarinah as Mille drove off. "He told me his mother and many women in the village are excellent seamstresses. Sounds like it could be a good place for the business."

"Several international fabric and clothing companies have partnered with local firms and set up there. Nearby Jatiluhur Lake provides clean water. There's a reliable power supply and skilled labor. We should check it out."

Laura took comfort in Sarinah's use of the inclusive "we."

***

Laura went to the kitchen to talk to Nissam. "I'm going to Purwakarta with Sarinah in a few days. She thinks it could be a good spot for the casualwear business. Can you come with us? I'd like to meet your mother."

"My mother save my life."

Taken aback by his comment, Laura waited.

"When I five years old, my family live in east Java. My father a farmer. My mother make *jamu.*"

Jamu was traditional medicine widely used throughout the country. Women attired in long batik skirts and long-sleeved blouses walked the hot dusty streets mornings and evenings, going door-to-door selling to their regular customers. On their backs they carried heavy baskets with bottles of remedies for a variety of ailments — headaches, liver problems, and osteoporosis, as well as potions for virility. Laura noticed the jamu woman who walked by the gate every day. Despite the weight on her back, she always had a smile.

"My family poor but happy," Nissam continued. "Then big problem in Jakarta. New president. Soldiers come to my village looking for communist. Then everybody looking for communist. Bad people come take my father from bed. He not communist. No matter. They tie him to tree. They push bamboo stick through his heart."

When Nissam choked up, Laura got him a glass of water.

"My mother afraid they kill me too. She take me to west Java. Soldiers not come there. We live with her sister. She marry again. Once she tell me story. Then never say anything more. Many people killed. No one talk about what happened. Everyone afraid."

***

With Mille driving, the group set out on the narrow road headed for Purwakarta. Though clearly reluctant to come along, Nissam joined Laura and Sarinah on their trip. Laura suspected that growing up in Purwakarta, he was bullied. In small towns anywhere it could be difficult for those who were different to find a place to hide. She was glad he overcame his fears and went with them.

They wound their way over the mountain following a slow-moving truck with oil drums piled high. Mille, eager to speed ahead, fidgeted. But blind curves and the truck forced him to creep along. Laura watched the drums wobble. She prayed one didn't roll off and crash through the windshield.

"So what does Jack think about all this?" Sarinah asked.

"He's supportive," Laura said, though she wondered if that was true.

"You sound doubtful."

"I know he wants me to be happy. But sometimes he doesn't act like it."

"Maybe he's jealous."

Laura laughed. "Of what? It's still just an idea." She paused to glance out the window. "I think he's preoccupied with problems at the bank."

"Wouldn't surprise me. It's tough for foreign banks trying to do business here."

Laura regretted her comment. She forgot that Sarinah's fiancé Harold was a banker. She hoped Sarinah didn't mention anything about Jack to him. She didn't want Jack's problems to become expat gossip.

"The co-op may be an idea now, but it will happen. You are one of the most determined women I know," Sarinah said. "Where does that come from?"

"My parents, I guess. My mother was a teacher. She brought biographies of famous women home from the school library — Rosa Parks, Mother Theresa, Margaret Thatcher. I read them all. And my father encouraged me. And after I fell out of a tree onto a picket fence, I lost a lot of blood and almost died. I was determined to do something meaningful. I just never figured out what that would be."

***

Laura looked out the window, recalling the day she came home from the hospital. She was in her bedroom, seated on the floor and putting toys into a cardboard carton when the door opened.

"Laura, what are you doing?" her mother asked.

"Packing my dolls to give to Sally. She can still have babies. She can pretend."

Her mother dropped to her knees and hugged her. She leaned back, gripped Laura with both hands and looked her in the eye. "Now you listen to me, Laura. You don't go feeling sorry for yourself. I'm glad I had you and Richard Jr., but not being a mother isn't the end of the world. There are women out there who have kids and shouldn't. They realize too late that it's not for them and the children suffer. You are smart and compassionate and persistent. You can do anything you want with your life. If someday you want children, there are plenty of kids out there who need someone to love them."

***

Laura glanced at Sarinah and said, "I've been thinking about adopting."

"An Indonesian child?" Sarinah asked, surprise in her voice.

"Nationality's not that important, though I question whether it's a good idea for a child to be raised in a culture different than its own."

"Depends on whether the culture can care for its people. In your country nationality is hardly an issue. America is a melting pot. No one stands out as different."

Laura knew the United States was a melting pot; she also knew pockets of discrimination existed.

"And Jack's okay with this?"

"We haven't really discussed it. In New York he said we were both too busy for a family. Now he's still busy and more preoccupied. It's hard to talk to him about anything."

"You two should take a romantic weekend and go to Bali. It's so beautiful and relaxing. It could be a second honeymoon."

"Odd you mention that. We stopped there before coming to Jakarta. I had a strange experience. I couldn't sleep. I had this feeling someone died in the room. We went to a cremation ceremony earlier. Jack said that had something to do with it."

"Where did you stay?"

"The Seminyak Kebun Resort."

Sarinah stiffened. "Indonesians would never stay at that hotel. It's built over an old graveyard."

Laura didn't understand. "I thought Balinese were cremated."

"Those elaborate cremation ceremonies are expensive so the dead are buried temporarily until enough money is saved. Sometimes that takes years."

Laura sat in silence, pondering Sarinah's explanation. Now it all made sense.

***

Mille braked and everyone pitched forward. "You okay?" he asked. He jerked his head around to check. "Sorry. Goat ran across the road."

Laura ran her hand through her hair. "How much further?" she asked.

"Just over hill."

Nissam, in front, remained quiet for most of the trip.

As they came over the rise, Laura spotted a dam, a sparkling blue lake and a bridge over a winding river. In the distance she spotted a town.

"Purwakarta," Nissam said. He wrung his hands.

They drove through a village similar to those in Jakarta, though less congested. Nissam directed Mille down a rutted red-clay road. Ahead he pointed to a weather-beaten wood frame house. Chickens scratched in the dirt, and a woman sat on the porch. When they stopped in front, she rushed out.

"My mother," Nissam said. He smiled for the first time since they left Jakarta.

As she approached the car, tears welled in his mother's eyes. Nissam had inherited her sweet features and warm smile. Her hair, pulled back, showed streaks of gray. Like most Indonesian women's, her skin was flawless. "*Saya* Peni," she said.

"*Ibu*, saya nama Laura." Laura addressed Peni as ibu, a term of respect.

The woman stared at Laura and then turned to speak to her son.

Nissam listened to her and smiled. "My mother like your hair. She say it remind her of red hibiscus, her favorite flower."

"Terima kasih," Laura said with a laugh. She preferred to think of herself as strawberry blond.

The women sat in a semicircle on the porch. Nissam settled on the steps at his mother's feet and translated.

"Nissam is oldest of my five children," Peni said. She looked down at him. "He is a good boy, but I worry about him in Jakarta. So many people." She patted her son on the shoulder. Laura imagined how mortified she would have been if she had seen Nissam after the police beat him. Fortunately she would never know about that.

Laura handed Peni several casualwear sketches and watched her study them. She relaxed seeing Peni nod her head, seeming to be pleased by what she saw. She spoke to Nissam.

"My mother say dresses easy to make. Women in the Purwakarta good at sewing. She say she good too."

Peni got up and went inside. She returned with several garments, evidence of her handiwork. Laura held up a skirt and checked the stitching at the waist and the hem. Well made, she thought. She had previously had concerns about the quality of local workmanship. Cheap apparel from Third World countries flooded the U.S. market. Laura thought the co-op should aim for the higher end with better profit margins. There, contemporary design and attention to detail mattered.

"The best place for fabric is Yogyakarta," Peni said via her son. "Many batik artists work there. I know someone to help you. The clothes, we sew here."

Sarinah mentioned setting up a co-op. Peni listened yet looked pensive. "There's a problem. Only two sewing machines in our village. We share."

Laura remembered the expensive machine she purchased to make the orangutan costume. Two machines for two hundred dresses would indeed be a problem. She penned *Sewing machines?* on her notepad while wondering where she would get the money.

Peni was a wealth of helpful information. She told Laura how much the women in the nearby garment factories earned and gave her an estimate for fabric costs. Laura knew professionals would be appalled by her research. She doubted they would consider data obtained in a village from a woman who shared a sewing machine reliable. But Laura had confidence in Peni. She put more value in her knowledge gained through practical experience than in the knowledge of the consultants who gathered information seated at a desk in New York.

"I know woman who manager at Bank Rakyat. They make loans for small amount. Maybe she help with money for sewing machines. They like women. They repay." Laura remembered Jack mentioning that Imee, the credit manager at the bank, had said something similar.

Nissam went inside and returned with a tray, a pot of boiling water, and cups. He poured for Laura, Sarinah, and his mother. Laura took a sip to be polite. For the second time, she was ignoring the warnings about not drinking local water. She had had tea with Dewi's grandmother in the kampung without incident. Here a clear lake glistened nearby.

The women passed an hour in conversation. Laura listened, asked questions, and became more confident. Peni knew where to source workers and get money. She seemed to possess the instincts of a good leader. She had endured one of the toughest management jobs of all — mothering five children. And she was a survivor. Laura remembered Nissam's story about his mother escaping the genocide. It seemed like the perfect partnership. Laura would help with design and contacts in New York. The business would be local. It would belong to Peni and the women in the village.

Laura and Sarinah said goodbye to Peni and walked to the car, where Mille stood staring at the right front tire.

"Flat," he said. He shook his head.

Laura looked at the rubber blob hugging the ground. Putting her hand to her mouth, she took a step back. She interpreted the scene as an omen — a sign the co-op was destined to fail. She walked away and watched from a distance, not returning until Mille had finished changing the tire. She got back in the car and berated herself for letting an inconvenience cloud her hopes.

***

Back in Jakarta, Laura gathered the information she needed to prepare a quote for the sundresses. She used prices she knew similar high-end dresses sold for at the retail level in the States. She backed out a 50 percent wholesaler margin, the freight estimate she got from a shipper, and a 10 percent donation for a rainforest conservation fund. The remainder, more than adequate to cover local expenses, would provide a decent return for the co-op. In the proposal, Laura asked for a 50 percent advance payment.

She knew that wasn't standard practice, but she needed up-front money for sewing machines and fabric. In time she would have Peni introduce her to the manager at Bank Raykat, but knew she couldn't rely on quick loan approval.

"*Semoga beruntung*, good luck," she murmured as she sealed the envelope.

With a spring in her step, she moved across the room to the front door. Outside she asked Mille to drive her to the post office.

On her return, she called Sarinah. "The proposal is on its way to New York."

"Carolina Josefina would be proud of you."

Laura hung up and leaned back against the wall. She hoped she hadn't set herself, and Peni, up for a letdown.

Chapter 30

The week following Doreen and Billy's farewell dinner, Jack sat in his office fiddling with a pen. He hadn't heard anything about the $40 million loan proposal. He expected approval by now. He thought about Laura also waiting for news from New York, but did not share his frustrations with her. There was no use doing so because she clearly didn't think his bank should finance a logging project in the home of the orangutan.

"There's an Angela Krauter in the reception room," Wati said standing at the door. "She doesn't have an appointment. Says you know her."

Jack dropped the pen he held. His muscles tensed. Angela Krauter — the bank's toughest, meanest auditor. "What the hell?" he muttered. He knew Angela had been transferred from New York to the bank's office in Hong Kong, but what was she doing in Indonesia?

He put on his jacket, adjusted his tie, mustered a smile, and headed down the corridor. Angela sat on the couch, flipping through a magazine, her long, shapely legs on display. Middle-aged and attractive in an unusual way, she had short, dark, heavily gelled hair and too-bright red lipstick that gave her the appearance of severity. Her presence struck fear into the hearts of bank managers everywhere.

"Greetings, Angela. What brings you to the tropics? Vacation?"

"I'm here for a surprise audit. Sorry for the lack of notice, but they're not supposed to be scheduled."

Jack's throat went dry. His mind swirled. "But Bank AmerIndo is a joint venture. Our Indonesian partners have responsibility for internal audits. They're done locally."

"As a foreign shareholder we have the right to inspect the books and records. Inspection, audit — call it what you want. The process is the same. Check the joint venture agreement. It's quite clear." She cocked her chin, her eyes focused in on him.

Son of a bitch. He'd check the agreement, though he knew she had to be correct. She wouldn't fly all the way from Hong Kong without knowing what she had the right to do.

"Don't worry; I won't get in the way. You won't even know I'm here. All I need is a workspace. I'll be spending most of my time with the controller."

"Sure," Jack said, his mind on the fraudulent invoice in the file. "Let's go to my office, and I'll have Gunadi come down."

She followed him down the hall. In the office she walked over to the expanse of windows. "Beautiful view," she said.

"Beats New York," Jack said as he dialed Gunadi.

"So how're you enjoying Jakarta? You've been here now, what, six or seven months?"

The J. H. Legal Advisory invoice looked authentic, yet the request to be paid in cash might raise suspicions. He could retrieve it. No invoice would be better than one that might draw attention. And yet there was the chance Angela might not even notice. Thousands of invoices filled the Accounts Payable file, though none for such a large amount. He had to stall her, but he couldn't think of a legitimate reason.

Jack realized she had asked him a question. "That's right. It's challenging but I like it," he said, irritated by her banter.

"And what about your wife? I remember she had a fabulous job in New York. How's she coping?"

"Laura's fine. She didn't want to come here, but now I may have to drag her back to the States. She's found a number of interests."

"Good for her."

Gunadi walked in, a pad of paper and pen in hand. "Hello, Gunadi. Good to see you again," Angela said.

"I didn't realize you two knew each other," Jack said.

"We met at the controllers' regional meeting in Hong Kong. Back before you came," Gunadi said.

"Gunadi and I are old friends," Angela said with a smile.

Gunadi looked uneasy. Jack wondered if the controller had firsthand knowledge of Angela's penchant for bedding younger men. In New York rumor had it that she worked her way through the newly hired batch of trainees. Once, after an evening at the theater, she invited a fresh-faced recruit back to her apartment. The next morning he appeared at work bent over, his face a grimace, his back a victim of Angela's long legs. Jack had a hard time imaging Gunadi and Angela in the throes of lust. Both were accountants.

"I don't need to take up any more of your time, Jack. I know you're busy," Angela said.

"I'd like to hear what you'll be doing while you're here."

"It's the standard audit. I'll be reviewing bank statements, reconciliations, loan loss provisions, petty cash controls, check signing authorizations, monthly receivables and payables, and backup documentation. The usual."

Backup documentation — the words resounded like a clarion call. Though only a single piece of paper among many, Jack decided he couldn't take the risk she might discover the J. H. Legal Advisory invoice and ask questions.

"Sounds thorough," he said, standing. "I'll check in with you later."

He hoped Angela wouldn't have time to get to the backup documentation file on the first day. He planned to stay late and remove the damaging piece of paper. Though already recorded in the bank's P&L, the transaction would merely appear there as an innocuous number. The invoice with the request for cash would be more obvious. He had to get rid of it.

During the day Jack sat through several meetings, his thoughts never far from tough Angela. He overlooked the possibility of an outside audit, a serious mistake. He should never have paid the bribe, an even worse mistake. He should have let the bank take the write-off. New York would not have allowed the bank to fail. Indonesia was too strategic to the bank's long-term strategy. They would have invested more capital to avoid public recognition of weakness, a crack in the façade of invincibility. He wouldn't have gotten his bonus, but he could have started over without having to deal with his predecessor's bad decisions. But there was no time for second guessing. He had to get himself out of the mess he created.

Early in the evening, Jack glanced at his watch — seven o'clock. Angela should be gone by now. He walked down the corridor past rows of empty desks and the irritating sound of janitors vacuuming the carpet. He let Angela have an office next to Gunadi. He peered through the glass front to make sure the room was empty. With a quick glance over his shoulder he stepped inside. His eyes raced over stacks of files. Where to begin? His fingers trembled as they wandered the tabs.

"Jack, what are you doing in here?" The suddenness of Angela's harsh voice startled him. Preoccupied, he had failed to hear the door open.

"Sorry, I thought you left."

"I went to the restroom."

"I need information from one of the folders," he said. "But that's okay; it's late. I'll get it tomorrow."

"The audit has started. You're not supposed to touch anything in here. If you want something, ask me first," she said, her voice stern.

Irritated, Jack struggled to keep his temper in check. "You're right. I was working on a project and wanted to finish this evening."

"What is it you need?" She stood, her feet apart, her hands on her hips.

"It can wait," he said. "And it's getting late. Can I invite you for dinner? You're staying at the Kediri. We can go to the restaurant there."

Angela looked at him as if questioning his motives. Jack didn't flinch. Though he didn't relish dinner with the tough auditor, he planned to resort to charm and flattery. He might need her support later on.

"Give me five minutes to tidy up. I'll meet you at the elevator," she said as she walked off.

With his head aching from stress, Jack slumped against the doorframe for a moment. Once back in his office, he called Laura to let her know he would be home late.

***

Jack chose the restaurant at Angela's hotel not for the food, but for its convenience. They entered the large room with its low arches, dimmed lighting, and an ambience of romance and intimacy. Angela looked around while Jack approached the maître d'.

"A quiet table where we can discuss business," Jack said.

They followed the maître d' to a table in the corner.

"You seem uptight," Angela said as they sat down. "Are you all right?"

"Just worried about the $40 million loan proposal I sent to the credit committee. It would be the biggest deal the bank has done in Southeast Asia. It'll be hard to relax until I hear back."

"I don't know anything about it," Angela said, toying with her necklace. When she picked up the menu, Jack glanced at her. With her severity and hostile manner, he sensed that in bed she would be a tiger.

"It's a sweet deal. The bank will make a lot of money."

"Good," she replied with obvious disinterest.

"So how long will you be here?"

"As long as it takes." She continued to peruse the menu. "What's good?"

"Rice."

Angela laughed. "Ah yes, rice. When I get back to the States I'm going to have the biggest, juiciest burger I can find."

"Would you care for wine?"

"A crisp white please."

"They do have white." Jack glanced at the wine list. "Not so sure about 'crisp.'"

"Whatever. I know it's not like living in Hong Kong. Fewer choices. That's why you guys get that large hardship allowance."

Jack chuckled to himself. He wondered how many would consider living in a huge house with a cadre of servants a "hardship." He'd heard of expat bankers who drove their visiting bosses by the reeking canals to make sure they didn't get the wrong impression and reduce those coveted extra monies.

"Yep, the limited selection of decent wine does make life tough." *It was going to be a long dinner putting up with Angela's inanities.* "So what made you decide to go into auditing?"

"It was that or being a detective."

Jack raised his eyebrows. He waited for more.

"They're similar; both involve ferreting out crooks." Jack flinched. He didn't think of himself as a crook. She continued, "But detectives deal with murders, and I faint at the sight of blood. So now I check numbers for clues."

After the waiter poured the wine, Jack raised his goblet. "It's good to see you," he said. They clinked glasses. "How long has it been? Probably two years ago at the bank's holiday party?" He pictured Angela on the dance floor shaking her butt, her trainee partner eager for his initiation into banking later that evening.

"I don't remember you being there."

"I remember you. You looked super in that silver dress." Absentmindedly, Jack put his hand on her arm.

"Are you hitting on me?" she asked, her look hard and accusing.

Jack drew back. "Sorry, don't get me wrong. I'm Southern. We touch and hug a lot. It's cultural."

Angela took a sip of wine.

"I know you guys at the bank gossip about me and my young trainees. I find it amusing." She smiled smugly. "Don't get any ideas," she said with a sideways glance. "You don't fit my profile. And I've learned my lesson. No more pen-dipping in the company inkwell, as the saying goes. Too bad there's not an equivalent expression for women."

Jack couldn't help but admire her. Smart, she didn't take any crap. Unlike most bankers, there were no pretenses with Angela.

"Let's order," Jack said. He picked up his menu.

***

The next morning, exhausted after a night of little sleep, Jack arrived early at the office. He tossed his briefcase onto a chair and hurried down the corridor, headed for the accounting department.

Damn! He saw Angela already there, busy looking through files.

"Good morning," he said. He forced an attempt to sound jovial. "You're an early bird."

"A good night's sleep, a cup of Sumatran coffee, and I'm ready to go," she said, her tone chipper.

In no mood for her high energy, Jack turned to leave.

"Wait. Didn't you need something from one of these folders?"

"I have other things to do now. I'll get it later."

"Thank you for inviting me to dinner. I appreciate that. Most nights I eat alone."

On his way back to his desk, Jack pondered Angela's comment. She sounded vulnerable. He never imagined she might feel lonely.

At his desk, Jack waited for Gunadi.

"I planned to take you and Angela to lunch today," Jack said to the controller when he came in. "But I'm busy. Perhaps you can take her." He knew Gunadi would be more than happy to go. The pair could discuss the latest FASB accounting practices, and he would be dining at an expensive restaurant — an experience he couldn't afford on his own.

Most importantly, Angela would be out of the office.

"Sure," Gunadi said. As Jack predicted, he beamed at the prospect.

"Make reservations at Layang-Layang across the street. Angela will enjoy that." Jack knew the food was good, the service slow.

Later Angela appeared in his doorway. "I hear you won't be able to join us." She was heading to lunch with Gunadi who stood beside her.

"Sorry. I have a couple meetings this afternoon I need to prepare for," he said, coming out from behind his desk. He escorted them down the hall to the elevator and pushed the button.

"How're things going?" he asked.

"Making progress. I hoped we might discuss a few things. Guess we'll have to do that later."

Jack cleared his throat. He wondered what she meant by "a few things."

The elevator arrived, the doors opened, and Angela and Gunadi stepped in. As soon as the doors closed, Jack hurried to the accounting department.

He entered the empty office and left the door ajar so as not to attract attention. He rifled through the stacks until he found the one he needed — payables. With the papers arranged in chronological order, he thumbed through to February but couldn't find the J. H. Legal Advisory invoice. Exasperated, he kept searching. His heart raced. If Angela returned and caught him with his hand in the files again, he would be in trouble. Then, wedged between other papers, he found it. He took it out and smiled at the judge's handiwork. The letterhead looked official. After all the trouble he had locating it, he doubted Angela would even notice. He decided to leave it there and take the risk.

***

The following morning, Angela strode into Jack's office. "I finished and would like to meet with you before I leave. My flight's later this afternoon. Are you free at one o'clock?"

"No problem." He tried to sound upbeat, though he dreaded the session.

Promptly at one, Angela entered. She took a seat and Jack braced himself.

"Most of the audit was straightforward. We don't need to spend time going through each item unless you want to. Everything will be in my report," she said. "But there are a couple of things that disturb me."

His hands clutched atop his desk, Jack leaned forward.

"There's a $575 credit card charge for damages to a hotel room in Samarinda. What's that about?"

The question caught him off guard. He had forgotten he had used the bank's credit card to pay for the broken mirror, and Gunadi never mentioned it.

"Must be an error. We haven't had any wild bank parties in Samarinda recently," he said in an attempt at humor. "I'll check into it." He jotted a reminder on a notepad.

"This next item is also odd. We made a Rp. 25 million payment to a J. H. Legal Advisory." She held up the invoice. "Gunadi says he gave the money to you." She paused to stare. "It's highly unusual to pay cash. Care to explain?" She looked confident and smug.

"I know it must seem strange," Jack said. He slowed his cadence and selected his words with care. "Things are different here. The legal firm that did the work is small. They only take cash. Maybe it's a tax thing for them. I don't know."

"The bank shouldn't be helping companies avoid paying taxes, if that's what you mean."

"That's not what I mean," he said. He grappled to maintain the upper hand. "Many companies here still do business on a cash-only basis."

"Which brings up another thing," she said. "There should be an approved vendor list. The bank needs to know who's behind the companies we do business with. We shouldn't be engaged in business with a legal firm that only takes cash. It sounds suspicious. I suggest that Gunadi draw up a list of vendors and have it approved." Her voice, the barrage of comments, and the questions came at Jack like the staccato of a machine gun. In a futile attempt to dodge her verbal onslaught, he leaned away.

"And last," Angela continued. "No reserve has been set up for a possible loss to cover the $1 million loan default in Bandung."

When will this end? "The case is being heard next week. The company has substantial assets. We expect repayment."

"Prudent accounting requires that a loss reserve be set up now. When a loan is in litigation, that's enough to establish reasonable doubt with regard to repayment." Angela crossed her legs, and her blue skirt hiked midthigh. Jack took it as a taunt.

"That's not your decision," he said, his voice rising. "The board will determine what needs to be done."

He needed to get Angela out of his office. "Is there anything else we need to talk about? I wouldn't want you to miss your flight." She was trying his patience as she verged on discovering what he had done.

"We've gone over everything I wanted to discuss." She stuffed papers into her briefcase, stood, and stiffly shook his hand. "I'll be waiting to hear who's behind J. H. Legal Advisory."

She stood, turned and strode through the door.

Chapter 31

For weeks, eager for a response from New York, Laura would greet Jack at the door when he got home, hoping he'd be bringing her a letter. But this particular evening he looked distraught and she forgot about the mail.

"Are you okay?"

"I met with Angela before she left. Didn't go well. But nothing I can't handle."

"You said she's tough. I'm sure she's like that with all the banks." Her comment was meant to comfort him, though she suspected there was something else going on she knew nothing about. "So now what?" She hoped that finally he might open up and confide in her. They had barely spoken in ages.

"Not sure." He turned to go upstairs. "I'm going to change clothes."

Disappointed, Laura watched him walk off. She picked up the stack of mail he tossed on the table and spotted a letter addressed to her. It had a New York return address. She ripped open the envelope and a check fluttered to the floor. She picked it up and gasped. *Two thousand dollars!* They accepted her proposal.

She ran to the kitchen. "Nissam, we're in business," she shouted, tossing her arms in the air.

Busy at the sink, he spun around. She held the check for him to see. "My mother be so happy. And busy," he said, his eyes wide, his hands clutching his face.

Laura glanced at the check amount again. She couldn't believe the good fortune. For a second she fretted, thinking she might have underpriced the order, but quickly dismissed the thought. Excited, she read the letter. They looked forward to a long-term relationship and planned to order more dresses.

***

When Jack came downstairs, Laura could hardly suppress her excitement. She dangled the check and hugged him.

"Wow, you did it. Two thousand dollars,"

"And they'll be ordering more." Laura's enthusiasm was in overdrive.

"Are you sure you can pull this off?" Jack looked dubious.

"Thanks for the confidence," she said, though she too had doubts.

"Don't get me wrong. This is all great." His enthusiasm sounded less than genuine.

"I already called Sarinah. Tomorrow we're going to Purwakarta to help Peni fill out paperwork for the women's co-op."

"Remember, you're not allowed to work."

"I know. The co-op is for the seamstresses, and maybe Sarinah wants to be a part of it, though we haven't spoken about it. Peni will be president." Laura wasn't even sure if a co-op had a president. For now, it didn't matter. Despite Jack's cautionary comments, she was caught up in the moment and wasn't about to climb down from her cloud.

Jack followed her out to the terrace, pulled up a chair and sat beside her. "What are you getting out of this? You're doing most of the work."

"Right now the business is mainly for the poor women in the village and to raise awareness for environmental causes. Maybe I can get paid for consulting. I haven't really thought much about it."

"I see."

"Don't worry, you're still the breadwinner." She put her hand on his arm to reassure him.

Jack got up and walked toward the kitchen. "This breadwinner needs a beer."

After he left, Laura went to sit by the pool. She suspected there was more going on at the bank than he let on. And she wondered if perhaps his problems had made him envious of her success. For the sake of her marriage, she decided to temper her enthusiasm.

With a cool breeze blowing across her face, she took a deep breath, closed her eyes, and began to meditate. She tried to find time to do that every day. When she first began, she found that her mind tended to wander. Now she was more able to focus. And she found the practice calming. She wished Jack would give it a try, though she knew he wouldn't.

***

The following day Laura and Sarinah, along with Nissam and Mille, drove to Purwakarta.

As on their prior visit, Peni waited on the front porch and rushed out to greet them. When Laura told Peni about the order, she clapped. Nissam translated, "I so happy," though her emotion needed no translation.

"What's a good name for the business?" Laura asked her. "Any ideas?"

"*Harapan,*" Peni said with no hesitation.

"Means hope," Sarinah said.

So totally perfect. Harapan for the poor women, harapan for the rainforest, and harapan for the orangutans.

"When New York want dresses?" Peni asked in halting English as she hesitated searching for the English words.

"In six weeks."

Peni's face clouded. Now, unafraid to use her broken English, she said, "That be a problem. Ramadan coming. Nobody eat sunrise to sunset. Everybody tired. No one want to work."

Laura grimaced. She had forgotten about Ramadan, the Islamic holiday where Muslims fasted for thirty days and little got done. She drummed her fingers on the armrest of the chair as Sarinah, Nissam, and Peni conversed in Bahasa too rapid for her to understand.

When the trio finished talking, Nissam said, "Tidak apa apa, no problem. During day, women sleep. After sunset, they eat. At night, they sew dresses."

In an attempt at maintaining an air of confidence, Peni cocked her chin. But her flitting eyes betrayed her giving Laura scant confidence. She visualized the business evaporating before it got started.

Chapter 32

With Angela closing in, Jack needed someone to talk to. By default, Judge Hartono became his confidant. Jack arranged to meet the judge, and he arrived at the now all-too-familiar scene — an empty Barong Bar with a gamelan playing discordant music. He decided to sit somewhere other than the table in the corner. He didn't want to meet where he lost his integrity.

"You're back," the pretty waitress said.

"A Bintang." He needed a drink and didn't want to wait.

When he arrived, the judge said, "Always good to see you, Jack." He sat down, and the waitress came over with a beer for each man. She, and they, had settled into a comfortable routine. "What's happening? You sounded worried when you called."

"The bank had a surprise audit, a tough woman from Hong Kong."

"I don't see how this concerns me."

"She wants to know who's behind J. H. Legal Advisory."

"I never thought that invoice was a good idea, but you insisted." The judge wrinkled his brow. Though he usually spoke in a monotone, he now sounded defensive.

"Without it I could not have gotten the money to you. I hope you're planning to hear the case soon. Angela might relax once the $1 million is repaid."

"Why don't you just have Tom call her off the audit? He can do that."

"You know Tom?" Jack asked, jolted by the mention of his boss.

"We met once. When he was in Indonesia for a board meeting."

Jack sat upright in his chair. "You two talked about the problem loan in Bandung? You told him you wanted money to hear the case?"

"He said it would have to wait, that the new bank president would deal with it."

Jack slumped in his chair. His boss set him up.

"Actually, I'm glad you called, I was about to call you. I have bad news."

Jack placed his hand on his stomach. He felt nauseated.

"I was prepared to hear the Bandung case and give your bank a favorable ruling, but now I hear the defendant is going to appeal. Then it will no longer be within my jurisdiction."

"Wait a minute," Jack jabbed his finger at the judge. "You said you'd take care of it. You said you 'could make life difficult for him' if he didn't pay up. Those were your exact words."

"Yes, I did say that. It's unusual for defendants to appeal."

"Then give back the money," Jack said though he already knew what the response would be.

"It's gone. But Jack, listen. We can work with the new judge. The bank will get its money. It may just take more time."

Jack glanced around the dark room. He squirmed as the noose tightened. "And pay him $25,000 too. There's no more money."

"I doubt if he would want that much. I will talk to him."

"You don't understand. There is no more money. Not one more rupiah."

"You're a smart man, Jack. I'm sure you can figure something out."

Jack gritted his teeth.

"I'm sorry, Jack. I know this is disappointing." The judge stood up. "I have to leave for an appointment. Perhaps we can get together again next week."

When the judge left, Jack went to the men's room. He looked in the mirror. Tired eyes glazed back at him. He splashed water on his face and rubbed the back of his neck. When he walked out he almost collided with the waitress standing outside the door. She handed him the bar tab.

***

In the car, Jack thought about his dire situation and he gazed out the window at images too fleeting to notice. He should never have given the judge the money. He considered himself an honest man.

Growing up, he achieved the rank of Eagle Scout, a symbol of leadership and all things good. Now he found himself in big trouble. He squirmed in his seat and clutched his hands.

"Let's make a quick stop at Blok M," Jack said to Haroon. Once they got there, he walked around the complex. With darkness approaching, the store windows blazed in garish neon colors. Over the heads of shoppers, he spotted an electronics store, went in, and bought a voice recorder. "To the office," he said on returning to the car.

As Jack rode the elevator to the sixth floor, his ire built. At his desk he inhaled deeply then dialed New York on speakerphone. When Tom answered, Jack turned on the recorder. "We don't have a good connection," Jack said. "Can you speak louder?"

"How's that?" Tom asked, his voice clear and distinct. "Better?"

"Much better," Jack said. He watched the recorder reel spin.

He pictured his boss with his feet propped up on his desk, a thumb hooked around his suspenders.

He inhaled again before starting. "You son of a bitch. Why didn't you tell me you knew Judge Hartono and that he wanted a bribe?"

Jack pictured Tom sitting bolt upright and rolling forward in his chair. For a moment, silence prevailed. "Well, Jack, I'll be frank. I didn't want that to sway your decision about taking the job."

"In other words, you set me up."

"I can see why you might think that. But you're a smart guy I knew you would know how to handle Hartono."

"You gave me the nod to pay him the money. Guess that makes you smart too."

"Hold on a minute. Let me close the door." Jack waited. "In those places you do what you've gotta do," Tom said when he came back to the phone. "And I assume Hartono's happy and everything's taken care of. By the way, how much did you have to give him?"

"There's a big problem, two problems in fact. The borrowers are going to appeal. And Angela Krauter was here. She wants us to write off the loan or set up a reserve to cover the possible loss."

"Angela was there? That is bad news, but I'm sure you can figure out a way to deal with her too." Jack knew what Tom implied, and it angered him even more. Still, he held his emotions in check.

"Call me later," Tom said. "And don't worry. You did the right thing. We'll figure it out." Tom's voice sounded shaky.

Jack turned off the recorder, removed the tape from the machine, and put it in his desk drawer. He was surprised Tom had been so open. He thought his boss was smarter than that.

Chapter 33

On Saturday morning, Jack showered, shaved, and headed downstairs to the kitchen. He poured himself a cup of coffee and put a slice of bread in the toaster. He hadn't slept well and didn't trust his nervous stomach to eat much. Outside he saw Laura meditating. He envied her serenity.

He waited until she opened her eyes before going out to join her. "So how's the Buddhist?" he asked. He pulled up a chair alongside.

"Meditation isn't easy. My mind wanders but not as much as it used to. Sarinah's Buddhist friend said that happens to everyone. I find it relaxing. You should try."

"No thanks." He glanced at the small Buddha statue perched precariously in the crook of a tree. "Why's Buddha up there?"

"Just temporary until I find a better place. I had him on the ground but Diablo mistook him for a fire hydrant."

Jack laughed.

"Peeing on Buddha is not a good idea. Could bring bad karma. In Diablo's next life he might end up in Korea, where dog meat is a delicacy."

Jack mustered a smile. "So what's happening in Purwakarta?"

"The village women are fasting through the day and working at night. Peni's remarkable. She's a natural leader."

"I'd like to meet her sometime."

"Actually, I owe Maya a debt of gratitude."

"How's that?" Jack asked much too quickly.

"If she hadn't left I wouldn't have found Nissam. His dressmaking skills gave me the idea for making casualwear. And his mother turned out to be the perfect person to run the co-op. Odd how things happen sometimes, isn't it"

"It is odd," Jack said, his voice without emotion.

"Are you okay? At dinner last night you seemed pre-occupied." She reached out, entwining her fingers through his.

He leaned forward and gave her a kiss. "Not your problem. Think I'll take a swim. Be back in a flash."

***

Laura walked across the lawn to the table by the pool.

"Join me," she said when Jack came out in his swim trunks. She decided not to press him about his troubles — at least not yet. She'd start with a lighter topic. "I haven't had a chance to tell you. The female parrot is sitting on eggs. The nest box Suparno made worked."

"That's exciting. How long before the chicks hatch?" Despite his words, he sounded disinterested.

"About twenty-eight days. The female sits on the nest, and the male feeds her. It's so sweet."

Laura, her motherly instincts aroused by nesting birds, the baby orangutan, and her work with children in the literacy program, intended to ask Jack about adoption. But now she hesitated. He seemed so distant, so unaware.

"Jack, you worry me. Please tell me what's wrong."

He looked away.

Laura stood up and glared. "Couples are supposed to talk things through. That's what keeps a marriage strong." She paused, then added, "And lasting."

"I'm sorry. It's just that I put up with so much crap at the office. The weekend's my downtime."

Laura didn't let up. "You're not being fair. I'm a wreck wondering what's going on. Whatever happened, it's my problem too. Can't you understand? We need to face it together."

He stared down at his hands in his lap. His silence angered her.

"You used to be full of energy. Have you glanced in the mirror lately? Have you noticed the dark circles under your eyes and the sallow cheeks? You're not the man I married."

"Maybe I need to see a dukun," Jack said. He looked at her with a half-smile.

She strode away across the lawn.

Diablo, asleep under the tree, sprang up. She squatted and wrapped her arms around his neck and buried her face in his fur.

"At least you love me."

He nudged her with his nose. "Where's the ball?" The dog scurried off and returned, a dirty tennis ball in his mouth. "Good boy!" she said. She pried the ball loose and tossed it high. Diablo ran out, snatched it on the fly, and scampered back.

"I wish I had a treat for you," she said, petting him. She threw again, this time in Jack's direction.

Jack glanced up and ducked as Diablo hurtled over.

"He wants you to play with him," Laura called.

"Can't you be more careful?"

"Sorry," she said though she wasn't.

When Laura tossed the ball a third time, it rolled into a clump of bushes at the far corner of the garden. The dog raced over, hesitated, and then plunged into the thicket. He didn't come back out.

"Diablo, Diablo," Laura called. "Jack, not sure what Diablo's up to. He's disappeared in the bushes.

"Hope he's not tangling with a cobra," Jack said from the lounge chair where he reclined reading a magazine. He didn't bother to look up.

The dog finally emerged, an old boot clutched in his mouth.

"Where did you get that?" Laura asked. She took it from him and walked to where he entered into the bushes. She parted the branches and discovered a well-worn path. Crouching she slowly made her way to the wall at the end. Through an opening she saw a lean-to on the other side. Odd, she thought. She backed her way out.

"Jack, come over here. Take a look."

Though Jack seemed disinterested, he got up and followed her into the brush.

"Hello, hello?" Laura called as they emerged into a clearing with a corrugated metal structure.

"Wonder who lives here," Jack said.

A small table, chair, and clothes on a hook were inside. A lone boot stood beneath the cot. Laura set the other alongside it. A photograph tacked to the wall showed Suparno beside the pool with Diablo. She remembered taking the picture and giving it to him. Another photo, yellowed with age, was of a much younger Suparno with Kartini and Maya. They stood on the bank of a river, a smoking volcano in the background.

"Suparno lives here," Laura whispered.

"Suparno! That explains it."

"What?"

"It's why he's always around."

"No one mentioned he lived on the other side of the wall."

"The servants don't think it matters to us where they live."

"But I care. He shouldn't be living in a place like this. Must be awful when it rains."

"There's no room for him in the servant's quarters. And he's not living any differently than most of the poor in Jakarta. Matter of fact, he's better off. He doesn't have to commute, he has a place to wash up, and he can eat with the others."

"Still, I feel bad." She pointed to the photograph of Suparno with Kartini and Maya. "Maybe they're related."

"I doubt it. They don't look alike."

Laura and Jack retreated out into the garden. Still puzzled, Laura spotted Mille up by the house, surprised he would be there on his day off.

"Mille," she called.

"Selamat pagi," Mille said, trotting over. He stopped in front of her, thrusting his shoulders and bouncing on the balls of his feet. Laura smiled. Not only had he learned English from watching Rocky movies, he had picked up the boxer's stance. "I forget something in car. Nyonya want to go somewhere today? No problem."

"That's kind of you to offer, but I just wanted to ask you something. Did you know Suparno lives over there?" She indicated the clump of bushes and the wall.

"I know," he replied.

"Why didn't anyone tell us?"

"No one ask."

"Is he related to Kartini and Maya?'

"He is."

"How?"

"Suparno father of Maya."

Jack edged closer.

"I don't understand. Why didn't he leave when they did?"

"He send money to them in Sukabumi. Not many job for people who no talk. No place else for him to work."

"Do you know why he can't speak? Has he always been like that?"

"Kartini say before Maya born, he talk."

"What happened?" Laura asked.

"Very sad. Suparno marry Kartini sister. Baby inside but upside down. When baby not come out, mother scream all night. She ask Suparno to kill her. Take baby. But he love her, he cannot kill his wife. He sit in dark and listen to her scream. Next day Maya born, mother die. Suparno never speak again."

Laura cradled her face in her hands. "You're right. So very sad."

Chapter 34

Monday morning, on his way to the office, Jack rushed out of the house. Too late he saw Suparno rounding the corner, a bundle of sticks on his back. The men collided and the gardener fell to the ground.

"Sorry," Jack said. When he bent to help, Suparno backed off. He cowered and crouched. Fear and loathing showed in his eyes. Jack knew the depth of the anger wasn't just related to their collision.

He wanted to explain he was sorry for what happened with Maya, that he had been drunk with remorse, that he made a mistake. But he knew Suparno wouldn't understand. And he doubted Suparno would view drunkenness as an excuse for anything. As Jack helped the gardener pick up the scattered sticks, he regretted bringing anguish to one who had so little. When Suparno jerked the bundle onto his back and moved on, Jack ran after him.

"I'm sorry," he said. Suparno kept walking.

As Jack returned to the car, he recalled waking up the morning after Laura left. He had a hangover and had panicked when he realized that Maya lay alongside him in the bed. When he aroused her, she grabbed her uniform off the floor and shyly crept away. He had quickly taken a shower, dressed and rushed off to work. All day he regretted returning and having to face Laura. Then he was surprised, and relieved, to learn that Kartini and Maya left abruptly. He fabricated the cover up about an argument over fly-covered chicken. Though Laura was skeptical at first, she ultimately seemed to believe him. He didn't like lying to her. He didn't like lying to anyone.

***

At the bank, Jack passed through the outer office, thankful the receptionist hadn't arrived. He wasn't up for social interaction. Then he saw Wati seated at her desk.

"Your boss called. Wants you to call him. Said it's urgent."

Shit, Jack thought. Now what?

When he was about to call Tom, Gunadi rapped on the door. "Any word on when we will be getting the $1 million repayment?" the controller asked.

"Nothing yet," Jack said.

"And the $40 million loan. Has it been approved?"

"No news on that either. I do have a message to call Tom. Maybe that's what he's calling about."

"Sorry to bother you." Gunadi looked disappointed.

Jack cupped his head in his hands. He had let down so many good people who counted on him.

He dialed New York.

"I got a call from Angela's boss in Hong Kong," Tom said. "They're concerned about a cash payment you made for twenty-five thousand to a small company. Angela complained you haven't given her the details."

Damn, Jack thought. She didn't waste any time.

"She's a pain in the butt. It pisses me off she's making such a stink about this. If she's implying I took twenty-five thousand of the bank's money and put it in my pocket, that's bullshit."

"Jack, you know that, and I know that, but you have to admit it sounds unorthodox. It will certainly raise a few eyebrows around here." Tom paused. "And you didn't tell me you paid the judge that much."

Angry and about to respond to Tom's comment, Jack bit his lip. Instead he said, "This isn't New York. Working in Indonesia requires flexibility."

"Okay. I'll hold them at bay. But sounds like you've gotten yourself into a real mess."

Jack sensed Tom backpedaling. If things got tough, he knew Tom would side with the auditors. He tipped his head back for a moment, thankful he had recorded his boss's complicity.

"Let's talk about the $40 million loan," Tom said. "There's a problem."

Jack rose from his chair.

"The credit committee has a new requirement. They want an environmental-impact study done on all project financings, particularly anything related to logging."

"They can't do that," Jack said his voice full of alarm. "They can't change the rules in the middle of the game."

"A die-hard conservationist joined the board. He's causing problems. I'm as pissed as you but we have to deal with it. Get an environmental study, and I'll get the deal approved. That's a promise." Jack gritted his teeth. He knew he couldn't rely on Tom's promises.

"No other bank requires an environmental study. Wibawa and Johnny will just go somewhere else."

"Talk to them. They're resourceful. I'm sure they can do something. Tell them it's just a formality."

Jack hung up. He sensed he was about to be Tom's sacrificial lamb. He needed to preempt the sacrifice, and he had to be quick about it. He opened the desk drawer and took out the recording of Tom implicating himself and condoning the bribe. He addressed a note to the president of the bank in New York, put it and the reel in a manila envelope, and set the envelope on Wati's desk in the outgoing mail.

***

Jack didn't want to meet Johnny and Wibawa at the Barong Bar, the place where nothing good ever happened. And he didn't want to face them together. He picked Johnny as the lesser evil.

But when Haroon pulled up in front of the sleek modern building Johnny owned, Jack flinched. Wibawa's black Mercedes was parked at the curb. *Damn, so much for divide and conquer.*

With his palms sweaty and his blood pressure on the rise, Jack walked into the lobby — and stopped midstride. Ari sat on a couch filing her nails. Her red dress matched the color of her lips, and a gold chain dangled from her neck. "Hello, Jack," she said. "Surprised to see me?"

He grappled for something to say.

"I have a meeting upstairs," he replied.

"That night at your welcoming reception you flirted with me and led me on. If you hadn't been so clumsy and knocked the alarm clock off the table, we would have made love. Instead you humiliated me and made me angry. When I got back to the room, Wibawa woke up. He beat me."

"You told him I tried to rape you. You know that's a lie."

"Perhaps I should talk to your wife. She will wonder how I know about that purple snakelike birthmark on your butt."

Jack took a step toward her. About to explode, he backed off and headed for the elevator.

At the third floor, breathing hard, he tried to get a grip on himself. The secretary ushered him into an elegant office. A full-length portrait of Johnny's father in military regalia presided over the setting. Johnny sat behind a large desk. Wibawa, his face grim, sat on the opposite side. Johnny directed Jack to the empty chair.

"Our project is moving ahead. The equipment for the pulp plant has been ordered," Johnny said.

About to put a damper on that upbeat message, Jack squirmed.

"We're negotiating with a Japanese firm to buy its plywood operation. Without access to logs from Indonesia, they will have to shut down. We expect to get the factory cheap and ship it to Kalimantan."

Another problem, Jack realized. The bank didn't finance used equipment.

"The world price for plywood has increased in anticipation of the export ban. Buyers doubt we will be able to ramp up in time to meet demand. If the higher price holds, the financials we gave you will look conservative."

Jack drummed his fingers together while the two men looked at him.

"You wanted to meet?" Wibawa finally said.

"I spoke to New York. The bank is keen on your project and eager to do business." He glanced from one man to the other. "But there is a new requirement. For loans related to logging, the bank needs an environmental impact study. It's just a formality," he quickly added. "Then you will get the forty million."

Johnny got up, came around the desk, and stood beside Jack's chair. His black eyes cold, he dropped his normal cordiality. "You led us to believe the loan would be approved, and now you're requesting something new. We've been waiting patiently, expecting the money."

"You will get the forty million. We just need an environmental assessment."

"You have let us down," Wibawa said. He leaned forward in his chair and stared across at Jack.

"I'm just as disappointed as you." Jack gestured with his hands for emphasis. "It doesn't have to be much of a report." He cursed New York for putting him in this predicament.

"That's going to be difficult. Orangutans live in the logging area," Johnny said.

Jack grimaced. *Orangutans!*

"The government granted your bank a license with the expectation you would support Indonesian business. What you are asking is unrealistic. Your bank is being uncooperative," Johnny said. He stood beneath the portrait of his famous father, his message clear.

Now even more uncomfortable, Jack shifted in his chair.

Johnny stepped closer. "I heard you paid Hartono money to get yourself out of a jam, but he hasn't been able to deliver. The borrower owes me a favor. You come up with the loan, and I can take care of your problem."

Jack winced. There was a time when Johnny's offer might have gotten his attention. Now he glanced at the two men and drew back.

"Your delays have made it difficult for us to start over with another bank, so we will get you the study you need. It will say the project is environmentally sound."

233

Now a veteran of Indonesian business, Jack wasn't surprised — a fraudulent invoice, and now a fraudulent environmental impact study. When would it end?

Tom set him up, and he succumbed to the corruption of the locals. He even lied to Laura but no more. Disgusted with himself, he got up and headed for the door. Before he walked out, he turned to face the two men. "Fuck it. Find your forty million somewhere else."

Jack strode past the elevator and took the stairs to the ground floor, relieved to see that Ari no longer lurked in the lobby.

"To the Barong Bar," he said to Haroon, waiting outside. He wasn't yet ready to go back to the office. He needed time to think alone. He was in big trouble. No one told the president's son to "fuck it."

***

Jack entered the bar and looked around. He didn't see the usual waitress, so got a beer from the bartender. He walked to a table to sit and ponder.

He thought about Laura. She quit her job to follow him. And against the odds, she managed to carve out a meaningful life for herself, whereas he lost his moral compass.

He felt low, no that was too mild. He felt like the scum in the old Dutch canals. He finished his beer and considered having another, but knew getting drunk wouldn't solve his problems. He tried that once before when Laura went to Borobudur and he was home alone with Maya. He had to get his life in order. He owed it to Laura; it was her life too. He just hoped it wasn't too late to make amends.

A dark-haired woman in a stylish floral-print dress entered. Jack glanced up and watched her take a seat at the bar. He heard her order a Singapore sling. On other occasions her beauty would have fascinated him. This time he knew better. He got up and went to pay the tab.

"Leaving so soon?" the woman asked. She swirled her drink, her smile overt, the invitation obvious.

She was exotic; he was tempted. She was a test of his resolve, and he knew it. He reached into his wallet, pulled out more bills, and handed them to the bartender. "The lady's drink is on me," he said. He walked out.

At the bottom of the steps of the hotel Jack breathed in deeply and exhaled. Determined and resolved, he was beginning to feel better about himself. He glanced around but didn't see Haroon. Instead a black car with two men inside was parked nearby with the engine running. The driver had a sparse mustache and wore dark glasses. He took a puff of a cigarette and flipped the butt out the window. Jack couldn't make out the features of the man in the passenger seat. The driver stared.

About to bolt back up the steps, Jack saw Haroon pull up to the curb. He rushed over and hopped in.

"Where we go, tuan?"

"The office," Jack said, his voice anxious. As they drove away, he turned around. The black sedan followed.

"That car behind us," Jack said. "Do you know those men?"

Haroon glanced in the rearview mirror. "Never see them."

Jack considered heading for the police station but doubted he would get much help there. The U.S. Embassy would be a better bet. Yet when he turned around again, the car was gone. At the bank, Jack glanced up and down the street. Not seeing anything suspicious, he got out and hurried inside.

In the security of his office, he wiped perspiration from his forehead. He suspected the men following him must work for Johnny and Wibawa. They were the logical suspects, though Ari, Tom, and Angela all threatened him. He had to set it right.

He took his personal account checkbook from the desk drawer, made out a check to PT Bank AmerIndo for $25,000, and walked down the hall to find Gunadi.

Stacks of files and brown manila folders lined the walls of the controller's office. Gunadi sat there, punching numbers into a calculator, his back to the door. When Jack cleared his throat, he wheeled around, startled.

Jack handed him the check. "It's for the money you gave me to pay J. H. Legal Advisory."

"I don't understand." Gunadi looked at Jack.

"I handled this badly, Gunadi. I tried to cover things up. The $25,000 went to pay a bribe. You needn't worry. None of this is your fault. There's a chance the million dollars won't be paid back. We need to set up a loan loss provision. It will have a major impact on our earnings, and New York won't be pleased. I'll deal with them." About to leave, Jack extended his hand. "Thank you, Gunadi, for all your help."

Unaccustomed to praise Gunadi smiled modestly.

"I'll be leaving the office in a few minutes, going home," Jack said. "But first, I'm stopping by the Kediri to buy a gift for my wife."

"Special occasion?"

"You might say that."

Before he left, Jack called Angela in Hong Kong. He didn't want her or anyone else to think he took bank money for his own purposes.

"That Rp.25 million cash payment you discovered. The money went to pay a bribe to a judge to get a favorable ruling on the Bandung loan. I've repaid it out of my own funds. And Tom was in on it."

"Really?" she said, her tone doubtful. He couldn't tell which part she didn't believe.

"Yes." He hung up. Jack knew he wasn't off the hook. Though he reimbursed the bank for the squandered money, there was still the fact that he facilitated the bribe of a government official, and that was a crime. But now, prepared to deal with the consequences, he no longer cared.

He called Laura. "Hi, honey. I'm on my way home. Break out a bottle of champagne. We're celebrating."

"Celebrating what?" she asked.

"Life. Our life together."

"What's going on? You don't sound much like celebrating. You sound exhausted."

"It's been a long day. We have a lot to talk about. There's so much I have to tell you. See you soon. I love you."

***

Jack walked across the lobby of the Kediri. He passed the Barong Bar. Never again, he thought.

Through the window of the jewelry store he saw a matronly woman seated behind the counter. A bell jingled when he opened the door. The woman glanced up, peering at him over the reading glasses perched at the tip of her nose.

"I'd like to buy a gift for my wife. Something special," Jack said.

"Tell me a bit about her," the woman said, obviously accustomed to dealing with clueless husbands.

"You may have seen her. She's the only redhead in Jakarta."

The woman nodded. "I did notice her walking through the lobby once. Tall and attractive?"

"That would be her." The description brought Laura's image to mind and Jack smiled.

"I just received a few items from Italy. Superb design and workmanship. I haven't even had time to display them." She went to the back room, retrieved a box, and set it on the counter. She lifted the lid and inside jewelry dazzled — a bracelet, a ring, and several necklaces.

"This one is unique." The woman held a bracelet up to the light. "I've never seen anything like it." Tiny gold wires resembling paper clips interlocked in an intricate pattern. Jack took it and glanced at the price tag.

"It's perfect. My wife will love it. Can you gift wrap it? And I'd like to include a card." Jack inscribed a note to Laura and paid the woman. Gift in hand, he crossed the lobby, his strides long, his chin high. He could hardly wait to see the look of surprise on Laura's face when she opened the box. Outside, light on his feet, he bounded down the steps — and froze at the bottom. The two men in the black sedan waited. Haroon pulled up in front and Jack jumped into his car. They drove off, and the men followed them out the gate.

Petrified, Jack gripped the gift in his lap.

"I try to lose car behind us," Haroon said. "Those men no good." He floored the accelerator and roared past the car ahead. He zipped in and out of traffic, skirting around several more vehicles. At the intersection, the light turned red. Haroon glanced in the rearview mirror and sped on through. Jack looked off to the side and saw a truck barreling toward them. "Haroon!" he yelled. Too late. The truck hit with the resounding crunch of metal striking metal and the shatter of glass.

Chapter 35

Laura strolled into the kitchen humming the musical score from *Out of Africa.* She rented the videocassette and watched the movie the night before while Jack worked late. She could relate to the main character, Karen Blixen, who in the film and in real life established a school for poor children in Kenya. Like Laura, Karen couldn't have children, her infertility the result of syphilis contracted from her husband, infected by a native woman. In the film, Karen came across as forgiving. Laura wondered if she would react the same if Jack did that to her.

"Nissam, let's have lime chicken for dinner. It's the tuan's favorite," she said, her mind back from Africa. "We haven't had it for a while.'

"Nyonya, you look worried."

Though she was worried, Laura managed a weak smile. Jack sounded odd on the phone, and he never came home early. He said something about a celebration. She wondered if New York had decided to call him back sooner than expected. She hoped not. Though reluctant to come here, she now found the country comfortable and familiar. If Harapan completed the dress order on time the co-op had a good chance of becoming a success.

She glanced at her watch. Where is he? In the garden, Laura sought distraction. She inhaled the now familiar sweet fragrance of white jasmine. She watched bees gather pollen from the red blossoms of the flamboyan tree. After a while she wandered back inside, sat on the sofa, and picked up a book.

At her feet Diablo growled, then he sprang up and rushed the door. He barked, and a knock followed. Laura stiffened; no one ever knocked. How would they have gotten in? Suparno wouldn't have opened the gate — except in an emergency.

Nissam came out from the kitchen and shoved Diablo aside. He opened the door a crack and spoke with whomever stood outside. When he turned around, his face had lost its color.

"Polisi," he said.

Two uniformed men of the same height stood in the doorway with their eyes downcast. They resembled bookends.

"Mrs. Harrison?" one asked, looking up.

Laura nodded and ran over.

"Your husband in automobile accident."

"Where is he?" Frantic, she attempted to peer around them.

"We sorry. He dead."

She grasped the doorframe for support, but her knees buckled and she slid to the floor. "No, no!" she cried. "It's not my husband. He doesn't drive."

Nissam helped her to her feet. "Where's Haroon? I want to talk to Haroon." Her hand at her throat, she struggled to speak.

The policemen shuffled from side to side. The older one spoke. "Driver dead too. The car run red light and crash with truck. They not suffer."

"He's not dead!" Laura sobbed. "I want to see him. Where is he?"

"He at the morgue."

***

Laura followed the policemen into a low-level austere building. An unsmiling older woman sat behind a reception desk in a room of empty metal folding chairs. Bare walls added to the gloom. A man attired in a blue shirt, black tie, and knee-length white coat came out. He introduced himself as Burundi, the coroner.

In a daze, Laura followed him through large double doors into a cold, windowless room. She hunched her shoulders and folded her arms across her chest. The air reeked of chemicals. Rows of stainless-steel cabinets with large handles lined one wall. Opposite, white sheets over gurneys contoured corpses underneath. Pairs of feet protruded, a tag attached to a toe.

Laura walked beside the coroner to the gurney at the end, the gurney set apart. Her hand over her heart, she held her breath. Burundi glanced at her, his eyebrows raised in question. She nodded. He lifted the edge of the sheet and pulled the cloth back partway. Laura gasped. She looked at a face, bruised and swollen, the mouth crusted with blood. She collapsed across Jack's battered body.

Laura sobbed. After a while, she raised her head and wiped the dried blood from his cracked lips with a tissue. She ran her hand along his shoulders and moved her fingers over the features of a face no longer handsome. From behind her came the coroner's voice. "He hit his head on the windshield."

On the way out Burundi handed Laura a brown paper bag with Jack's personal effects.

***

Back home Laura climbed the stairs, went into the bedroom and closed the door behind her. Out on the balcony, she glanced up at a sunset too beautiful for the grief she felt. She missed Jack and sought gloom. Her head down, she walked back inside and moved across the room. She stopped to pick up a threadbare sock on the floor. Jack dressed impeccably — except for the worn socks. Opening the closet, she ran her fingers along the fabric of the business suits hanging inside. She picked a rumpled T-shirt off the bed, the one Jack had worn the night before. It was heavy with his scent; she pressed the fabric to her face. A tear ran down her cheek. He couldn't be dead. The door would open and he would walk in. They would make love like before. She lay back and fell asleep clutching his shirt.

Much later Laura opened her eyes to a room of shadows. Disoriented, she tried to remember where she was. Alongside her on the bed, she heard breathing. Afraid to move, she lay still. Then something sprung up and licked her face. Diablo. She wrapped her arms around his neck. He had never ventured upstairs before. The dog whimpered and pawed the pillow, and the pair lay together in the dark.

Eventually Laura got up and went to the bathroom, where she splashed cold water on her face. Her stomach announced her hunger. She ventured downstairs, Diablo close at her heels. In the living room, lights blazed. Nissam slept on a mat in the corner. She called out, and he jumped up.

"Nyonya, you okay? You asleep long time." His bright face and expression of concern made Laura feel better. "Sorry about tuan," he said.

"I'm sorry too, Nissam. But he'll be back." She still hadn't gotten used to him not being there. His presence was everywhere, especially in her mind.

Nissam gave her a questioning look, but didn't comment on her odd remark. "You need to eat. I made you dinner."

In the dining room the long table was set for one. Though pictures adorned the walls, the space had the same feel as on that first night — empty and impersonal. Nissam brought out food and dished some onto her plate. She picked at the rice. Uncomfortable in the silence, Laura got up and turned on the CD player, something she rarely did. It was Jack who listened to music. With a disc already in the machine, she pushed play. The familiar lyrics of "I Will Always Love You," the bittersweet Dolly Parton song filled the room.

Laura remembered Jack had played that song several times over the past weeks. She wondered if he'd had a premonition he was about to die and intended the heartfelt lyrics as a message. But she knew better. Jack didn't believe in premonitions; the song had to be a coincidence.

Laura hadn't spoken to her family. She needed to let them know. Now it was morning on the East Coast in the States, so she phoned her father.

"I'll fly right out," he said.

"Thanks, Dad. You don't need to do that. I'll be okay." But having said that, she burst into tears, dropped the phone, and curled into a whimpering ball on the floor.

Her mother advised her to take pills to help her sleep. Denise, her best friend, cried. Laura attempted to locate her brother, but he was salmon fishing in Alaska and couldn't be reached. Jack's sister in North Carolina was home baking a pineapple upside-down cake. She said she could help with arrangements at Magnolia Cemetery.

Laura wasn't sure Jack wanted to be buried there. He had never said what he wanted. He expected to live forever.

She wandered through the quiet of the house. She knew if she sat down she would think about Jack and cry. She missed Doreen and thought of calling her. But Doreen, a font of practical wisdom, had her own problems — a philandering husband and a son in the penitentiary.

***

An arrangement of white orchids arrived from Pak Wulundari, the director of Jack's bank, and his wife. And several women from the American Women's Auxiliary stopped by to drop off casseroles.

Sarinah came over, and together the women sat in the living room. Laura turned the pages of her wedding album, showing Sarinah pictures of her and Jack on their special day.

"What wonderful memories. You and Jack look so happy and in love." Sarinah pointed to a photograph of the couple, their heads slightly tilted forward and facing each other, their eyes downcast, their profiles silhouetted in the glow of candlelight.

Laura studied the picture, and tears welled. She shut the book. "Jack was murdered. He wasn't killed in an automobile accident. The coroner lied."

Sarinah stiffened.

"Cars can't go fast in Jakarta; there's too much traffic," Laura said, her voice rushed, a fist clenched. "Plenty of fender benders, but people don't get killed. And Jack always wore his seat belt. He couldn't have hit his head on the windshield. His wounds were severe. He was beaten."

Sarinah put her arm around her friend. "Laura, you're under a lot of stress. I know this is tough. But why would anyone want to kill Jack? Doesn't make sense."

"Things weren't going well at the bank. Maybe something happened. I want to see the car."

Sarinah looked puzzled. "How is that going to help?"

"Just a hunch. Who knows, maybe there was no car crash at all. I'm going to the police station. Maybe his car's still there."

"I'll go with you."

"Thanks, but I had better go alone. I don't know what I'll find. And you're Indonesian. I don't want you to get in trouble."

***

Mille drove Laura across the city to the old section of Jakarta. He stopped in front of an imposing colonial building fronting a cobblestone square.

"I wait by the car," Mille said. His dark eyes rolled across the police headquarters' intimidating façade. A large wooden entry door stood ajar. Laura stepped into a rotunda, its aged paint peeling from the walls. A policeman sat behind a table in the center of the cavernous room. He wore a khaki, short-sleeved shirt with epaulettes and a hat with a prominent silver medallion above the visor. A brass lamp with a green glass shade cast a glow over his folded hands. Laura approached, and he glanced up.

Tempted to blurt out her husband had been murdered, she paused, reminding herself she couldn't say that. She had no proof, only a hunch. She gave the policeman Jack's full name and the date of the accident. She requested a copy of the police report for insurance purposes. The police officer made a note in his ledger and asked her to wait. He pointed to chairs lining the wall, and she took a seat. She expected to be there awhile and was surprised when he returned in a few minutes and motioned her over.

"Report not finished," he said. "Come back tomorrow." She suspected him of stalling. "I'd like to see my husband's car," she said.

"It not here." He glanced over her shoulder at the lengthening line behind her.

"Where do they take cars after an accident?" He penned an address on a piece of paper and handed it to her.

Outside she gave the note to Mille. "You want to go there?" He shook his head. "It is far."

"I want to find the tuan's car." She felt robotic, like someone moving through a checklist.

Mille was right. The place was far, the traffic heavy. Laura considered turning back but hoped the dump would be just ahead. After an hour Mille turned onto a side road. A foul odor permeated the air.

"*Berbau*, stinky," he said. He pinched his nose.

Mille pulled up to the gate that blocked the road. Several men in uniform stood conversing. Behind them, a mountain of trash loomed. Scores of pickers with open-weave baskets strapped to their backs sifted through the refuse of other people's lives. The women wore large cone-shaped bamboo hats to protect them from the scorching sun. Some had on gloves; most did not. A yellow earth-moving machine lurched back and forth, its metal scoop lifting garbage high into the air. Pieces dangled and dropped to the ground, and scavengers rushed in, hoping to retrieve discards of some value.

"Mille, I don't think this is the right place."

"It address on paper." He showed her what the policeman wrote.

Frustrated, she hoped the man hadn't purposely sent her off with the wrong directions in an effort to dissuade her. Mille got out and spoke to the men at the gate. Laura's hopes rose when one of them pointed further down the road.

They drove another half mile. Directly ahead Laura saw many wrecked vehicles scattered about. How would she ever be able to find Jack's car in the maze? Disheartened, she and Mille got out and began the search. She thought she might have been wrong about no deadly collisions in Jakarta; most of the cars were badly smashed, and all were stripped. Inquiring faces peered from empty hulks and women wandered past carrying crying babies. Others cooked on open fires as if at a campground. The dump had been turned into a village where many lived. Though Laura had been in Indonesia for nearly a year, she still was not accustomed to poverty on this scale. She doubted she ever would be.

"I don't think we find tuan's car here," Mille said.

"Let's not give up." Laura hoped they might stumble onto the spot where cars had been recently dumped — those not rusted or lived in.

245

"Nyonya, over here," Mille shouted. He indicated a dark-blue sedan; its chrome gleamed like a beacon in the sun. Laura balanced on her toes, trying to get a better look. The wreck resembled Jack's car, but she couldn't be sure. She moved closer and she spotted green worry beads dangling from the rearview mirror. The beads belonged to Haroon.

The left rear side of the car was smashed, but the driver's seat and the right rear passenger side where Jack always sat remained intact. There had been an accident, but the impact could not have thrown Jack through the windshield. She was right. He wasn't killed in the crash.

Someone murdered him.

Chapter 36

Laura returned to the morgue. The bored receptionist sat at the desk and the rows of chairs still empty. "Please tell the coroner Mrs. Harrison is back."

The woman picked up the phone and spoke in hushed tones. With a hand over the receiver, she advised Laura that Burundi was in meeting. "Tomorrow's better."

Though not normally confrontational, Laura seethed. There was a cover up and people were lying to her.

"Tell him I'll wait. Tell him it's urgent."

After a few minutes the coroner came out. "Mrs. Harrison, I am surprised you are back. Did you forget something?"

"Can we can talk in private?"

He led her down the hall to an unoccupied office, which he motioned her into.

"I found my husband's car at the dump," she said. "He wasn't killed in the automobile accident. You didn't tell me the truth." Her voice cracked; she struggled to keep her composure. From her purse, she took rupiah notes, folded them, and extended her hand.

"Please keep your money, Mrs. Harrison."

She felt foolish and stuffed the rupiah in her pocket.

"I was trying to protect you from the truth. But as you have persisted, I will tell you what happened. You are correct; your husband was not killed in the crash. I do not know the whole story. I only know what forensics tells me, or what I have heard or surmised. Two men in a black car followed him. His driver tried to elude them. He ran a red light and collided with a truck. The men following ran over, pulled your husband and driver from the wreck, and beat them. They tied your husband's hands behind his back and dislocated his shoulder in the process. He cried out, and they stuffed a rag in his mouth. They tossed him in the trunk and instructed the driver to go back to his village and keep his mouth shut."

He continued, saying he doubted if the men meant to kill her husband. They had been hired to rough him up, scare him. "Your husband choked on the rag and suffocated on his vomit."

The prior day the coroner sounded sympathetic. Now, perhaps irritated by Laura's return and persistence, he no longer seemed inclined to temper what he had to say. Laura wasn't sure she could take any more. But the coroner kept on. He said the men, probably frightened by what they did, dumped the body on the steps of the morgue. Laura reached to steady herself on the edge of a desk.

"Who hired those men?"

"That I do not know."

***

Laura considered going to the police but knew that would be a waste of time. She wouldn't be taken seriously. She would be portrayed as a distraught, fragile expat woman who lost her husband in an automobile accident and couldn't cope. And should the police question the coroner, he would deny all that he told her. She decided to go to the U.S. Embassy.

Concrete barricades blocked easy access to an imposing white building set behind a high, black, iron fence. At the entry visitors were searched, their passports scrutinized. Laura was ushered into a small office where books on U.S. history filled the shelves. A photograph of President Reagan hung on the wall.

A man with a shiny baldhead and fringe of white hair got up from his chair and came around the desk to greet her. He wore a bow tie, rimless round glasses, and suspenders holding up wrinkled trousers

"Joe Freeman, deputy consul," he said. He led Laura to a matching pair of navy-blue upholstered chairs.

Laura sat down. "My husband was murdered," she said, her voice forceful. After seeing the car and realizing that something terrible had indeed happened to Jack, she was energized and determined to learn the truth.

Joe leaned forward.

"Harrison. The name's familiar. Isn't your husband president of Bank AmerIndo?"

"Was."

Laura told him about her visit to the morgue and the car at the dump. Joe took notes.

"You are very brave, Mrs. Harrison. Few could have endured so much distress alone." His kind voice and sympathetic manner gave Laura hope. "Any idea as to why someone would want to kill your husband?"

"The coroner said they meant to scare him."

"Why?" Joe cocked his head, an eyebrow lifted.

Laura hesitated. She wondered if she ought to mention Judge Hartono. She never heard what happened to his request for a bribe. Maybe that had something to do with it.

"When we first came to Jakarta, my husband was approached by a judge who asked for money under the table to settle a case. As far as I know he never gave him anything. And I doubt if it's even relevant. I'm sure other businessmen have been involved in bribery without being murdered. It seems to be part of the culture." She glanced away. She had made it sound like she condoned bribery when she didn't.

"The judge's name?" the deputy consul asked, his pen poised.

"Hartono."

"Mrs. Harrison, I need to ask you some questions you may find uncomfortable. I hope you will bear with me."

Laura, unsure as to what he had in mind, flinched.

"Was your husband involved with other women?"

She had always wondered about Maya. And then there was Ari. Jack never seemed the same after the trip to Kalimantan. She shook her head.

Joe's gaze penetrated, and Laura looked away.

"Just a few more questions," he said. "Then we will be finished."

Laura shifted in her chair. Her spirits flagging now, she felt ready to leave.

249

"What about your husband's dealings at the bank, and his Indonesian business associates?"

"He was working on a big loan for a logging project. Wibawa and Johnny were involved."

Joe cleared his throat. "Johnny, the president's son?"

Laura nodded.

Joe took off his glasses and set them aside. "Did he say anything about problems with these men?"

"He didn't tell me much about his work. He was under a lot of stress." At the mention of Wibawa and Johnny, the deputy counsel stopped taking notes.

"Mrs. Harrison, I am so sorry for your loss," he said, standing. "Here's my card. I know this must be very difficult for you. If you should think of anything after you leave, please call me."

Laura thanked him for his time. She made her way back out through the labyrinth of security. The deputy consul would fill out the required forms and create mounds of paperwork in the process. Laura doubted anything would happen. She suspected that along the way, Jack's file would get misplaced. The U.S. government wasn't about to confront powerful interests and put a strategic global relationship at risk because an American banker was murdered.

Outside Mille waited. "Let's go home," she said.

But she knew she couldn't rest yet. Jack's body lay in the morgue, and she needed to make arrangements. She knew he had a will, though she couldn't bring herself to look at it. What was the point? He was gone.

Tom's secretary in New York had left messages. Laura didn't want to talk to Tom, though she knew she would have to at some stage.

Laura was in Indonesia on a spousal visa, and she no longer had a spouse. Soon she would have to leave. Trying to cope while worrying about the future, she called Grace, her former boss in New York. Disturbed to hear what had happened, Grace gave condolences. Though Laura didn't inquire about her old job, Grace said the position had been filled. She suggested Laura stop in when she got back and she would see what she could do. Laura regretted making the call.

***

The next morning when Laura came downstairs, she spotted the brown paper bag from the morgue still by the front door. She had lacked the courage to look inside and so left it there. Though still unwilling, she brought the bag to the sofa and opened it. Inside, scuffed shoes rested atop a folded tan suit. She set them on the floor. On pulling out Jack's bloodied shirt and crumpled tie, she gasped, dropped the items, and rushed outside.

She walked around aimlessly, wiping tears from her eyes. She passed the frangipani and remembered Hugh's comment about it being the flower of graveyards; she stiffened and moved away.

After a while, Nissan came out of the house with a cup of tea. She sat in the shade and sipped it.

More composed, Laura went back inside and returned to the bag on the sofa. She took out Jack's wallet, empty except for his New York driver's license, a few of his business cards, and a snapshot taken of them on their honeymoon. She put the picture in her pocket and set the other items aside.

She looked for his Rolex watch and was surprised to find it still there. A folded piece of paper lay on the bottom. She opened it — a receipt for a gold bracelet purchased from Kediri Jewelers. It was dated the day he was killed. Why would he be buying jewelry? It wasn't her birthday or their anniversary. She grabbed her purse and went outside to find Mille.

"To the Kediri," she said.

***

Laura crossed the lobby, passing the Barong Bar. Her pace quickened at the sight of a jewelry store at the end of the colonnade. Inside, an Asian woman sat behind the display case. Reading glasses dangled from the chain around her neck.

251

Laura greeted her and reached in her purse for the receipt. She laid it on the counter. "I believe my husband was in here a few days ago."

"You must be Mrs. Harrison. I recognize the red hair. Your husband told me about you." Her smile initially warm, faded. "I am so sorry. I read about the accident in the newspaper. A terrible thing; he seemed like such a nice man."

"Did he say why he was buying a bracelet?" Laura asked, though afraid to hear what the woman might say. Maybe the gift wasn't for her.

The saleswoman went over and locked the door. She flipped the sign in the window to *CLOSED*.

"I owe you an apology," she said. "I am so absentminded. Your husband wrote you a note to go with the gift, but when I wrapped the box I forgot to put it inside. I noticed my mistake after he left. I called his office and left a message. Then I saw the article in the newspaper."

The saleswoman opened the drawer, took out a white card and handed it to Laura. *I am sorry for hurting you and for my mistakes. I hope you will forgive me. I love you. Jack.*

Laura lowered her head. The saleswoman put her arm around Laura's shoulders. "Are you okay? Would you like a glass of water?"

"Thanks, I'll be fine." She took a tissue from her purse.

"A strange thing happened yesterday," the woman continued. "I went to the Hotel Indonesia to drop off a package and saw one of my customers in the lobby. The woman is not Indonesian Chinese like me. She's from Hong Kong. There is a difference, if you know what I mean." She rolled her eyes and looked at Laura as if waiting for a sign of confirmation. But Laura had her own thoughts.

Ari!

"She had on the bracelet your husband bought for you. I am not mistaken. It is so distinctive, one of a kind."

Laura's heartbeat quickened.

"Odd," the woman said. "I cannot figure out how she got it."

Laura slung her purse over her shoulder. "It is odd, isn't it? Thank you for being so kind." She made her way to the lobby and took refuge in a large chair in the corner. Why would Ari hire thugs to beat up Jack?

Laura remembered when they met at the welcoming reception. She instantly disliked Ari. She thought her an irritant, a harmless flirt. Now it appeared she might have been complicit in Jack's death. Laura suspected something happened in Kalimantan. Underneath the expensive jewelry and the flash, she sensed an insecure woman — a woman who could tolerate anything except humiliation. Still, she doubted Ari would harm Jack, though she didn't put it past Ari's husband Wibawa — or Johnny.

Back at the house Laura called Sarinah and asked if she could come over.

When Sarinah arrived, the women sat in the garden. Laura told Sarinah about Ari, the bracelet, the note, and the meeting at the embassy. "I can't let them get away with what they did," she said.

Sarinah put her hand on her friend's arm. "Don't," she said. "You start prying and you will end up like Jack. Forget Wibawa and Johnny and Ari. Their day will come. You aren't the one to make it happen."

Laura continued with her brave front. "The police are too afraid to take on the son of the president or Wibawa. And even if they ended up in court, a judge would be there with his hand out. Someone has to do something."

I accused Jack of being naïve. Am I the same?

"This is not the time for revenge," Sarinah said.

Chapter 37

Sarinah left, and Laura called Tom. Though reluctant to speak to him, she couldn't put it off any longer.

Mildred the secretary answered. When she found out it was Laura, she said, "I wept when I heard about Jack. Such a nice man. And so smart."

Laura thanked her and asked to speak to Tom.

"Oh, I guess you haven't heard," Mildred said. "Tom's no longer with the bank."

"Gone?"

"It happened right after your husband's tragedy. The president summoned him to his office. Tom came back upset. He packed all his things and left. Didn't even say goodbye. I slaved for that man for ten years and not a word of thanks. How rude. Your husband wasn't like that. He was considerate. There's a new head of international, Stan Rosen. I know he wants to talk to you. I hope you get back that designer job you had. Call me. We'll have coffee and a Danish. Probably been a long time since you had a decent Danish. My treat. After all you've been through, that's the least I can do. You take care, dear." She patched the call through.

"Stan speaking," came a heavy New York accent. "Sorry for your loss, Laura. Be assured the bank will do whatever it can to assist with your return to New York. I've asked one of the Hong Kong bank wives fly to Jakarta to help you. You shouldn't have to go through this alone."

"Thanks, but I can manage," Laura said though she wondered about that.

"I have good news, if that's even possible. It's about Jack's insurance. You'll be getting a check for two million dollars."

"Two million?"

"Double indemnity," Stan said.

***

On the terrace, Diablo lay at Laura's feet. The dog never ventured far from her.

"I will miss you when you go back to the States," Sarinah said.

"I haven't decided what I'm going to do." The windfall complicated Laura's life. Now she could do anything she wanted. She hadn't anticipated that. In a similar situation, most would have been elated by a sense of freedom. Laura felt some of that. But mostly she felt alone.

"I thought you wanted to return to New York," Sarinah said.

"I'm not sure. I might stay here."

Sarinah eyes widened. "You don't have a visa."

"With a handful of rupiah, anything's possible. I know it sounds crazy. Why would a woman want to stay in a place where her husband was killed? I'm not sure I have a good answer. My father thinks I'm suffering trauma and not thinking rationally. He has threatened to come and take me back to Connecticut."

"I can see why."

"I don't have anything to go back to." She sounded wistful. "Here I found compassion, a side of myself I never knew. I love helping the kampung children. The batik business shows promise, and village women will have decent jobs. There's already a large order for more dresses. I'm passionate about the rainforest. No one else seems to care." And Laura knew that if she left, Jack's murderers would go unpunished. She didn't mention that to Sarinah, however.

Laura sought strength in her marriage. She came to Indonesia hoping to bring Jack and her closer together. Yet their relationship deteriorated, and then he was gone. And though she missed him, she was beginning to gain strength in her solitude

"I would love it if you stayed," Sarinah said. "But I should caution you. Your goals might be too ambitious for Indonesia."

Laura got up went to the window and looked out at the garden. Jack too expressed doubts and cautioned her. She chose to ignore him. And she would ignore Sarinah, too.

***

Laura was finishing breakfast when Nissam entered.

"Sorry to bother you, nyonya. Kartini and Maya outside. They want see you."

Puzzled, Laura pushed the plate of papaya aside. She couldn't imagine they would want to express condolences. They left almost a year ago without an explanation.

Maya stood at the gate, a basket balanced on her hip. Kartini, beside her, brushed a wisp of gray hair from her forehead. Suparno, broom in hand, vanished around the corner of the house when Laura came out. They must have come to visit him she assumed, recalling that he was Maya's father.

"Selamat pagi, nyonya," Kartini said. "We sorry about the tuan."

"Terima kasih," Laura replied. "You came all the way from Sukabumi?"

"On the bus. Three hours, many stops."

"How nice of you to visit. I'm sure Suparno's happy to see you. It's been quite a while." About to ask Kartini why they left, she decided otherwise.

Laura looked at Maya. She didn't detect the insolence that bothered her before. The girl appeared serene, her face a lovely glow.

Yet when Maya exchanged glances with her aunt, she seemed nervous. Her eyes questioned, and Kartini nodded. Maya drew back the cloth that covered the basket. The baby inside opened its eyes and squinted in the bright sunlight. Its skin was fair, the hair sandy. Laura felt faint. Jack had betrayed her from the grave.

"A boy," Maya said proudly. "Maybe you want hold him." She held the basket out to Laura.

Laura stepped back. Her worst fears were confirmed. Jack had cheated on her.

"Take him back to Sukabumi," she said, angry and defiant.

"Maya need help," Kartini said. "She need rupiah take care of baby. Tuan not know. Now he dead."

"He's not my baby," Laura said. Her voice trembled

"Your husband good man, nyonya. He not mean hurt you," Kartini said. "He tell Maya he do something wrong. He say he pay

256

money to bad people. He feel sorry. He get drunk. He need comforting. If you been here…" Her soft voice trailed off.

Though Kartini was careful not to offend, her message and the implication were clear.

"Maya not able to sleep. She afraid *kuntilanak* the ghost come and steal baby. He know Maya not have money for baby food."

"Not my problem. Take him back to Sukabumi."

Laura could take no more of Indonesian superstition. She fled into the house. She grabbed the wedding photograph of her and Jack from the table. In the kitchen she tossed the picture into the trash. Upstairs, empty cardboard boxes for Jack's belongings sat in the corner. She grabbed his things out of the closet and threw them in. More framed photographs of her and Jack in happier times sat on the bedside table. She hurled them in too.

Chapter 38

Laura had Jack's body cremated. She put the urn in the linen closet, a place where she wouldn't be reminded of his betrayal.

Her family expected her to return to the States. They argued it was safer there. But safety was no guarantee anywhere. And she no longer considered the place where she grew up to be her home. She couldn't imagine her new Buddhist beliefs in Episcopalian New England. With Jack's insurance proceeds, she no longer had to work. Though her family had money, her father had always encouraged her to be independent, to make it on her own. Now she could live anywhere. She could do whatever she wanted. She had always envisioned that one day she would have her own fashion business. That didn't necessarily mean it had to be in New York. She could help Peni launch Harapan. She hadn't wanted to come to Indonesia; now she wanted to stay — at least for a while.

She didn't expect problems getting a resident visa. She had the money. And Sarinah had recommended an influential lawyer. Laura would assume her maiden name and move to Purwakarta. She hoped Mille and Suparno would join her there, though she doubted Nissam would want to leave the city.

When Laura entered the kitchen, Nissam was busy preparing the next meal.

"I'm moving to Purwakarta," Laura said.

Nissam stopped stirring the rice. "Why you want to live in Purwakarta? Even people in Purwakarta not want to live in Purwakarta."

"I think it's beautiful."

He looked unconvinced.

"I plan to rent a cottage and help your mother with the business."

"I not going back," Nissam said, his tone defiant.

"I know. I will help you find another job with an expat family. They will be lucky to have you."

***

The following day Laura was busying herself putting books in a box when Nissam came in with a small package. "Boy on motor bike drop this off."

Puzzled, she took it. No return address: only her name and address were written in a feminine scroll. She opened it and gasped. A gold bracelet! She took out the card and quickly read it.

I am sorry for what happened to your husband. Wibawa went too far. I am leaving him. I am going back to Hong Kong. Ari.

Laura fastened the gold bracelet around her wrist. She silently thanked Ari for sending it to her. She admired the unique design and the beauty. Jack bought it for her the day he died. She would treasure it forever. She dropped her head in her hands, and wept.

Chapter 39

Laura went to the kampung for her final tutoring session before moving away, though it wouldn't be the last time she visited. She intended to stop by whenever she came to Jakarta. The kampung and Dewi were now part of her life. She said her goodbyes and left early to go finish packing.

As she walked back she thought about Jack's child. And about Eko and Wayan and all the other boys she tutored. Jack's child would grow up to be like one of them. They seemed happy, though their futures were uncertain.

As she approached the house, she saw a man wearing a white shirt and dark trousers loitering at the gate.

"Mrs. Harrison?" he asked.

Laura nodded, her eyes narrowed. His official manner reminded her of the coroner.

"Can I see your resident visa?" he asked.

Laura caught her breath. "Who are you?"

"My name Rama from Immigration." He pulled a card with a photo from his pocket and waved it in the air.

Laura's heart beat rapidly. "My visa's inside," she said, her voice hesitant.

"Visa no good. Your husband dead. You have to come with me."

"Leave me alone," she said in a panic. Laura pushed open the gate and dashed toward the front door. Inside she went to the window and watched the man walk to a black sedan parked at the other side of the road. Two men wearing dark glasses, one smoking a cigarette, waited. The man climbed in and the car slowly crept away.

Laura sat on the sofa to catch her breath. They had to be the same thugs who had killed Jack. The coroner mentioned two men in a black sedan. Now they were after her. Sarinah warned her about seeking revenge, but she had no time to plan that. Perhaps they suspected Jack confided in her, that he told her things they didn't want divulged. She twisted her hands in her lap. He kept his Indonesian life a secret from her.

Laura knew she couldn't stay in the house any longer. They would be back and the next time she might not be so lucky. She had yet to begin the process of getting her own visa and was vulnerable. She wondered if perhaps the man really was from Immigration. Perhaps he planned to take her to the airport and have her deported. Or maybe the men had something more ominous in mind — like binding her hands and feet, taping her mouth and shoving her into the trunk as they had done to Jack. She couldn't leave her fate to chance. She had to leave, and she had to leave fast.

She stood in front of a mirror and grimaced. As a redhead, she wouldn't be able to move about the country undetected. She found her purse, took out a fistful of rupiah and went to find Mille. "I need you to go to Blok M and buy a bottle of black hair dye and a pair of rubber gloves," she said handing him the money. As a brunette, she hoped to blend in.

"My *nenek* use for gray," Mille said pointing to his head. "You do not need. You young."

"I'll explain later." Laura went back in to pack an overnight bag.

***

Shortly Mille returned with a small bottle and yellow plastic gloves. Laura ignored his questioning face, thanked him and went upstairs.

She stood at the washbasin in the bathroom with a towel draped over her shoulders and began to cut her hair. She winced as she watched her long locks fall to the floor. She hadn't had short hair since high school. Once finished, with a comb she parted her hair into quadrants. Noting the time, she began to apply dark liquid to the roots, and then all over. The instructions on the label had been in Bahasa. She hoped she had translated correctly. She dared not make a mistake. After the prescribed number of minutes, she rinsed out the dye, shampooed and dried her hair. On glancing in the mirror, her jaw dropped. Dark short hair accentuated her pale skin and emboldened the freckles across her cheeks and the bridge of her nose. The dye did not conceal her Irish heritage. She considered getting a headscarf and trying to pass herself off as Muslim but thought that might get her into even more trouble. Disappointed with her new look, she grabbed her overnight bag from the bed and rushed downstairs.

Mille's eyes widened. "You look Indonesian," he said. She suspected him of being facetious, but realized that was not an Indonesian trait. She climbed into the car and fluffed her hair. Perhaps she looked more local than she thought.

"Where we go?" he asked.

"Purwakarta," Laura said, her voice now shaky. "We have to be careful. There may be two men in a black car outside. I think they're after me."

"Nyonya do something bad?"

"I think they're the men who killed the tuan."

"No worry nyonya. They not get you," Mille said, his voice shaky too.

Laura got down and lay rigid on the car floor. With her hands folded across her chest, she resembled a corpse in a coffin. And as the car moved slowly down the driveway and out through the gate, Laura held her breath. Through the window she watched a cloudless blue sky and the tops of trees move past. Though concerned as to what was happening, she dared not speak or sit up.

"I not see them," Mille said.

Though reassured, Laura couldn't relax. The two men had followed Jack's car, and caused Haroon to have an accident in a chase as he tried to elude them. Though she changed the color of her hair, her red Kijang would be a beacon.

As Mille drove over the rutted roads, Laura bounced along uncomfortably. She considered asking him to take her to the airport where she could flee the country and be safe. But she couldn't desert the women of Harapan. The business had begun to show promise. She couldn't walk away from her commitment to saving the rainforest. Like Peni twenty years earlier, she would seek refuge in West Java, far from the corruption of the capital, and from there she would safely plot her revenge.

***

In Purwakarta, Laura located a bungalow close to where Peni lived. The house had Western plumbing, a garden and view of the lake. As her life passed like a blur she eventually began to settle in and feel optimistic. Lured by the promise of steady jobs, Mille and Suparno joined her. They brought Diablo and all her birds with them. Sarinah closed up the big house and had the rest of Laura's things transported over the mountain. Nissam stayed behind and Sarinah found him a job with an Australian family.

The dress order for New York shipped on time and Harapan received more orders. Peni proved to be a good leader. She took charge. She rented warehouse space, purchased more sewing machines, and hired seamstresses. Bank Rakyat granted Harapan a loan, and Laura opened an account for The Harapan Rainforest Trust. She made an initial deposit from Jack's insurance proceeds. Sarinah too invested in the business and took an active role in marketing.

Laura hoped the women of Harapan might take an interest in conservation. But when she mentioned the plight of the orangutan, their eyes glazed. Laura suspected that conservation might only be a concern of those with means. The poor had their own survival to contend with. Yet to succeed, conservation needed everyone's participation. Laura's hopes lay with the young. She started a literacy program in Purwakarta. The books in Bahasa and English had vivid illustrations of Indonesia's natural world, the flora and fauna found nowhere else.

"Only in Indonesia," she would say as she turned the pages.

***

Laura sat in her small garden in the shade of the banyan tree. She took the plastic card from her pocket and stared at the photo of a woman with short dark hair named Laura O'Malley. Sarinah's influential lawyer friend helped her get the visa. Now with the sun warming her face, Laura closed her eyes and meditated. Within, darkness prevailed, and then the steady peaceful rhythm of her breath. The minutes passed, and she opened her eyes. She sat still, stretched, and glanced at the small Buddha statue in its new home on a pedestal. The Buddha reminded her of Borobudur and the Wall of Good and Evil. *Good comes to those who do good.* She recalled Kartini's words. *He pay money to bad people.* Jack paid the bribe — he had held so much back from her. *Your husband good man. He not mean hurt you.* And then there was the tenderness of Jack's note. *I am sorry for hurting you…I hope you will forgive me.* He asked for her forgiveness, not realizing he left behind a child that would cause her more pain than he could have imagined. She got up and went to find Mille.

"I want to go to Sukabumi," she said.

"Why you want to go there?" he asked with a puzzled look.

"I want to find Kartini and Maya. Suparno can go with us. He must know where they live."

"No need. Tomorrow they come to visit him here."

"With the baby?"

Mille shrugged.

The next day Laura waited on the front steps. She toyed with the collar of her blouse, ashamed of the way she had treated the women when they came to her for help and unsure what to expect. She spotted Kartini and Maya with the baby in her arms. She rushed out to greet them. "Nyonya, you look Indonesian," Kartini said repeating the now familiar refrain.

"Thank you for the compliment." Laura directed her attention to Maya.

 "I'm sorry. I will help you."

"I sorry too," Maya said. She held the baby out for Laura to hold. Laura took him and cradled him to her breast. The infant grasped her finger with his tiny hand. Laura caressed his cheek, and as she held him, her heart beat with the love of a mother. She put her face close to his small head. It smelled all things special and good — baking bread, clothes drying in the sun, soft soap, and rich fresh-turned earth. She drew back and noticed the infant's uncanny resemblance to Jack.

"What's his name?"

"We call him Lesmana," Kartini said. "It mean foolish night."

Laura flinched. She looked at the aunt, certain she must be joking. But the woman showed no humor. Laura couldn't just change the name. He wasn't her baby. She would call him Les and hope the nickname stuck.

The infant gurgled. He gave her a toothless grin. Perhaps I should buy a book on parenting, she thought. I don't know the first thing about raising a baby.

Chapter 40

Kartini, Maya, and the baby moved to Purwakarta. Maya learned to sew and took a job as a seamstress working for Harapan.

"Maya a good worker," Peni said as she and Laura sat on her front porch late one afternoon. Laura smiled as she recalled Maya, the sullen sultry maid. The responsibilities of a child, a better paying job and maturity really changed her.

Kartini opened a restaurant with lime chicken as the specialty. The women settled into their new lives — all except Laura. She had unfinished business. She needed to find a final resting place for Jack's ashes. And Wibawa remained unpunished.

Laura recalled the visit to Bali with Jack a year earlier and the elaborate Balinese cremation they witnessed. There, death was a joyous occasion, a celebration of the loved one departing to a better place. Laura wanted a similar ceremony for Jack. Off the coast of Jakarta lay a chain of islands. The coral reefs and pristine beaches resembled those in Bali. She would take his ashes there.

Before the sun rose, Laura and Mille left Purwakarta and drove over the mountain. The headlights of the car cut through the darkness. A rooster's crow announced their arrival to the outskirts of Jakarta. She considered crouching down on the car floor as she had done before. Instead, she fingered the visa card in her pocket for reassurance. She heard the familiar, haunting call to prayer. The capital was beginning to stir. There was something magical in observing the dawn of a new day in a big city where defused light and muted sounds prevailed. She watched expressionless men push carts piled high with foodstuffs. The scene brought back memories of Pak Hajji and the tofu operation. She suspected that he and his family would soon be heading to the morning market with a fresh batch.

At Tanjung Priok, Jakarta's old port, wooden seagoing vessels languished at the breakwater, their red, yellow, and blue colors muted by salt and sun. Debris sloshed in the brackish water, and the pungent odor of marine decay hung heavily in the humid air. Mille drove past the old vessels and stopped near a white cabin cruiser that ferried scuba divers to the reefs. A middle-aged man, his solid girth perched over low-riding stained shorts, swabbed the deck. As they approached, he looked up and greeted them. His friendly face had been darkened and creased by years spent on the water.

After Laura negotiated the fare to Pulau Seribu, the group of islands sixty miles out in the Java Sea, she and Mille boarded and took their seats. Laura cradled the urn in her lap. The man cranked the engine and reversed out of the slip. Slowly he maneuvered the craft past the channel buoy markers and into open water. Once underway, he added power and the hull rose. Wind whipped Laura's hair and spray splashed her face. She recalled how Jack loved the sea. She pictured him riding the waves in Bali and the moment she spotted him tumbling in the surf. Frightened, she raced over, fearing the worst when he didn't move. Then he flipped over and grinned at her, saying, "I'm alive." A tear ran down her check as she recalled his playfulness and spontaneity.

She had sworn revenge against Wibawa for taking Jack from her. But she couldn't live with hate. Now her heart was full of love for little Les. She couldn't put her life in jeopardy. She needed to help raise and support him. And Ari had already exacted the best revenge of all: Wibawa would grow old and die alone.

Though angry at Jack for the way he treated her, she forgave him. She stared out across the open sea. She never loved him more than she did at that moment.

For hours they skirted the waves. Hunkered down, Mille turned pale. Laura braced and winced each time she was lifted up and slammed back down on the hard seat. Gradually the deep blue indigo turned an emerald green and then crystal clear, as sunlight reflected off the shallow, sandy bottom. A large turtle swam past, and a school of small, silver fish flitted just below the surface.

When they dropped anchor the boat bobbed in place. Mille jumped over the side to help Laura. With the urn under her arm, she waded ashore. A breeze blew a strand of hair across her face, and the sand warmed her feet. So beautiful, so peaceful, she thought.

Laura and Mille walked to the other side of the tiny island, and Mille shinnied up a palm to retrieve a coconut. His feet found the invisible ridges of the trunk, and he worked his way down. Once at the bottom, he slashed off the top of the coconut with his machete. Laura placed Jack's ashes inside. She waded out until small waves lapped her thighs. She set the coconut in the water and whispered, "I will always love you, Jack." And she walked back to sit on the beach.

As the sun hovered at the horizon, the sky evolved into a brilliant, fitting eulogy of color: streaks of crimson and deep purple, cobalt blue, burnished gold, and swaths of yellow.

Twilight fell, and the silhouetted coconut drifted away.

Epilogue

Politics

President Suharto's thirty-two-year autocratic reign ended in 1998, his downfall brought about by student demonstrations and economic crisis. Joko Widodo became president of Indonesia in 2014, the first person to be elected from outside the military or political elite.

Corruption

The Komisi Pemberartasan Korupsi (KPK) was formed in 2002 to tackle the country's corruption. Supported by the public, the commission and its mandate are under constant threat from police and politicians.

Rainforest

Palm oil has replaced timber as the biggest threat to the rainforest. In 2015 slash and burn, an inexpensive method of clearing for new palm oil plantings, caused forest fires that unleashed a vast amount of smoke into the atmosphere. The hazardous haze affected millions in Indonesia and neighboring Singapore and Malaysia.

The Banks

Despite sustainability pledges that specifically address deforestation, American, European, Japanese, and Indonesian banks continue to finance projects that put the rainforest in peril.

The Orangutan

The orangutan remains in crisis. In the last decade, 80 percent of its habitat has been lost. The primate has been listed as critically endangered. In 2017, an unknown species of orangutan, the Tanapuli, was discovered on the island of Sumatra. There are believed to be only 800 of them. It is the rarest ape on the planet.

CPSIA information can be obtained
at www.ICGtesting.com
Printed in the USA
BVHW030038060419

544799BV00002B/4/P

9 781945 181504